Burn Me From the Outside

Scorched Memories
Book 2

Laci Mae Wyld

This novel contains material that may be distressing for some readers. Themes and scenes include strong language, explicit sexual content, corruption and abuse of power, references to the death of a parent, arson, and threats of violence.

Reader discretion is advised.

I want to dedicate this book to the most inspirational person I have ever met, Matty. The happiest and most beautiful person in the world, who, no matter what challenges life throws your way, never lets it bring you down. You are a beacon of love and light, and everyone who has the privilege of meeting you loves you.
Love you, Matty.

Contents

1

Red Flag

LUCAS

The surveillance room is a coffin, barely big enough for the metal desk, three ancient monitors, and the odor of every man who's ever done a twelve-hour night shift with nothing but cigarettes and burnt coffee for company. I lock the door behind me and pull the chain. The bulb overhead hums with electricity and threat.

This is where the ghosts live. Old calls, old fights, the faces of people you thought you'd already buried, stuck forever in grainy black and white, shuffling through the same twenty-four frames per second.

I load the feed for the previous week, fast-forward through days of nothing: empty halls, a janitor pushing a mop like he's doing penance, the endless parade of men and women killing time at the vending machine. I know what I'm looking for, though I pretend I don't. That's the only way to survive in this job. You tell yourself it's just routine, just due diligence, even as your hands start to sweat on the mouse and you taste copper in the back of your throat.

The clock reads 2:14 a.m. when the screen flickers, then freezes on a figure I know too well. Even in the distorted glow, I'd recognize that walk: long stride, shoulders set like rebar. A man I'd trusted with my life, more than once. A man who'd pulled me out of a fire with half his own arm on fire and never spoke of it again.

He moves through the rear hall, checks both corners with the precision of a drill sergeant. Not paranoia—practice. I watch, transfixed, as he disables the archive room alarm with a code only three people are supposed to know. The digital clock in the lower corner ticks: 2;15, 2:16, 2:17. He's in the records vault for exactly two minutes and thirty-eight seconds. Long enough to get exactly what he wants.

I slow the playback, frame by frame. His hands work the shelving, grab a stack of blueprints and a heavy-duty aluminum case—my case, I realize, the one I used to log specialty tools after a response. Forensics kit, maybe, or the new set of rescue saws. He tucks everything under one arm, relocks the door, and vanishes down the side corridor.

I can hear my own heartbeat, drumming out a countdown I don't want to see reach zero.

The next camera picks him up on the ground floor. He moves fast, head down, steps measured but urgent. Out the side exit, past the trash compactor, into the parking lot where every angle is blind except for the last, distant lens aimed at the lot's back corner.

That's where I see the handoff.

Rowe is already there, waiting in the shadow of the old water tower, face tilted just enough to keep it out of the light. My guy—my brother in arms—passes the blueprints and the case in a smooth, practiced gesture. Rowe accepts them with a nod, then turns and walks away like he's got all the time in the world.

But that's not what kills me. What kills me is the moment just before they separate, when my colleague slips a folded note from his breast pocket and tucks it into Rowe's palm, the way a man might pass off a communion wafer. Intentional, ritualistic.

I rewind the footage three times, slow it until the frames blur together. I want it to be a misunderstanding, a glitch, a shadow. But it's not.

My hands are shaking now, and my jaw's locked so tight my molars ache. I force myself to breathe. In, out. Nothing's changed except what I know.

I load a blank drive, check the ports, and drag the footage over. Every second feels like an hour. I keep glancing over my shoulder, expecting the door to rattle, the chain to snap. I've worked the job long enough to know the real danger always comes from behind.

As the files transfer, I go back to the video, watching every detail: the angle of the handoff, the line of sight for each camera, the way my colleague keeps his face averted. He knew where every lens was, every blind spot. He knew because I taught him.

The progress bar ticks to 99%, then sticks, then jumps to done. I yank the drive, pocket it, and kill the lights. For a second, I stand there in the dark, eyes shut, letting the afterimage of the betrayal burn into the backs of my lids.

When I open the door, the corridor is empty. I move fast, head down, walking like I've got somewhere else to be. On the way out, I pause at the breakroom, listening for voices, but all I hear is the hum of the fridge and the whisper of the ventilation system.

I hit the street and walk a full block before I stop and breathe. The morning is cold, the kind of cold that wants to live inside your bones.

I want to go back and confront him. I want to scream, punch a wall, do something to make it hurt less. But I know the rules of this world.

You gather evidence. You watch your back. And you trust no one, not even the man who once pulled you out of hell.

By the time I reach my car, my hands have stopped shaking.

I drive home in silence, replaying the footage over and over in my head.

It's after midnight, but I don't even bother with sleep. I run the shower until steam forms a ripple of fog on the bathroom mirror, scrubbing my face until I almost recognize myself. Then I head out to the kitchen table in just my towel; the drive is sitting on the table. I stare at it as if it might sprout fangs and bite.

The house is quiet except for the tap-tap of Sophie's phone as she prepares emails for her lawyer or maybe the DA. She has been so busy and determined since taking on an investigator role with the County. I'd ask, but right now I don't want to talk. I just want to not think, not feel, not be the guy who got played by his own crew.

She comes in quietly, pads across the tile in old sweats, a mug of peppermint tea cupped in her hands. She sees the drive and the stack of printouts and knows, instantly, that I've found something bad.

"Was it him?" she asks, voice just above a whisper.

I don't answer. I just cue up the footage, the frame already frozen on my guy in the archives. I play it once, full speed. She doesn't flinch. She just watches, jaw set, eyes laser-locked on the screen.

I play it again, slower, then pause at the moment the note changes hands. Sophie leans in, and I see her fingers twitch like she wants to reach through the monitor and throttle both men right then and there.

I slide the zoomed printout of the frame across the table. She studies it, then flips it over. The note is partly visible, one corner folded over, and there's a spatter of what might be coffee on its edge. Sophie takes a pen and traces the handwriting, as if she can conjure the words through sheer will.

"Let me see it," she says, gesturing to some of the other papers I have compiled.

I hand her the envelope—extracted from the evidence locker, chain of custody all but blown up now that I'm running my own investigation. She turns it over, runs a thumb across the crease, then narrows her eyes at the scrawl on the outside.

Her lips move as she deciphers it. "This...this is Bennett," she says, voice tight. "It's his penmanship. I'd know it anywhere. Look at the way he slashes the T. The double loop on the Y." She jabs the note with a finger. "He's still calling the shots. Even from lockup."

The words hang in the air, more corrosive than bleach.

My hands clench and unclench on the table, the splintery Formica biting my palms. "He's not just calling the shots," I say, "he's got half the department on a leash. Maybe more."

I can see the exact moment the betrayal hits Sophie—not as a slow burn, but as a hammer blow. She pushes her mug aside, lays out the rest of the evidence: the drive, the photos, her own annotated maps of the last few weeks of fires. The table is an autopsy slab now, and we're the ones with the scalpel.

"We missed something," she says, and it's not a question. "Look here." She overlays the parking lot blueprints with the pattern of Rowe's last three sightings. "He's using the old water tower as a dead drop, and every time he makes a delivery, there's a spike in radio silence across the central district. Your comms logs—they're full of blackouts and static." She points to a cluster of dots. "That's not coincidence. That's coordination."

I want to feel proud, vindicated, but all I can taste is bile.

"So what's the play?" I ask. "Call the state boys? Leak it to the press? We do either, and the whole department gets torched. Every rookie, every retiree, everyone who ever believed in this job, they'll be radioactive for years."

She looks at me, and the pity is almost worse than the anger. "You can't save the building if the foundation's rotten. You know that."

I think of my father, of every old bastard who ever sat at this table and lectured me about loyalty, and I want to scream. I get up, pace the room, run my hands through hair still damp from the shower. I want to throw something, break a window, light a match, just to see what happens.

But I don't.

I stop, stare at the wall, at the crooked diploma, the faded group photos, the brittle paperbacks nobody's read in years.

I turn to Sophie. "We take it to the chief. Everything. We demand a full shutdown—no shifts, no calls, nothing until every man and woman gets vetted by the state. Even if it means we're out of work tomorrow."

Sophie smiles, but it's a hard, mean smile. "You sure you want to be the whistleblower, Lucas? The stuff I've told the lawyers about Bennett and Rowe is one thing, and I haven't been a part of the Willow Creek Brigade for a bloody long time; they will see it as you turning on your brothers."

I think of the footage again—the handoff, the handshake, the look on my "brother's" face. "It's the only way," I say. "Bennett thought he was the last one standing. He's not."

She stands, walks around the table, and puts a hand on my shoulder. Her palm is cold, but her grip is steel. "You're not alone in this," she says.

I nod, even though I don't believe it yet.

We spend the next hour prepping: duplicating files, printing every page, cross-referencing every scrap of handwriting. Sophie annotates the evidence with an archivist's precision, making sure there's no way anyone can sweep it under the rug.

When we're done, the table looks like a war zone.

Sophie leans in, her eyes fierce. "You ready?"

I swallow, taste adrenaline and regret and something like hope. "Let's burn it down," I say.

And for the first time since this nightmare started, I almost want to watch it burn.

When I walk into the chief's office, it's like stepping onto a bomb range. The usual morning light is blocked out by hastily taped newspaper over the windows, the kind that promises "maintenance" but delivers only paranoia. There's a folding table at the center of the room, scarred and crowded with coffee cups and battered laptops, every inch screaming emergency command center.

Every senior officer is there. Some I've known since rookie days; others are new, brought in to plug holes left by scandal or burnout. Most avoid my eyes, but the captain gives me a single, sharp nod—permission or warning, I can't tell.

Chief sits at the head, his posture military, hands flat on the table as if holding down a corpse that won't stop twitching. His uniform is immaculate, but his face is gray and drawn, bags under his eyes deep enough to drown in.

I don't knock. I don't announce. I walk straight up to the table and drop the folder with a thud that startles even the hardcases. The printouts, USB drive, and Sophie's annotated maps spread out like the opening hand of a very bad poker game.

Chief doesn't flinch. "Hayes," he says, voice calm as always. "This is a closed session."

"Not anymore," I say. My hands are shaking, so I grip the edge of the table until the knuckles go white.

One of the senior officers—the deputy chief, I think—tries to interject. "You got a grievance, Hayes, file it with—"

"I've got more than a grievance," I say, and my voice cracks like a branch. "I've got proof this department is compromised from the inside out."

A hush falls. Even the coffee machine, ancient and usually wheezing in the background, seems to stop breathing.

Chief gestures at the folder. "Walk us through it."

I pull out the first photo—my colleague, my friend, walking the archives after hours. "This is from two nights ago," I say. "Surveillance shows him entering the restricted file room, disabling the alarm. He removes blueprints and equipment, then meets with Caleb Rowe outside. Handoff's right there." I lay out the still frame of the exchange.

Another officer tries to cut in. "That could be—"

"It's not a setup," I say. "The alarm code was his. The blueprints match what's missing from the vault."

I open the next printout—Sophie's handwriting, the map of radio blackouts. "It's coordinated. Every time there's a break-in, a fire, a bomb threat, there's a communications blackout in the central district. Someone's running interference from dispatch, and it's happening on our watch."

Chief lifts the note, stares at it. "This is Bennett's script," he says, almost to himself. "He's still running the show."

I nod. "From the inside, or from jail. Doesn't matter. The point is, we're compromised. We can't protect anyone if we don't burn it out, now."

There's a crackle in the air as the officers shift, lean in, whisper to each other. I watch them all, every gesture, every microexpression.

Chief leans back, pinches the bridge of his nose. "You're asking for a full shutdown."

"I'm demanding it," I say. "Every crew off shift. Every badge surrendered. We call in the state boys to audit the entire department. If we keep running, we're just making it easier for them."

Deputy Chief blusters. "You realize how this will look to the city? The insurance, the liability—"

Chief silences him with a look. Then, to me: "What makes you think we'll survive the fallout?"

"We won't," I say. "But the department might. If we don't, we're just another story on the ticker."

Chief is silent for a long time. The kind of long that's usually filled with death or regret.

Then, finally: "Play the tape."

I do. I connect the USB to the battered Lenovo and cue up the footage. There's a collective flinch as my guy walks through the archive; another when Rowe appears in the lot. The moment the note changes hands, Chief's jaw locks so tight I can see the muscle jumping.

When it's over, nobody speaks. Chief stands, slow and heavy, and picks up the phone. He dials the state fire marshal's office, recites his name and badge number, then says: "We have an internal breach. I'm requesting immediate external oversight. Yes, full shutdown. No, I don't care about PR right now."

He hangs up, then faces the table, every man and woman staring at him like they're waiting for a death sentence.

"Effective immediately, Willow Creek Fire Department is suspended from duty," Chief says. "All personnel will turn in their badges and gear to the front desk, then report for debrief with the oversight team. No exceptions. No leaks. Anyone breaks silence, they're gone for good."

He doesn't look at me as he says it. He doesn't have to.

I should feel triumph, but all I feel is the hollow silence that comes after an explosion. My brothers and sisters are stunned, numb, angry, but there's no mutiny in their eyes. Just loss.

As I leave, Chief calls after me. "Hayes. Stick around. You'll need to brief the state team."

I nod, not trusting myself to speak.

The hallway outside the office is deserted, the echo of my footsteps the only sign I still exist. I lean against the wall, breathing in the institutional cleaner, and listen as one life dies so another can begin.

Somewhere, out there, Bennett's laughing.

But in here, at least, there's nothing left to burn.

SOPHIE

The community center smells like Lemon Pledge and fear. The folding chairs are set up in crooked rows, the old basketball banners above the stage drooping like flags at half mast. Every seat is filled, and then some—people standing in the back, crowding the exits, phones out, waiting to see if I'll combust under the klieg lights of public shame.

The press has brought their own electricity, a static charge that bounces from lens to lens and settles on my skin. I stand behind the podium in a suit borrowed from my mother's closet, the hem two inches too short and the color an atrocity against my hair. I left my glasses at home; I want them to see my eyes.

I clear my throat and adjust the mic. It squeals, then dies.

"My name is Sophie Grant," I say, and the crowd goes silent.

I don't have a speech, just bullet points and the stubborn certainty that I'm the only person willing to say the thing out loud.

"The Willow Creek Fire Department has been suspended, effective immediately," I begin. "The investigation is ongoing, but I can confirm that multiple members of the department participated in a conspiracy to conceal and facilitate arson for profit, at the expense of public safety."

A gasp ripples through the room. Someone in the back yells, "Bullshit!" but another shushes him fast.

I keep going, heart pounding so hard I worry the mic will pick it up. "I know this hurts. I know some of you have loved ones on the force. I know what it's like to see someone you trusted—someone you called family—fall from grace."

I look down at my hands, then back up. "But this isn't about destroying trust. It's about rebuilding it—on a foundation of truth. We cannot heal if we lie to ourselves."

The crowd stirs, a rolling boil of whispers and low-grade fury. I spot the mayor, arms crossed and jaw tight, flanked by two city councilmen in suits that cost more than my car. A row of wives and kids sit in the front, some with faces set like stone, others already brimming with tears.

I breathe in. "The people sworn to protect us have been compromised. But I believe we're stronger than the worst things done in our name. I believe in redemption. And I believe in justice."

There's a beat, a kind of hush where I can see the words land, scatter, and take root in a hundred different ways.

A local reporter in a yellow windbreaker shoves her phone in my face. "Are you afraid for your safety, Ms. Grant? There are rumors that the whistleblower has received threats."

I square my shoulders. "Let them try," I say, and the words come out harder than I intend. "I don't burn easy."

It gets a laugh—a real, nervous laugh from the back rows—and I feel the energy shift. Some of the faces soften; some just harden further.

I wrap it up with a promise: "The investigation will continue. No stone will be left unturned. And I promise you—every fact I learn, I will share with you, in person, just like this. No secrets. No shortcuts."

I step away from the mic. The applause is scattered and awkward, but it grows. I force myself not to cry, not to flinch, not to shrink.

As the room empties, I catch sight of three little kids with their mother. The youngest is still in pajamas, hair in cowlicked tufts, clutching a toy fire engine. He's crying, but his mother kneels and whispers in his ear, and the boy looks up at me, eyes wide and searching.

That's when the guilt hits—bigger than any shame, heavier than the loss of the job, the family, the whole way of life. I want to go to them, to explain that it's not their fault, that I'm trying to make it better. But the mother just shakes her head, gathers the kids, and leaves.

In the hallway, a line of cameras waits. I duck past, find the exit, and step out into the cold. Lucas is there, leaning against his truck, arms folded across his chest. His eyes are dark and unreadable.

"You did good," he says.

"I don't feel good," I admit.

He shrugs. "That's how you know it mattered."

I want to reach for him, but I'm not sure if I still have the right. Instead, I jam my hands in my coat pockets and stare at the parking lot, watching the reporters chase after the next headline.

"It's not over," I say. "Bennett, Rowe—they'll push back."

"They will," Lucas says. "But so will we."

He opens the passenger door, gestures for me to get in. I hesitate, then slide onto the cracked vinyl seat. It smells like him, like coffee and ozone and the faintest trace of sweat. It's the only place I've ever felt safe.

He starts the engine and cranks the heat. We sit in silence, the world outside moving in slow motion.

After a while, I look over at him. "You think we'll make it through this?"

He glances at me, then at the road ahead. "We've already survived worse."

I laugh, and it's a real laugh this time. "I guess we have."

He puts the truck in gear and pulls away from the curb, the headlights slicing through the early morning fog.

We drive toward whatever comes next, side by side.

And for the first time, I believe we'll actually make it.

LUCAS

It's almost midnight by the time I stumble back to the house. My body's running on nothing but caffeine, adrenaline, and the stubborn refusal to give the bastards the satisfaction of watching me break. I close the door behind me, fumble with the deadbolt, and drop my keys onto the counter. The place is dark except for the kitchen light, which flickers in a way that makes the shadows look alive.

I take three steps before I notice the trail—a slow drift of clothing, each piece a deliberate clue. First a scarf, coiled on the stairs like a snake. Then a shirt, balled up and tossed at the baseboard. Then her jeans, legs inside-out, leading straight into the living room.

I follow the breadcrumbs, pulse already starting to pound in anticipation. The sight of her—barefoot, legs folded under her on the threadbare rug, wearing nothing but my old department shirt—nearly stops my heart. The shirt drowns her, sleeves past her fingertips, but the hem barely reaches midthigh.

She looks up, and even in the dim light, her eyes catch mine with a force that's almost physical.

"I thought you could use a distraction," Sophie says, her voice soft but sure.

For a second, I forget everything: the betrayals, the shutdown, the pile of statements I still have to give. There's only her, and the way she sits with her knees tucked in and her hair wild around her face, and the slow, sly way her hand slips up to undo the top button of the shirt.

She doesn't stand. Instead, she waits for me to cross the room, her gaze never leaving my face. I kneel beside her, reach out and run my hand along her cheek, thumb skimming the line of her jaw. She turns into the touch, and I feel her sigh, low and shivery.

"You're freezing," I say, and she laughs—a sound that shivers through me.

"So warm me up," she whispers.

I lean in, kiss her, slow at first, then hungrier. Her mouth is fire and ice at once, urgent and demanding and absolutely sure of what it wants. I can taste the peppermint from her tea, the tang of adrenaline, the residue of the day's battles.

She drags her hands up under my shirt, nails grazing my skin. I shudder and pin her wrists above her head, just for a second, feeling her twist and arch into the hold. Then I let go, and she claws at my back, pulling me closer, mouths crashing together hard enough to bruise.

There's no time for finesse. We yank at each other's clothes, desperate for skin, for proof that we're real and still alive. I lose the shirt first, then my jeans, then she's naked beneath me, every inch of her radiating heat. I want to memorize her, every scar and freckle and shadow, but I can't slow down, not now.

We don't make it to the bedroom. Instead, we collapse on the rug, her back arched against the floor, my hands everywhere at once. I run my mouth down her neck, her collarbone, her chest, biting at the places I know will make her gasp. She writhes under me, fists in my hair, nails raking my shoulder blades.

When I finally push inside her, it's a relief and a shock all at once. We move together, hard and frantic, the edge of desperation in every thrust. I lose myself in the feel of her—slick, tight, greedy—and the way she clings to me, legs wrapped around my waist, holding me so close I might never break free.

The living room fills with the sound of our bodies, wet and raw and alive. I feel her come apart under me, the stutter of her breath, the clench and release. I follow, unable to hold back, hips bucking as I spill inside her.

For a long time, we don't move, just breathe, bodies entwined and slick with sweat. The world could end, and I wouldn't care, not as long as I have this: the weight of her on my chest, the tangle of our limbs, the heartbeat thrumming against my skin.

Eventually, I roll to the side, pulling her with me so we're spooned together on the rug. I stroke her back, draw lazy circles over the curve of her hip. She hums, content, her cheek pressed to my shoulder.

"You're not my weakness," I whisper, lips against her hair. "You're the reason I fight."

She twines her fingers with mine, squeezes. "You're a sap," she says, but the words are softer than I've ever heard them.

I nuzzle the top of her head, let my hand drift down to cup her ass. "You make it easy."

She laughs again, then turns over, so we're face to face. Her eyes are tired, but there's a light in them I haven't seen in weeks.

"Promise me something," she says.

"Anything," I reply, and mean it.

"Don't let them put the fire out," she whispers. "Not if it means you lose yourself."

I think about that, about the job and the rules and the city that never really cared about us in the first place. I think about her, and how she's the only one who ever saw the real me—the burn scars and the broken parts, the need to save people even if it kills me.

I kiss her, slow this time. "I promise."

We lie there for a long time, listening to the radiator clank, the wind rattle the windows. At some point, we fall asleep, limbs knotted and mouths pressed together, the kind of sleep that only comes when you know you're safe.

In the morning, the light through the window is soft and forgiving. I wake with her still wrapped around me, her breath warm against my neck, her hand on my heart.

Whatever comes next, whatever burns, I know we'll face it together.

That's all I ever needed.

2

Fireline Breach

LUCAS

THE TEMP OFFICE IS A FORMER INSURANCE CUBICLE FARM on the second floor of a strip-mall plaza, the kind of place that would be a discount urgent-care clinic if it weren't already outbid by the local methadone dispensary. The air's just as sterile as the last one, but every time the heat kicks on it brings the ghosts of carpet shampoo and a little bit of mildew. I sit at a desk meant for a much smaller man, knees knocking into the drawer, the legs shimmied with a stack of printer paper to keep it from wobbling. The only light is fluorescent, and it bathes everything in the sickly optimism of a crime scene.

I'm three cups deep into the kind of coffee that comes in foil packs and tastes like plastic regret, but it's not helping. The stack of files in front of me is two feet high, the result of an all-nighter of background checks and internet rabbit holes.

Sophie's handwriting litters half the pages, sharp block letters and flagged sticky notes in radioactive orange. I read the same five pages over and over until the lines blur, then I try a different stack.

It's almost four when I hit the lead.

Buried in a sheaf of scanned juvenile court records, right between a busted shoplifting charge and a court-ordered psych eval, is the name: Caleb Thomas. No mention of Rowe, not even in the aliases. The mugshot is fourteen years old, but the eyes are the same, looking at the camera like they're reading a secret in the lens. The rest is boilerplate, a dozen censored lines, a birthdate, and a parent's name, and then—on the last page—a single signature I'd know anywhere.

Troy Bennett. As bold and precise as every memo he ever sent.

The note reads: "Juvenile record sealed by order of the court, per recommendation of Det. Bennett. Subject to name change and sealed status upon completion of probation." There's a case number and a date—exactly one month before Caleb "Rowe" joined his first fire company in a town three counties over.

My hands go numb. I flip through the whole bundle again, fingers digging into the edges of the paper. The signature repeats, more desperate each time. There's no doubt now.

Bennett didn't just know Caleb Rowe. He built him. Shielded him from everything. Created a ghost.

I have to stop and breathe. The heat in my shoulders tightens until it feels like a tourniquet. If I let go, I'll start shaking, so I make myself go slower, force myself to see every line again.

I don't know how long I sit there, staring, but at some point, I become aware of my phone buzzing under a stack of old firehouse rosters. It takes three tries to pull it free without scattering everything to hell. The screen reads 3:51 AM, and the message is from Sophie:

"You still alive?"

I debate lying for a split second, then just text back:

"Found something. Come now. Bring coffee."

The moment after I hit send, I realize it sounds more urgent than I wanted it to. Doesn't matter. The office is empty, security long gone, nobody but the janitor and maybe a rat colony for company. I have thirty minutes, maybe less, before the sun comes up and someone expects me to act like a functioning human being.

I print two copies of the files, staple the bundle, and write "READ THIS" on the top sheet in ballpoint that tears through the paper. The coffee has congealed into something I could use as grout, but I drink it anyway.

Sophie shows up in less than twenty minutes, hair a mess, mascara smudged, wearing the same hoodie from last night but with different sweats. She looks at me, then at the file, and doesn't bother with greetings.

"What is it?" she says, voice husked from lack of sleep.

I push the file across the desk, watching her eyes as she scans. She's faster than me, or maybe just less attached to the illusion that there's still a good explanation for any of this.

It takes her all of sixty seconds.

She stops on the signature. "Troy," she says, not a question.

"Buried everything," I say. "Not just the record, the whole fucking identity. I don't think there's a single real document for Rowe after age fourteen."

She flips a page, finger running down the line. "Why did he do it?"

"Why does anyone?" I say. "Favors. Leverage. Maybe he thought he could steer him straight, or maybe he was always planning on using him as a weapon. Doesn't matter."

She sets the file down, but her hands stay on the pages, flattening them as if she can press the truth deeper into the paper.

"Look at this." She taps the date. "That's the same week my dad died. He was busy that month."

Her voice is flat, but her jaw ticks.

I don't know what to say, so I let the silence stretch. The room is so small it makes even the air between us feel sharp, like the edge of a snapped-off knife.

Sophie slides the file closer, studies the margins, every annotation, every crossed-out line. I watch her face, the way it changes as she reads. Hardens. The softness that I sometimes catch when she thinks I'm not looking is gone; all that's left is the predator, the part of her that survived.

She looks up. "You know what this means, right?"

I nod, but she says it anyway:

"He's been protecting him all along. Not just hiding evidence, but grooming him. Feeding him every step."

"Yeah," I say, and my voice sounds like it belongs to someone else. "Bennett was running two jobs. Cleaning up the town's fires, and creating someone who'd make sure they never stopped."

Sophie stares at the file, then at the wall behind me, as if trying to burn a hole through both.

She pulls her phone, thumbs a number, waits.

When the call picks up, her voice is cold and professional. "This is Grant. I need a full copy of the Bennett personnel jacket, including psych evals. No, I don't care if it's sealed. You get it, or I come down there and do it myself."

She hangs up before the other side can argue.

We sit in the silence, listening to the heater rumble through another cycle.

Finally, Sophie speaks, voice low: "You ready to end it?"

I think about the years wasted chasing the wrong ghost. About every night spent pretending the bad guys were on the outside, not in the same room, drinking the same coffee. I think about Rowe, and Bennett, and what it means to burn your own house down to save a single secret.

"Yeah," I say. "Let's light the match."

The heater cycles off. The only sound is the hum of the lights and the slow, even breathing from the other side of the desk.

We don't look at each other. We don't have to.

Tomorrow, there will be fire.

Tonight, we prep the kindling.

SOPHIE

The coffee shop is one of those converted gas stations with too much character, chrome stools with the foam coming out, a wavy counter, and an open kitchen where the fry oil has become a kind of air. I pick the booth farthest from the window and order a black coffee, the kind that comes from a glass carafe that's been in service longer than the staff. The place hums with 6 AM energy—a couple of retired cops talking about how the world used to be, two high-schoolers doing SAT flashcards, a single mom haggling with a toddler over a donut. I try not to think about how normal everything looks from the outside.

The man I'm meeting is already there. He wears a faded state corrections windbreaker and the kind of khakis you get at a retirement party. He's built like a boiled egg—thin gray hair, skin like he's allergic to sun—and he drinks coffee the way a man drinks water after a long walk through hell.

He doesn't stand when I approach, but he gestures to the seat. I set my notebook on the table, tap a pen against the margin, and try to look less desperate than I am.

"You're the Grant girl," he says, voice like a bark. "I didn't expect you'd look so much like your father."

"Depends on the lighting," I say, and immediately hate myself for wanting to win the first volley. "Thank you for meeting me."

He shrugs, takes a sip. "Couldn't sleep anyway."

We sit in a weird truce for a minute. I flip open the notebook, scribble the date and his last name—Burke—at the top. "I just have a few questions," I start, but he cuts me off.

"You want to know about Caleb," Burke says. "Not much I remember, but I'll try."

He lies, and we both know it.

I set my phone to record and slide it onto the vinyl between us. He glances at it, then at me, and then the file opens. "He came in at thirteen," Burke says, voice gone flat. "Set fire to a chicken plant. Wasn't even mad about the place, just wanted to see what would happen to the feathers. Insurance wrote it up as vandalism, but the kid got two years in juvie."

He drinks, continues. "He didn't talk much. They sent him to my office once a month. Every time, he just stared at the clock. Said he was counting down. 'Until what?' I asked him. He never answered."

I jot the quotes. "When did you notice the obsession with fire?"

Burke smirks a little. "Not much to notice. Kid drew flames on every sheet of paper. Used to light the edges of his math homework, just to see how far the burn would go before it caught the desk. Got so we had to check him for matches before every meeting."

I nod, try to keep my hand from shaking. "Did he ever mention my father?"

"Not by name," Burke says. "But he talked about Willow Creek. Always said he'd go back and finish his fire. 'Finish the fire, finish myself'—that's how he put it."

The words take a second to land. I feel them hit the base of my skull and radiate out. I glance at the phone, make sure the tape is rolling.

Burke looks me dead in the eye. "There's more, you know. It's not in the files, but sometimes he'd talk about what comes after. He said the only way to be free was to erase the thing that made him. That's what the fires were, for him. Erasing."

He leans forward, voice lowering. "I think he hated your dad, Miss Grant. I think he hated what your dad built. He said if he ever got out, he'd burn the last thing that mattered. Said it was his destiny."

My hand freezes on the page. "The last thing that mattered," I echo.

Burke nods. "Your old man's legacy. You, the house, and the station."

The shop keeps pouring customers through the front door, someone orders pancakes, a waitress giggles behind the counter, but the whole world tunnels down to Burke's tired face and the note of finality in his words.

"He's here," I say, barely more than a whisper. "He's going after the station."

Burke shrugs again, like he's seen every play before. "It's where I'd look."

I want to ask more, but I already know the rest. Rowe didn't just want to burn things; he wanted to turn himself to ash. To finish the story.

My mouth tastes like copper and old pennies. I throw a five on the table, thank him with a nod, and fumble my phone as I dial Lucas.

He picks up on the first ring. "Tell me you have something."

I watch the world tilt and slide by the window, a mom corralling her kids, the air outside already burning off the morning fog. "It's the station," I say. "He's going to torch the firehouse."

A pause, then Lucas's voice, steady as a metronome. "I'm on my way."

I stand up too fast, knee cracking on the table's edge, coffee splashing up and over my notes. I don't bother to mop it up. I just grab my stuff and head for the door, nearly plowing into a guy holding a tray of breakfast sandwiches.

"Sorry," I say, but I'm already gone.

Outside, the sky is that brilliant, blank blue you only get after a night of hard weather. I sprint for my car, hands shaking as I unlock it, a sick electricity under my skin.

The engine turns over, and I peel out of the lot, the diner's neon OPEN sign reflected in my rearview until I hit the light and it vanishes behind the curve of the road.

I fumble for the next call, the last number Dad ever taught me to memorize.

"State Fire Marshal," the woman answers crisply.

"Grant, Sophie. Code red. Repeat—code red for Willow Creek Station. Probable arson attack. Suspect Rowe, Caleb. Subject obsessed, likely suicidal. Advise immediate evac."

She asks for a callback, but I'm already merging onto Main, the town blurring into one long streak of siren-colored terror.

Every mile closer to the station feels like losing a year off my life.

Burke's words ring in my ears: The last thing that mattered.

He's going to burn it all, and he's going to do it now.

I just hope to God we get there first.

LUCAS

There's a kind of silence that only happens at the end of a long shift—the dead space before the alarms hit, the sense that everything in the world is holding its breath just for you. The firehouse smells like it always does: sweat, diesel, the faint ghost of burned toast from breakfast. I step through the side door, badge still clipped to my belt, and for a second I can almost pretend it's a normal day.

Then the first alarm sounds. Not the dispatch chime, but the harsh, local one—someone's triggered the emergency system from the main hall.

I break into a run. My boots catch on the slick tile, and I barely avoid colliding with a rookie coming the other way, face white as chalk. He's yelling, "Hazard in the bay, possible chemical!" and I can hear the old guard barking orders, their voices already climbing the panic scale.

This isn't a drill.

"Evacuate now!" I shout, voice ringing down the corridor. Every muscle in my neck feels like a steel cable. "Out, out, out! Take the back stairs—double time!"

Someone tries to argue—"But Chief—"—but I cut them off with a stare. The herd instinct kicks in, and within ten seconds everybody in sight is moving, some with more coordination than others, but none stupid enough to argue again.

I head for the engine bay. The overhead doors are already open, letting in the morning light, and there's an unnatural slickness on the floor—a puddle spreading out from under Ladder 1, shimmering blue-green with a rainbow slick of what I'm pretty sure is solvent. The air burns my eyes and scrapes my lungs raw.

I radio in, thumb pressed so hard to the button I hear it creak. "Dispatch, this is Hayes at Station. Level two hazardous. Evacuate all personnel. Suspected accelerant in the engine bay. Advise state hazmat, immediate backup."

"Copy, Hayes. State notified. What's your twenty?"

I'm at the edge of the puddle, trying to eyeball the source, when I see the canisters—three of them, unmarked, wedged between the trash compactor and the main pump. Whoever set this up knew the system, knew exactly where to place it for max effect.

I sweep the bay—no sign of Rowe, but I know his signature. I know it in my bones.

I grab the nearest fire extinguisher, pull the pin, and test the air. The stench is overwhelming, so thick it's almost sweet. Acetone? Paint thinner? Something volatile, something meant to go off at the lightest touch. I force myself to slow down, take inventory: two engines, both fueled; four crew lockers in direct line of sight; half a ton of equipment that'll turn to shrapnel if it goes up.

That's when the alarms shift from steady to wailing, the kind of sound that vibrates your teeth.

I hear the blast before I feel it—a low-frequency gut punch that knocks the wind out of me and tilts the world forty-five degrees. The floor lifts, or maybe I just lose my footing. The next thing I know, I'm sliding across the tile, extinguisher skittering away, air full of dust and glass.

The fire moves fast. Real fast.

It crawls the ceiling, catches the drop tiles, then fans out in a sheet of orange that erases everything. I haul myself up, lungs screaming, and run for the only exit not blocked by a wall of heat. The smoke is black and greasy, the kind that sticks to your teeth and nails and dreams. I can hear the rookies yelling from outside, can feel the pressure drop as the bay doors buckle and twist in the draft.

I don't look back.

I hit the door shoulder-first, bounce off, and go through it on the second try. Outside, the world is all blue sky and screaming. Firefighters—my team, my people—are scattered on the concrete, some coughing, some just staring. One guy is missing his helmet, and his hair is already singed into a kind of ducktail. Another clutches his arm, blood streaming through his fingers.

I spot Sophie by the curb, standing perfectly still, eyes locked on the side entrance. She's pale, but not from the smoke. I can see her mouth move, but I can't hear her over the noise.

She sprints forward, and the same instant, I see movement at the edge of the engine bay—a shape, too big to be a shadow, crawling out through the wreckage. It's one of the old-timers, Ellis, the guy who always brought donuts and never remembered to wipe the powder off his mustache.

He staggers, falls, gets up again. His sleeve is on fire.

Without thinking, I run back in. Someone grabs at my shoulder, but I shake them loose and barrel into the half-collapsed bay. The heat is incredible, like standing in front of a blast furnace. I can feel the eyebrows singe off my face.

I reach Ellis, yank him upright, and half-carry, half-drag him out. The air outside feels like ice in comparison. Ellis collapses on the ground, rolling and slapping at his arm, and the rest of the crew rushes over, smothering the flames with jackets and their own hands.

Now the engines arrive. Sirens, more urgent than any I've ever heard, were stacking up on the street with red and white and blue lights pulsing in a perfect sync. The hazmat team is on them before they're fully out of the cabs, hosing us down, screaming at us to stay put, don't go back in, don't breathe.

But I can't stop. I need to know who made it out, who's left. I count helmets, count heads, scan for anyone missing. I lock eyes with the rookie who first saw the leak, and I want to hug him, or maybe kill him for not yelling louder.

Sophie finds me, hands on my cheeks, forcing me to look at her. "Are you burned?" she says, over and over, until I realize I can't feel my face.

I shake my head, try to speak, but nothing comes out.

She pulls me into a hug, hard enough to bruise. Her hair is full of ash, and she smells like ozone and panic. I hang onto her because there's nothing else left to do.

The station—my second home, my only real family for years—is gone. It's not just the building. It's the lockers, the little Christmas lights we never took down, the polaroids from every birthday and prank and rookie initiation taped to the walls. All of it, blackened, melted, erased in a single, calculated hit.

I want to go back in, just to salvage a piece, a single thing that proves I was here. But the crew keeps me grounded, all of us together, for the first time ever, acting as if we might actually die if we split up.

The fire takes less than twenty minutes to finish its job.

When it's over, the walls are skeletons. The engines are just hunks of twisted metal. The rescue van is a blackened hulk. All the gear—axes, hoses, the commemorative ball from the station's first Little League win—is just so much debris.

The only thing that doesn't burn is the plaque on the front wall. "Willow Creek Firehouse—Est. 1924." The letters are half melted, but they're still legible. I stare at them until my vision goes blurry.

Sophie stands next to me, arm slung over my shoulder. Her hand shakes, but her voice is steady.

"We'll rebuild," she says.

I know she means the station. But maybe, just maybe, she means us.

I turn, brush the soot off her cheek, and kiss her. Not gentle. Not slow. I need to feel something that doesn't hurt.

She kisses back, just as fiercely.

In the background, the world is all sirens and shouted orders. But in that moment, I hear only the crackle of embers and the pounding of my own heart.

Rowe is still out there. But now, I know exactly what I'm fighting for.

And I swear to God, I'm going to finish it.

After a fire like this, the world slows down to a crawl. Every second is counted in lungfuls of smoke, the weight of wet gear on your back, and the small acts of survival that feel holy in the moment—someone handing you a bottle of Gatorade, a medic dabbing ointment on the burn you didn't even know you had, the simple fact of standing upright while the building you called home is nothing but a jagged shell.

The station's a total loss. The roof has collapsed, and the brick-work glows orange from the embers inside. The air is full of particulates and old regrets, and every time I blink, I see the afterimage of flames dancing on the backs of my eyelids.

Firefighters, city, county, even some volunteers, are still here, mopping up, hosing down hotspots, trading black humor about the "new open-concept design." The haze makes everyone look like a ghost.

A paramedic wraps Ellis's arm, chattering at him like he's a little kid, and for once, he just nods, docile. The rest of my crew stands in a loose knot, shivering, ash in their hair, every one of them running on fumes but refusing to leave until the last ember dies.

The fire marshal stands beside me, hands on his hips, watching the ruins with the thousand-yard stare of a man who's seen too many of these. His coat is spattered with soot, his boots flecked with melted rubber. He doesn't say anything, just hands me a bottled water and waits.

Sophie finds me at the edge of the perimeter, her walk determined but careful, like she's navigating a minefield. There's ash in her eyelashes, a streak of carbon down one cheek. Her hair is wild, and her clothes look like they spent the last hour in a fireplace.

She stops half a step from me and doesn't bother with small talk.

"He was here," she says. "Rowe. I saw him—he came in through the maintenance shed, right before the explosion."

I taste the urge to run back into the smoking pit, to tear the place apart with my bare hands and find whatever trace of him is left. But there's nothing left to find. He got what he wanted.

I clench my jaw until it hurts. "This isn't just arson anymore," I say. "It's a fucking declaration of war."

Sophie's mouth tightens, and I see the fire in her eyes—brighter and hotter than the real thing. "Then we burn him down. No more hiding. No more clean-up jobs."

I look at her—really look—and I see the full weight of what's happened. Her hands shake, but her voice is steady. She's lost everything, twice now, and all she has left is the mission and whatever I can offer her.

The world narrows to just the two of us.

The fire behind us is finally dying. The crews begin to pack up, the city's flashing lights giving the scene a funhouse glow. The station is nothing but rubble and black smoke, but in the clearing air, I see the future—ugly, uncertain, but ours.

I reach for Sophie, catch her by the wrist, and pull her close. She doesn't resist. Her shirt is already ruined, so I grip her by the shoulders, leaving sooty prints that look like battle scars. I kiss her, deep and rough, tasting the ash and adrenaline and a promise of something that still matters.

She melts against me, fingers digging into my arms, her breath warm and sharp in the cold night.

When we break apart, there's a hush around us. The other firefighters look away, pretending not to notice, but I know they see. They know what it means to need something so bad it's all that keeps you upright.

"We end it," I say. "Together."

Sophie nods, and for the first time in hours, maybe days, she smiles.

The sun is coming up behind the ruins. The smoke is thinning, but the smell of it will hang in the air for weeks, maybe longer. The next shift won't have a building to report to, but they'll have each other. They'll have us.

We stand there, arms wrapped tight, as the world keeps turning. And when the last engine leaves and the street is finally quiet, we don't let go.

Not even for a second.

Whatever comes next, we face it side by side.

And when the world tries to burn us again, we'll burn brighter.

3

Cold Smoke

LUCAS

THE PHONE WAKES ME AT 4:36 AM, VIBRATING SO HARD IT nearly skitters off the nightstand, and into the glass of water I forgot to finish. For a minute, I'm not sure whether it's the aftermath of the firehouse or the hangover of adrenaline that makes my hands tremble when I swipe the screen. The message is from an unlisted number, but I know the area code—it's the one the State uses when they want to be sure you pay attention.

"Lake Kestrel. 10 minutes ago. Your arsonist."

I don't say her name. I just nudge Sophie awake, and she's up before her eyes are open. She reads the text, and the change in her is chemical—every line of her body sharpens, and the softness of the night before is replaced by a purpose so old it might as well be instinct.

We dress in silence. The kitchen is still thick with the smell of burnt toast and old coffee from the day before, but I force down a mug anyway. Sophie checks her phone, then a second phone, then her watch, ticking through her list with a soldier's precision. I sling the go-bag over my shoulder, and we're out the door before the sun even thinks about showing up.

The world outside is blue and dead. The streetlights are the only things alive, and even they look tired, throwing long, useless shadows on the frozen pavement. The drive out to the lake is a study in tension—every radio report, every flash of headlights in the rearview, every dip in the road a new opportunity for doubt to creep in.

Sophie is stone-faced, but I know what's running through her head.

I want to say something comforting, something that will make it all less real, but there's no script for this. So I keep my eyes on the road, and when she finally speaks, it's like a glass breaking in a church.

"He's not going to let us take him alive," she says.

"No," I agree, voice thick with the taste of last night's whiskey. "But he doesn't get to decide how this ends."

She turns, and the look she gives me is pure Sophie—no pity, no false hope, just the kind of honesty that cuts straight through.

"We finish it," she says. "No more loose ends."

We ride the rest of the way in silence, watching the world go gray and then white as the fog rolls over the lake. The turnoff is just a break in the tree line, barely marked, the gravel road pitted and soft from a week of thaw and freeze. My boots sink three inches in the mud when I get out, but Sophie's already ahead, scanning the perimeter with her hands buried deep in the pockets of her dad's old field jacket.

The lake is a crater of stillness, ringed by birch and pine, the water black as oil and just as slick. Mist crawls over the surface, and I can smell it—the echo of smoke, but not firehouse, not even cigarette. This is the mineral sting of an extinguished campfire, old and recent at once.

We move together, steps in sync, circling toward the public picnic area. No cars, but footprints—one set, maybe two, stamped deep and messy into the mix of leaves and frost. Sophie crouches, studies the prints, then gestures me over.

"Think he's hurt?" I ask.

She shrugs. "If he is, he's used to it by now."

We follow the tracks to the edge of the dock. There, at the end of the planks, is a fire pit—freshly scraped, but the ashes are cold. I nudge the charred remains with my boot and see the shape of a phone, half-melted but still recognizable. The battery's been removed, smashed to bits.

Sophie kneels beside the fire, sifts through the ashes, and pulls out a lump of metal wrapped in what looks like a torn piece of turnout coat. She unwraps it carefully, hands steady. It's a badge, blackened but not destroyed. She turns it over in her palm, thumb tracing the number.

"Dad's," she says, quietly.

There's a pause, just long enough for the sun to break through the fog in a single, accusing beam. She holds the badge tight, then stands and surveys the rest of the clearing.

I spot it first—a gash in the bark of an old birch, fresh enough to still bleed white. Letters, carved with the point of a knife or maybe a box cutter.

So finish it.

Three words, six inches high, at heart level.

Sophie runs her fingers over the letters, slow and deliberate. She doesn't flinch, not even when the edge of the bark snags her skin.

"He wants a showdown," I say, stating the obvious.

"No," she corrects me. "He wants an audience."

I watch her process it—the way her jaw tightens, the way she stands a little straighter, like she's already rehearsed this a thousand times in her head. She steps back, studies the carving as if it might change if she looks long enough.

"My father faced him here once," she says, voice flat. "The night after the Linder fire. They never wrote it up, but I found the report in his desk. Dad drove out and waited, just like this, because Rowe couldn't stand the idea of anyone else getting the last word."

"And?" I prompt.

She smiles, but it's not a happy smile. "Dad let him go. Thought he was doing the right thing. Second chance, all that."

I see the question in her eyes, the challenge. "You think I'd let him walk?"

She shakes her head, soft. "No. But I need you to let me go in first."

The words hit like a slap. Every cell in my body wants to say no, to wrap her up and drive her ten states away, but I know it's not my call. It never was.

"He'll try to get inside your head," I warn. "He knows every trick."

She shrugs. "So do I."

We stand there for a minute, wind whipping off the lake, the air full of invisible things.

She turns to me, and the moment crystallizes—everything we've built, everything we've lost, boiling down to whether or not I can trust her to face the monster alone.

"Promise me you'll stay close," she says.

I nod, throat tight. "Closer than your shadow."

That gets a real smile out of her, for half a second.

We work the area—mapping the best cover, noting every angle, every possible escape route. Sophie marks the tree line with bits of orange tape, the same kind Dad used for fire drills. We set up a simple code: one whistle means all clear, two means trouble, three means get out and don't look back.

By the time the sun is a hand's width above the trees, the plan is in place. We sit together on the old picnic bench, sipping burned coffee from a Thermos and watching the mist lift from the lake.

She checks her sidearm, cleans her glasses, and takes out Dad's badge, rubbing the soot off with her thumb. I watch her, memorizing every movement.

"Don't do anything stupid," I say, and it's half a joke, half prayer.

She glances at me, eyes bright but steeled. "I've got too much to live for."

We both know that's new.

She leans in, and for a second, I think she's going to kiss me, but she just presses her forehead to mine. We sit like that, breathing in the cold, for a long minute.

When she pulls away, she's already a different person—the hero I always suspected she could be, the avenger Rowe never saw coming.

She walks down to the clearing, not looking back.

I hang back, just like I promised. But I'm ready.

Because when the fire starts, I'll be there to put it out.

Or die trying.

4

Burnout

SOPHIE

THE CLEARING AT THE NORTH LAKE IS EXACTLY AS I remember it from childhood—minus the choking veil of smoke and the evidence of recent war. The picnic tables are gone, burned or hauled away, and the ground underfoot is a slush of scorched pine needles, wet moss, and gray ash. The air clings to my skin, acrid and electric, the way it does in the first minute after the sirens stop.

I walk in slow, not because I'm afraid, but because I want every step to register. The badge at my throat catches the low sun and throws a thin, wavering beam through the haze. I can feel the weight of it, the way my father's hands would press on my shoulders when he wanted me to stand straight, not slouch, not cower. My hands are still bandaged from the station fire—a patchwork of white that's already black at the fingertips. They tremble if I don't lock them in place, so I shove them in my pockets and focus on the sound of my own breathing.

He waits for me on the far side, near the ruined fire ring, half-leaning against a stone slab that's blackened and slick with old resin. He wears the same denim jacket as always, sleeves singed at the cuffs, and he's shaved his hair down to fuzz, probably in a motel bathroom with nothing but a disposable razor and a half-pint of courage. The wound on his cheek is healing, but the scab is fresh. He looks younger in the morning light, almost a kid. It makes me hate him more.

"Didn't think you'd come alone," Rowe says, not moving. "That's not your style."

I shrug, take two steps closer, and let the badge show. "You wanted the Grant family. Here I am."

He smiles, ugly. "You're not your dad."

"No," I say, "I'm not."

He pushes off the rock, walking the perimeter with that weird, off-balance stride—half swagger, half limp. He's circling, looking for tells. He'll find them. I'm made of nothing but weaknesses, but for now, I keep my chin up.

"Nice memorial," he says, gesturing at the rings of burnt stones. "Was this your idea, or his?"

"My dad didn't waste time on shrines. He put out fires. He didn't start them."

That gets a laugh. "You say that like it's a good thing. All he ever did was clean up other people's messes. Sweep it under the rug." He pauses, scowling. "You really think you're different?"

I don't answer. I'm not here to debate history.

He stops at the old log bench, sits, and stares at me over his knees. "I expected a gun, maybe a wire. Not a family heirloom. Is that supposed to scare me?"

"Should it?" I say.

He shrugs, picks at a splinter on the log. "Depends on whether you want to kill me or just watch me go up."

There's silence, thick enough to slice. I let it expand until I can almost taste it—ash, old wood, the ghost of every beer can and cigarette ever snuffed out here. My hands itch to reach for the badge, to rip it off and toss it in his face, but I don't. I hold the line.

"What's your plan, Caleb?" I ask. "You torch the station, you try to kill half the city's crew, and then you come here and wait for me? Why?"

He leans back, hands splayed on the log behind him. "You're asking the wrong question. You should be asking what the town would look like if nobody ever put out a fire. If we just let it burn. Think about it, Sophie. Clean start. All the rot, all the secrets, gone in a night."

"You want to be the town's personal arsonist," I say. "A civic cleanser."

He grins, teeth white and sharp. "That's the best pitch I've heard in years."

I force myself to move, slow and steady, circling the ring. The debris crunches under my boots—broken glass, twisted aluminum, the melted remains of a bottle. My shoes are slick with lake mud, and every step is a reminder that this is the only ground that matters.

"You know what my dad would say?" I ask, stopping across from him, the stone fire ring between us.

"He'd say 'Call it in,'" Rowe says. "And then he'd try to be the hero. That's how he got dead."

I swallow, the old wound flaring in my chest. "He'd say you're a coward. All your fires, all your big plans—they're just excuses to keep running."

His eyes go flat. "Running from what?"

"Yourself," I say, and for a second I see the truth land. He flinches, barely.

He stands up, shaking, and for a moment I'm sure he'll lunge at me. But instead, he just spits on the ground and laughs.

"I used to think the Grant family was untouchable," he says. "Turns out you're just as fucked as the rest of us."

He's close now, closer than I want, but I hold steady.

"You could have been a firefighter, you know," I say, softer. "You could have been anything."

He stares at me, face twisted. "And miss out on this?" He sweeps his arm, taking in the carnage, the lake, the world on the brink.

I let him savor the moment. Let him see how little it matters.

"I read your file," I say, watching him. "All of it. The psych evals, the court records. You wanted to be a hero, too. But when nobody let you in, you burned it all down."

He steps forward, but I don't back up. The heat from his body is real, and I smell the accelerant under his nails.

"Why are you here, Sophie?" he whispers, like a lover. "Why not let the marshals take me? Why not let the cops do their job?"

"Because I wanted to look you in the eye," I say, "and let you know you're not special. You're just the last fire that needs putting out."

The words hit. He reels back, snarling, and I see the knife before he even moves. I clock the motion—the way he reaches for his belt, the glint of steel. But I'm ready. I always have been.

I sidestep, feet planted, and shout, "Now!"

The woods behind him ignite with white light—LED flashbangs rigged from the back of Lucas's truck. The marshals' team pours out of the trees, guns up, voices booming. Lucas's face is raw and naked in the light, and I see the way his eyes lock on me, making sure I'm still standing.

Caleb tries to run, but he's blinded, stumbling over the stones. He swings the knife in a wild arc, catching nothing but air. Two marshals hit him from behind, pinning his arms, forcing him down. He howls, animal, biting at the hands that hold him.

I watch, hands clenched, as they slam him to the ground. The badge at my throat feels hot, like it's burning through my skin.

Lucas comes up behind me, breathless, sweat cutting tracks through the grime on his face.

"You okay?" he whispers, hand on my shoulder.

I nod, eyes never leaving Rowe as they cuff him. The fight goes out of him fast—he's limp in their hands, breathing hard, eyes locked on the badge.

"It's over," Lucas says, squeezing my arm.

I shake my head. "No. Not until he pays for all of it."

Lucas doesn't argue. He just stands with me, both of us watching as the past finally gets dragged out into the light.

The smoke in the clearing starts to thin. The sun is almost up.

Somewhere behind us, the world starts to breathe again.

But I don't move. Not until I'm sure the fire is really out.

For a second, everything is still. The marshals' team drags Caleb to his knees, one hand twisted behind his back, his face pressed to the ash-choked ground. Lucas is at my side, heart pounding so loud I can hear it over the crickets and the distant whine of a city coming awake. The badge is hot at my throat, every inch of my skin prickling with the nearness of the end.

Then Caleb laughs—a single, animal bark that splits the morning air. He arches his back, and I see the motion before I register what it means: his free hand is already inside his jacket, pulling something out, palming it against his chest.

"Down!" I shout, but it's too late.

The explosion is white, not orange—no fire, just light and sound so sharp it needles every nerve in my body. I drop, arms up, but the concussion hits from behind, lifting me, spinning me in a spray of gravel and shattered pine cones. I'm airborne, then sideways, then—

Then I hit water.

The shock of the lake is nuclear. My body seizes, lungs slamming shut, the cold so complete I think my heart has stopped. For a second, I just float, stunned, feeling the world narrow to blackness and bubbles. Then training kicks in, the way it always did with Dad: keep your head, keep moving, don't panic.

But I am panicking. My hands are numb and useless, my boots drag me down. The water is black, and my ears ring so loud I can't tell which way is up. Something brushes my face—a branch, a line of weed, a dead fish—and I almost scream, but the sound is only bubbles.

I flail, desperate, try to kick, but my legs are tangled in something heavy. My mind is a whiplash reel: if I die now, all of this was for nothing. If I die now, Rowe wins.

And then, from the murk, hands. Two of them, strong, wrenching me by the shoulders, dragging me back to the surface.

I break through, coughing lake water and sunlight and the kind of raw, ragged scream that strips your throat. I can't see, can't hear, but I feel Lucas's arms around me, the hoarse cursing in my ear, the frantic slap of his hand against my back.

"Breathe," he says, voice shredded. "Breathe, dammit."

I breathe. I spit out a mouthful of slime and blood. The world snaps into color—blue sky, gray water, the red stripes of a distant marshal running the shoreline. The cold is a pain that clarifies everything, and the only thing I want is to feel the ground again.

Lucas hauls us to the shallows, both of us clawing at the mud, knees buckling with every step. We collapse on the bank, water streaming off our clothes, the cold already replaced by the burning in my lungs. I roll over, arms wrapped around my ribs, and just shake. I don't want to cry, but I can't stop.

Lucas is beside me, both hands braced on the ground, blood and water pouring from a gash above his eyebrow. He looks at me like he can't believe I'm real.

"Jesus," he says, voice gone soft, "you're a goddamn lunatic."

I try to laugh, but it comes out a cough. "You jumped in after me."

He grins, mouth red, and for a second the world is just the two of us, breathing, alive, still here.

Down the bank, I hear a commotion. Two marshals are pulling Caleb up the shore, his jacket and face half-melted, hair singed off in patches. He's barely conscious, but his eyes are open, locked on me even as they drag him past.

Lucas helps me sit up, his hand finding mine. "You okay?"

I nod, shivering. My hands are bleeding, the bandages gone, fingers raw and blue.

Together, we watch as the marshals cuff Caleb's ruined wrists, his skin blistered, mouth clenched tight against the pain. For once, he doesn't fight.

I want to say something—something grand, or righteous, or final—but the words are stuck behind my teeth.

Instead, I just watch, breath coming fast, as the man who tried to burn us all is finally, completely, put out.

The air is full of sirens, now. The smell of burning replaced by the sharp, metallic stink of victory.

I pull Lucas closer, lean my head on his shoulder, and let myself shake until the cold and the fear drain away, leaving only the bright, clean ache of survival.

The ambulance is a tomb, lined with steel and white plastic, the gurney bolted down like a coffin in a box made for shipping. I'm wrapped in a silver shock blanket, hands clenched so tight my fingernails cut the edge of my palm. The world outside is a blur of blue and red, the lake's edge crawling with uniforms and paramedics and news crews setting up just far enough away to pretend they're not ghouls. I count the beats of the flashers as if they're seconds of my life, each pulse a tiny explosion in my chest.

Through the open canvas at the back, I watch them haul Caleb to his feet. He can barely stand, his wrists double-cuffed and his head lolling forward. The marshals don't bother with a jacket; the burns on his arms are already oozing, the skin sloughing off in sticky ribbons. He looks like a deflated scarecrow, eyes pinched shut, mouth a flat, stubborn line.

Lucas sits beside me on the bench, a trauma pad slapped haphazard across his bleeding eyebrow, his shirt plastered to his chest in the shape of my handprint. He's so close I can smell the lake on his skin, plus a new note of singed hair and antiseptic.

He doesn't say anything at first, just lets our knees touch and our breathing sync. Eventually, he finds my hand in the folds of the blanket and threads his fingers through mine. His grip is hot, reckless, alive.

"It's over," he says, voice barely above a whisper. There's a tremor in it—shock, or relief, or the slow settling of a year's worth of adrenaline.

I watch the last of the smoke drift up behind the tree line. The sun is fully up now, but the air feels colder, the world peeled raw. In the hush of the ambulance, the only sound is the distant hum of news helicopters and the wet click of my teeth when I finally open my mouth.

"It's just beginning," I say. My voice is a ghost. "Someone always rebuilds."

Lucas smiles, the line of it fierce and battered. He squeezes my hand and leans in, his forehead pressed to mine. For a long, unmeasured minute, we don't move. We just let the rest of the world keep spinning, content to stay still for the first time in months.

The EMT checks my vitals, takes my temperature, snaps a light in my eyes. He tells me I'm lucky, that most people don't survive a blast like that, or a plunge into a lake in early spring. I don't correct him; luck has nothing to do with it. It's all stubbornness, all refusal, all the stupid, unbreakable will to make it one more day.

They don't make us wait at the hospital. We're VIPs, apparently, and besides, nobody wants the press getting a look at the walking wounded before we're cleaned up. They run us through triage, bandage my hands again, dab ointment on Lucas's face and give him a tetanus shot he pretends not to flinch at. They offer me a change of clothes, but the idea of wearing anything that isn't mine makes my skin crawl.

I take the hospital scrubs anyway, rolling the waistband until it doesn't swallow my hips. Lucas is right behind me, his own scrub pants an inch too short, a badge of shame he wears with a lopsided pride.

We're supposed to wait for the state investigator, but the urge to move—to breathe, to do something that isn't sitting under fluorescent lights—is too strong.

I grab his hand and pull him down the hallway, past the line of nurses at the station and into a service corridor marked "Staff Only." It's quiet back here, except for the hum of vending machines and the drone of a distant generator.

Lucas follows, no questions. He doesn't need to ask. We're running on the same charge, the same need to prove we're still here, still alive, still tethered to something real.

I find the first unlocked door—a supply closet—and drag him inside, slamming it shut behind us. The light is harsh, the air thick with the scent of bleach and latex gloves, but I don't care.

I reach for him, and he's already there, kissing me with a force that's all teeth and gratitude and the animal urgency of the truly desperate. His hands are everywhere at once, anchoring me, mapping the new landscape of scars and bruises. He pushes me back against the shelving, and the metal bites into my spine, sharp and welcome.

"You sure?" he asks, voice rough, eyes so blue it makes me dizzy.

"Shut up," I say, and pull his mouth to mine.

It's not gentle. It's not slow. We don't have time for patience or pretense or even the illusion of control. Our bodies collide, every movement a small violence, a test of what hurts and what still works. I hook my fingers in the elastic of his pants and drag them down, and he does the same to mine, fumbling the drawstring with hands that shake as much as my own.

He lifts me, easy as ever, and I wrap my legs around his waist, the cold edge of a shelf pressing against the backs of my thighs. He kisses down my neck, finds the spot below my ear that makes me gasp, then bites down, not hard enough to break skin but enough to leave a mark.

I want to tell him to slow down, but I can't. I want to memorize this, every second, but my brain is on fire, all the old controls blown out by the blast and the near-drowning and the months of wanting and not having. I grind against him, desperate, and he groans, low and guttural, his hands braced on my hips.

When he's inside me, it's a relief and a shock, the kind of pain that proves you're still alive. We move together, fast and brutal, the sound of our bodies echoing off the shelves and through the thin walls.

I come first, the release so sudden and fierce it almost knocks me out. Lucas isn't far behind, burying his face in my shoulder, his whole body shuddering with it.

For a moment, we just hang there, tangled and sweating, the

world reduced to the pulse in my throat and the taste of salt on his skin.

When the adrenaline finally drains, he lowers me to the floor, careful, his hands gentle now. I stand, adjust the scrubs, wipe the tears I didn't realize were leaking down my face.

He smooths my hair back, kisses my forehead, and just holds me. Neither of us speaks. There's nothing to say that matters as much as this.

Eventually, we stumble out of the closet, bodies wrecked but intact, and limp back to the waiting area. The news is already playing on the TV—a shot of the lake, the flashing lights, the ruins of what used to be the safe place in my head. The anchor calls us "heroes," but all I see is the way the sunlight breaks through the smoke, and the way Lucas's hand stays anchored to mine, as if he's afraid of letting go.

I lean into him, let myself be small for the first time in years. He holds me, and I believe, finally, that it's safe to let him.

There's always another fire. There's always a new beginning, too.

And for the first time, I want it.

We walk out of the hospital together, blinking into the morning, the world bright and unburned. His hand in mine, my badge shining at my throat, and the certainty that we can face whatever comes next.

Together, we set our own terms for survival.

And this time, no one gets to burn us out.

5

Aftermath

SOPHIE

The main street of Willow Creek is a wound that keeps reopening, no matter how many times the city workers come by with shovels and asphalt, or how many hand-lettered "We Stand Together" banners the Chamber of Commerce zip-ties to the lamp posts. This morning, the air is so cold it pinches the inside of my nose, and even though the sky is blue and raw above the ruined water tower, I can't shake the sense that someone is about to pull a gun.

But what they pull, mostly, is me.

I make it six feet from the corner of Main and First before the first local news van blocks my path, the painted logos bright as bruises against the slush-stained curb. The reporter is a woman I recognize from high school, now ten years and one on-camera nose job into her career. She shoves a mic at my chest and asks the same question I've heard twelve times in the past four hours: "What does it feel like to be called a hero?"

I want to say it feels like a second-degree burn—raw, tight, a little too pink at the edges—but I keep the script. "I'm just glad no one else got hurt. We were lucky."

Behind her, the camera guy gives me a sheepish wave and mouths, "Sorry," before zooming in. The mic stays there, planted and expectant, and I realize I haven't stopped moving my left hand in my pocket. I'm rubbing the surface of my father's badge so hard that the skin of my thumb is flaking.

"How are you holding up, Sophie?" the reporter asks, but her eyes are on the corner where the last fire took the bakery, and behind her, a parade of neighbors and survivors drifts closer, the way you might edge toward a car crash just to see who made it out.

"I'm fine," I say, and when she asks again, I try to put a little smile on it. "Really, I'm okay."

It goes on like that for a block and a half: reporters passing me down the line like a relay baton, every third person from the elementary school asking for a photo, a handshake, a quote for the town paper. They all want a soundbite. They want catharsis, or closure, or something they can post on Facebook and call it resilience. What they get is me—wrung out, hands bandaged, face tight from the cut above my eye that the hospital only half glued shut.

When I finally reach the intersection by the library, a group of kids with hand-painted signs clumps around my legs, chanting "Go Grant!" and "Our Hero!" in a rhythm that gets stuck in my teeth. One of them, a girl with thick glasses and a gap in her front teeth, holds out a fistful of construction-paper hearts. I take one, thank her, and then, because I can't help myself, kneel and tell her, "You don't need to be brave all the time, okay? It's enough to just be kind."

She blinks at me, then nods, as if this is both the most and least surprising thing an adult has ever said to her.

By the time I break free, my head aches from the noise, and I smell like a combination of road salt and the kind of cheap hair-spray that news anchors order in bulk.

I duck behind the side entrance of the library, cut through the narrow lot, and keep my hand wrapped around the badge, squeezing it until I can almost feel my father's hand closing over mine. The wind stings my face, and I realize that all the adrenaline in my system has burned off, leaving nothing but a thin crust of exhaustion and the taste of the last question I couldn't answer.

What now?

My aunt's house looks the same from the outside as it always has—white aluminum siding, cracked green shutters, one gutter hanging on by a single rusty bracket—but up close, there are new details. The front window has been replaced, the frame still raw and smelling like sap. There's a second deadbolt, recently installed, and a doorbell camera that blinks a blue dot every time someone walks up the path.

Inside, it's a museum of controlled chaos. The entryway is cluttered with half-emptied boxes, my boots lined up by the mat with military precision. The air is thick with the scent of cut pine, old smoke, and a faint undertone of antiseptic from the first aid station I set up on the dining room table. I keep the badge in my pocket even though I should hang it up—old habit, or maybe superstition.

I set my bag down and make a beeline for the kitchen, only to find that the coffee pot is empty, and there's a note in Lucas's handwriting taped to the fridge: "Back at 3, will bring food, don't shoot me." The time on the stove says 2:57.

On the table, next to a haphazard stack of manila folders and a legal pad covered in my own blocky handwriting, is an unopened envelope with the state seal. I stare at it like it might explode, then set the badge down and flip it open.

Inside is a letter, printed on cheap cardstock, with language so formal it might as well be Latin. I scan the first paragraph, skip the boilerplate, and land on the only part that matters:

"We are pleased to offer you the role of Regional Director, Community Fire Response and Prevention, effective immediately."

I read it twice, then fold it and slide it under the legal pad. My hands are shaking.

Lucas comes in exactly on time, as always, carrying a white plastic bag that smells like fried chicken and chili cheese fries. His face is bandaged at the eyebrow, but the cut is healing, the swelling mostly gone. He sets the bag down, takes one look at my face, and freezes.

"Which one was it?" he asks. "Reporter or town council?"

I shake my head, force a smile. "Both, and then some."

He grunts, tears open the bag, and sets a Styrofoam clamshell in front of me. "Eat. You look like a corpse."

I pick at a fry, let the salt burn the inside of my mouth, and try not to look at the envelope under the legal pad. Lucas stands on the other side of the table, arms crossed, scanning the room like he's assessing a breach.

"You want to talk about it, or just sit here until we both pretend it didn't happen?" he asks, not unkindly.

I shake my head, then nod, then laugh at myself. "I'm tired," I say. "I know that's not a real answer, but it's the best I've got."

He sits, leans back in the chair until it creaks. "You did good, Sophie."

I don't correct him.

"Did you ever think it would end?" I ask, voice soft.

He looks away, jaw flexing. "No. I thought we'd get Rowe, maybe. But the rest—"

He gestures at the files, the news vans, the world outside.

"It's never over, is it?" I ask.

He shrugs, then leans in, voice low. "You want it to be?"

I look at him, at the faint new lines at the corners of his eyes, the set of his mouth, the way his fingers drum on the table in perfect, silent sync with the heartbeat in my wrist.

"I got a letter," I say, pushing the envelope toward him.

He reads it, lips moving just enough to trace the words. When he finishes, he sets it down and meets my gaze.

"You want the job?"

I don't answer. Instead, I reach for the badge, close my hand around it, and let the silence build. The kitchen fills with the sound of the radiator clanking and the wind rattling the loose window pane.

Lucas doesn't push. He just waits, the way he always does, as if patience could fix a lifetime of bad timing.

"I don't know what I want," I say, finally. "But I think I need to find out."

He nods. "You don't have to decide tonight."

I try to smile, but it feels strange on my face. "What about you?" I ask, changing the subject. "You going to stay on with the county?"

He laughs, a rough, real sound. "They want me to train the next batch of arson investigators. Pay's shit, but the hours are worse."

"Perfect," I say, deadpan.

He grins, then stands and circles the table until he's close enough that I can smell the grease on his jacket and the faint, coppery trace of bandages. He kneels beside my chair, rests his hands on my knees, and looks up at me with the same intensity he used to reserve for bomb sites.

"You don't have to do this alone," he says.

I swallow, try not to let the words hit too deep. "I'm not very good at together."

He brushes his thumb across my kneecap, slow and deliberate. "Neither am I."

For a long minute, we just sit there, the only light in the kitchen coming from the overhead bulb that flickers every time the furnace cycles. Outside, a squad car glides past, slow and predatory, and I realize I don't even care if they're watching.

I lean forward, rest my forehead against his, and close my eyes.

"What if we just stopped for a minute?" I whisper.

He lets out a breath I didn't know he was holding. "We can try."

We eat the rest of the fries in silence, and when the food is gone, I gather up the files and sweep them into a single, uneven stack. Lucas helps, not saying anything, but his hand lingers over mine each time we pass a page, a pen, or a scrap of notepaper.

Eventually, I walk him to the door, and he pauses on the threshold, eyes searching mine for something I can't name.

"You'll call if you need me?" he says.

I nod. "Always."

He opens the door, but before he steps out, he turns and presses his mouth to mine, slow and sure, as if he's mapping out a future one cell at a time.

When he's gone, I lock the door, slide the chain, and watch him walk down the path. The blue of the security camera blinks once, then goes dark.

I stand there, fingers curled around the badge, and let myself feel the exhaustion, the relief, and the low, constant thrum of something like hope.

Outside, the world is still burning. But for now, I can breathe.

I flip the badge in my palm, once, twice, then set it on the windowsill where the morning light will hit it first.

Tomorrow, there will be more questions. More fires, maybe.

But tonight, I just want to rest.

And maybe, just maybe, I will.

We fall into a routine, the kind that forms out of necessity more than intention: coffee at 7, calls from the state investigator at 8, interviews with a parade of grief counselors and mid-level bureaucrats until noon. The afternoons are worse, full of errands that don't matter and paperwork that does. Evenings, though—those are ours.

Tonight, Lucas is already at my kitchen table when I get home, his coat draped over the back of the chair, the scar above his eyebrow red in the harsh light. He's poking through the stack of case files and clippings I left out, one hand splayed across the margin of a printout, the other drumming on the Formica.

"You ever think about just torching all of it?" he asks as I walk in, toeing off my boots.

I dump my bag in the hall and grab a glass from the cupboard. "We've had enough fires for a while."

He gives me a crooked smile, then pushes the files aside to reveal a sheaf of stapled pages, crisp and official: the advocacy program proposal. The letterhead is more impressive than the content.

I sit across from him, the table between us a neutral zone. I read the first page, then the second, and by the third I can feel my heart doing that weird, arrhythmic thump it only does when something is about to go sideways.

"They want me to chair the whole thing," I say, scanning for the catch.

Lucas leans back, chair rocking dangerously. "They want you to save them from themselves. Classic."

I flip to the last page. "There's a stipend," I mutter. "Not much, but..."

He shrugs. "Hero work doesn't pay."

We sit there, the silence more companionable than awkward. The hum of the fridge, the rattle of the radiator, the distant whine of a siren threading down Main. I glance at the badge on the windowsill; it winks at me, a reminder and a challenge.

"You're going to take it, aren't you?" Lucas asks.

I nod, once. "I think I have to."

He's quiet, but I can feel the tension. He's never been the jealous type, but this is different—it's not about me, or even the town, but about the thing inside both of us that can't let go.

"You don't have to keep burning yourself up for these people," he says, voice low. "You can just...live."

I shake my head. "That's not how it works. Not for me."

He runs his hand through his hair, frustration in every movement. "You're allowed to stop fighting, Soph."

I don't answer. Instead, I pull the proposal closer, mark a couple of notes in the margin, and try to act like I can already see a future where this fixes anything.

After a while, he stands, stretches, and walks over to the sink. He fills the kettle, sets it on the burner, and stands there with his back to me, the muscles in his shoulders tense and precise.

"There's something else," he says, finally.

I brace for it. "What?"

He turns, leans against the counter, arms folded. "They offered me a promotion. Permanent assignment, state level. I'd have to move to the capital. Next week."

I freeze, the coffee cup halfway to my mouth.

He watches me, eyes unreadable. "I haven't answered yet."

The room feels smaller, the air pulled tight around us. I set the cup down, hands steady, and focus on the patterns in the laminate.

"Do you want to go?" I ask, not sure I want the answer.

He shrugs, looks away. "It's better work. More money. Less..." He waves his hand at the window, at the whole town. "Less ghosts."

I think about what it would be like, waking up in a place where nobody knows my name, where the only history that matters is the one I choose to make. I try to picture it, but it's like staring at a blank page—no color, no lines, just space.

"I don't want you to go," I say, and the words crack on the way out.

He crosses the room in three steps, stops just short of touching me. His hands clench, then unclench, as if he's holding back something enormous.

"Then give me a reason to stay," he says, soft but desperate.

I look up, meet his gaze, and for the first time since the fire, I let the fear show. The fear of being left, of being too much, of never learning how to need something without destroying it.

"I'm not good at this," I say.

He smiles, sad and true. "Neither am I."

We stand there, the kitchen silent except for the soft click of the kettle as it starts to boil. The proposal sits between us, the edges curling from the heat of the overhead light. I want to reach for him, but I'm afraid if I do, the moment will break.

So we just stand, inches apart, caught between the thing that almost killed us and the thing that might save us.

The kettle whistles, sharp and bright.

I pour the coffee, hands shaking, and set a mug in front of him.

He takes it, wraps his hands around the cup, and lets the steam fog up his glasses.

We drink in silence, the kind that says everything.

Somewhere, just past the horizon, something is waiting for us.

But for now, we stay exactly where we are, held together by the simple act of not letting go.

I don't know who moves first, but it feels like the choice is made for us by every second we've spent pretending there was a safe way to want each other.

He reaches for the coffee, but I get there first, sliding the mug out of his hand and pinning his wrist to the table. For a split second, neither of us breathes.

Then I haul him forward by the collar, hard enough to pop the top button, and crash my mouth against his. He's still holding the cup, and the hot liquid splashes across my arm, but neither of us lets go.

We stumble backward, hips banging the table, then the counter. My feet lose contact with the floor as he lifts me, and I lock my legs around his waist. His hands grip my thighs, fingers digging through the old sweatpants I never bothered to change out of, and the next thing I know I'm sitting on the kitchen counter, the proposal sheets fanned out beneath me like a bad omen.

He buries his hands in my hair and kisses me like he's starving. The need is so sharp it's almost angry.

"Fuck," he says, voice gone thick, and he leans his forehead against mine, panting. "You don't have to—"

"I want to," I say, and mean it.

He doesn't argue.

I dig my hands under his shirt, find the line of his back, and rake my nails down hard enough to make him gasp. He shoves the mug aside, not caring when it rolls and shatters against the tile.

He tugs my waistband down, rough and efficient, and I kick the rest of the sweats off. The edge of the counter bites into my thighs, and I like it; I want to feel every part of this, every ache and scrape and bruise.

He goes for my shirt, but I pull it over my head first, bandages and all. His eyes are wild, full of the same panic and hunger I feel. He peels the medical tape from my hands, slow and careful, then kisses every raw patch of skin he finds.

"You're not leaving me again," I growl into his mouth, hands twisted in his hair. "I won't let you."

He smiles, teeth flashing, and bites my jaw just hard enough to leave a mark. "Then keep me here."

He unzips his jeans, fumbles with the fly, and I help, desperate, greedy, clumsy with need.

There's no finesse, no choreography. Just bodies crashing together, moving like we're trying to erase the memory of every bad thing that came before. The first thrust is so hard it knocks a spoon off the counter. The next one nearly topples us both to the floor, and we're laughing and groaning and cursing in the same breath.

I bite his neck, leave a bright red crescent. He shoves me flat on the counter, hair spilling over my eyes, and I pull him down to me, arms and legs wrapped tight.

When he slides inside, it hurts, but the pain is a relief—a proof that I'm still here, that there's something in this world that can fill the hollow.

He moves fast, desperate, and I match him, meeting every thrust. The world narrows to sweat and breath and the slick sound of skin on skin. The proposal pages crumple under my back, but I don't give a fuck. Let them see what real fire looks like.

He braces his hands on either side of me, gaze locked on my face. There's something close to wonder there, like he's amazed we made it this far without combusting.

We come together, our bodies shuddering; he holds me tight, biting down on my shoulder, and for a moment, everything is white-hot—a flashbulb behind the eyes—the kind of explosion you can only survive if you're willing to burn with it.

We collapse together, bodies tangled, sticky with sweat and each other. His chest heaves against mine, and I feel his heart hammering, wild and alive.

For a long time, we don't move.

Eventually, he pulls me upright, hands gentle now, and tucks my hair behind my ears. His thumb traces the scar on my collarbone, the one Rowe left me as a parting gift.

"You know you're a fucking maniac," he says, voice soft.

I grin. "You love that about me."

He kisses the top of my head, then my mouth, then the hollow just below my ear. "You're not wrong."

We sit on the counter, arms wrapped around each other, and let the world go quiet. The kitchen smells like sex and cold coffee and the lingering sweetness of fried chicken.

He leans back, studies my face. "So what do we do now?"

I exhale, let the question settle.

"Finish the work," I say. "Fix the town. Try not to kill each other."

He nods, lips curving in that wry, half-smile that used to drive me nuts.

"I'm in," he says.

We sit there, naked except for the dusting of ash and the bandages on my hands, and look out at the street. There's a hush to the evening now, the kind that feels earned.

"I don't want you to go," I say, softer this time.

He looks at me, really looks, and I know he's not going anywhere.

"Then you're stuck with me," he says.

I pull him close, and for the first time in a long time, I let myself believe it.

Tomorrow, the calls will start again. The news vans will come back. There will be more questions, more messes to clean up.

But tonight, we have this.

We have us.

And for once, it's enough.

6

Charred Edges

SOPHIE

The walls in Dr. Riley's office are painted that precise shade of eggshell you only see in therapist's waiting rooms and funeral parlors. The lights are low, not in the moody "bar at last call" way, but in the way that makes it hard to tell if it's morning or the end of the world. There's a couch, of course, upholstered in gray fabric that feels like the underbelly of a new puppy, and two chairs angled just so, with a little wooden table between them. Every sharp edge has been blunted. The whole place is a habitat for people who don't trust their own skin.

I'm already sweating through my t-shirt. The pit stains are a Rorschach for "failure to cope." I sit with my hands wedged between my knees, gripping so hard my fingers go bloodless. Dr. Riley, who is all cardigans and gentle vowels, has been talking for three minutes and thirty-seven seconds about "expectations" and "process" and "the safety of this space," and every syllable is a challenge not to bolt for the door.

"So, Sophie, what brings you here today?" she says, and I nearly laugh because it's the most cliche opener in the world.

I try to answer, but the air gets stuck in my chest. All I can manage is, "I don't know where to start."

She smiles, the corners of her mouth lifting just enough to read as human. "That's perfectly normal. Sometimes the hardest part is just showing up."

I want to argue, to point out that the hardest part was all the years of not showing up, of running headfirst into fire and thinking that was the same as therapy. But I keep my mouth shut, afraid the words will turn into a scream if I let them loose.

We sit like that for a minute, the clock ticking somewhere behind her. She lets the silence work, which is probably a technique she learned in school, but I'm already counting down until I break.

"I have nightmares," I say finally, eyes fixed on the seam of my jeans. "And I keep having these moments where I... snap awake and I don't know where I am. Even if I'm at home."

Dr. Riley nods, as if this is a diagnosis and not the world's worst horoscope.

"What are the nightmares about?" she asks.

I consider lying, or at least minimizing, but the energy it would take to construct a believable alternate trauma is more than I can muster.

"Fire," I say. "And sirens. Sometimes it's the station burning down, sometimes it's my old house. Sometimes it's just... smoke. I can't breathe."

Dr. Riley writes something in a little notebook, then sets the pen aside. "When did the nightmares start?"

I think about it. The honest answer is "forever," but she wants a date, a trigger, a neat little timeline.

"The night the water tower went up," I say. "But it was happening before that. I just didn't notice."

She waits, her hands folded in her lap, letting me decide how much to share.

I draw a breath, shallow and ragged. "I got used to waking up at the sound of alarms. For a while, I thought that made me prepared. But after the last fire, I started waking up even if there was nothing. Sometimes I wake up and I'm already outside, or I'm halfway down the block, and I don't remember how I got there."

She scribbles again, but doesn't interrupt.

"I started carrying a flashlight, like an old man," I say, forcing a laugh. "I check every room. I unplug everything before I sleep. I keep an extinguisher under the bed, just in case."

"Have you ever felt like you were in danger, even if you knew logically you were safe?" Dr. Riley asks, gentle.

I nod, teeth clenched.

"That's very common with trauma. Hypervigilance, they call it. Sometimes, the mind is trying to protect us, even when there's nothing left to protect against."

I hate the word trauma. It feels like a diagnosis for weak people, people who don't know how to get over it. But I can't deny the tremor in my hands or the way my voice keeps jumping octaves. I can't deny the feeling that every time I close my eyes, I'm back in the inferno.

She asks about my childhood next, and I stiffen so hard I nearly tip the chair. She doesn't push, just sits in the quiet, nodding, letting me pick up the thread if I want to.

"I used to think that if I could predict the next fire, I could stop it," I say, softer now. "I kept lists, made maps, even called in fake alarms sometimes just to see if anyone would show up."

She smiles again, sympathetic. "And did it help? Being prepared?"

"Sometimes," I say. "But when it mattered most, it didn't."

I want to stop there. I want to pack up the pain and leave it on the neat little end table with the lavender-scented candle and the dish of therapy pebbles. But there's a knock at the door, a soft triple tap, and Dr. Riley stands.

"Just a moment," she says, and I brace for some kind of intervention, maybe a wellness check. But when she opens the door, Lucas is there, standing awkwardly in the hall, holding a cup of gas station coffee and wearing a shirt with a wrinkled collar.

He looks at me, then at Dr. Riley, then back at me. "Sorry," he says. "I was just—I thought you might want backup."

Dr. Riley glances at me, eyebrows raised. "Would you like him to join us?"

I nod, once. "Yeah. Please."

He takes the chair to my left, far enough away not to crowd but close enough that I can smell his aftershave, the kind he only wears for court or funerals. He doesn't speak. He just looks at me, steady and sure, and I feel something in my chest unclench.

Dr. Riley resumes her seat. "Sometimes it helps to have a familiar face," she says, and I almost smile.

I expect Lucas to try to fix things, to offer a joke or some dumb anecdote about his own therapy experience, which, for the record, was mostly court-mandated and a total joke. But he just sits, elbows on his knees, hands folded in front of him, the way he does when he's waiting for a verdict.

Dr. Riley asks about the last fire—the night of the station. I tell her, in halting sentences, about the alarms and the smoke and the way the world went white, about pulling Ellis out of the bay and thinking he was already dead, about the moment I realized there was no going back.

I start to lose the thread halfway through, my throat closing up. Lucas reaches over, careful, and slides his hand into mine. He doesn't squeeze, just lets his fingers wrap around mine, solid and warm.

Dr. Riley waits until I catch my breath. "Sophie, you're doing incredibly well. It's very brave to confront this head-on."

I want to argue, to say that this isn't brave, that it's just another kind of failure. But Lucas squeezes my hand, just a little, and I find the words again.

"I don't want to be afraid forever," I say, voice barely above a whisper.

"You won't be," Dr. Riley says, gentle and certain.

We sit like that for a while, the three of us in the eggshell cocoon, the only sound the clock behind her and the soft rhythm of Lucas's breathing. I don't cry, not exactly, but something in me leaks out, slow and invisible.

By the end of the hour, I'm exhausted. The air in the room feels less heavy, like someone finally cracked a window. I let go of Lucas's hand and wipe my palm on my jeans, embarrassed, but he just stands and offers me the coffee.

"It's cold," he says, "but it's got three sugars, just how you like it."

I take it, and for the first time in weeks, I almost feel normal.

Dr. Riley sees us out, her voice soft and unhurried. "You did important work today," she says.

Lucas winks at me as we hit the parking lot. "Told you," he says. "You're fireproof."

I snort, but the sound is real. "You're such a dork," I say, and it feels good.

We drive home in silence, the road shining wet in the new morning sun.

The nightmares aren't gone, but they don't feel quite as big now.

And maybe, just maybe, I don't have to fight them alone.

The day the memo shows up, I'm halfway through a cold bagel and the fifth attempt at a grant proposal. I don't notice the envelope at first, because I never check my physical inbox anymore; it's a relic from when people cared about stationary, or about anything in a form that couldn't be deleted with a keystroke.

But there it is, wedged between an overdue water bill and a coupon for a car wash I'll never use. The envelope is county-issue, off-white and cheap, but what makes me pause is the coffee stain in the corner. I pick it up, sniff—hazelnut, the fake kind. The kind Bennett used to drink.

I freeze.

I glance around, as if someone might be watching me open it, but the office is empty except for the hum of the fluorescent light and the ancient printer doing its best impression of a dying cat.

Inside: a single sheet, heavy stock, folded once, printed in 12-point font. I flatten it on the desk, heart already picking up speed.

The header is blank. No letterhead, no date, just a list:

- Payments to contractors routed via offshore intermediaries

- Transfer of evidence from arson sites to off-site storage, unlogged

- "Incentive" structure for whistleblowers and non-disclosure

- Law enforcement collusion: see attached witness statements

There's no attached witness statement. There's not even an "attached." Just the facts, bare and ugly, with a line at the bottom that makes my skin go cold:

Bennett, Troy J.

No title. No signature, just the name, as if that's all it needs.

The coffee has bled through the last line, warping the paper and turning the B into a brown smudge.

I read it three times. My mouth goes dry. For a second I think about shredding it, then about photographing it and emailing it to every reporter in the state, but all I do is stare at the name.

It's not a confession. It's a threat, or a warning, or both.

I look at the badge on my desk, the one I started keeping there after the last fire. I want to call Lucas, or Dr. Riley, or literally anyone, but my hands won't stop shaking.

I fold the memo, slip it back in the envelope, and put it in the bottom drawer under an old phone charger and a pack of gum.

The rest of the day is a loop of distraction—phone calls I don't remember making, paperwork I can't focus on, a long meeting with city hall where I nod and smile and take fake notes until my pen runs out of ink.

All the while, the memo sits in my mind like a ticking grenade.

At home that night, I pace the living room, the letter in my back pocket. I haven't told Lucas yet. He's on the couch, feet up, watching a game show with the sound off. He's pretending to be relaxed, but I can tell from the way he keeps checking the street outside that he's ready to run or fight or both.

He waits for me to say something. I want to, but the words keep getting jammed in my throat.

Finally, I just hand him the memo.

He reads it in silence, lips tightening as he gets to the bottom. He doesn't look up for a long time.

"Are you sure it's real?" he says.

"No," I answer. "But I know it's meant for me."

He nods, slow. "You want to go public?"

I don't answer, not right away. Instead I start pacing again, hands in my hair, the world narrowing down to the soft drag of my socks on the floor and the thump of my heart.

"If I testify," I say, "I become a target again."

He says nothing, just watches me pace.

"But if I don't," I continue, "then everything my father died for stays buried."

Lucas rises, comes to stand in front of me, blocking my path. He's calm, but his hands are shaking, too.

"I'll back you," he says. "Whatever you decide. But you need to know what it might cost."

I search his face for a sign that he wants me to stay quiet, to bury it, to run. But all I see is the old stubbornness, the one that used to annoy me, now turned to something like hope.

"I'm tired of hiding," I say, and my voice is so raw I barely recognize it.

Lucas lets out a long breath. "Then let's do it. Together."

I nod, jaw tight, tears prickling at the corners of my eyes. I don't let them fall.

He pulls me into a hug, tight enough to crack ribs, and for a second I feel like I'm sixteen again, hiding in the back of the station, the world outside burning down but safe for just this moment.

We stay like that until the panic eases.

That night, I draft the email. I put all the evidence I have into a single file, label it with my name and badge number, and send it to the state investigator, the AG's office, and every major paper I can think of.

I hit send before I can change my mind.

Then I turn off my phone, crawl into bed next to Lucas, and let myself fall asleep without checking the locks three times.

In the morning, everything will be different.

But for now, I let myself rest.

The house is burning down and I'm inside it, again.

I can smell the carpet melting, the plastic of the window blinds curling into black ribbons. The air is thick with that blue-white smoke you only see in chemical fires, the kind that fills your lungs like expanding foam. Every doorknob I touch is red hot, every window sealed shut by a wall of fire outside. There's a siren in the distance—sometimes my dad's, sometimes the one from the night of the water tower—but mostly it's just the sound of my own breath, high and ragged, echoing off the drywall.

I run from room to room, calling for someone—my father, Lucas, sometimes a child version of myself. The furniture rearranges itself between blinks; sometimes the kitchen is first, sometimes the bathroom. There's always a clock on the wall, its hands spinning so fast they become a blur, and I know, in the deep, lizard part of my brain, that if it hits midnight, I'll die.

Every time, I wake up just before it does.

Tonight, I don't make it.

I get to the stairs, trip on the loose board (always the same one), and tumble down, hitting each riser with a slap that jolts the air from my chest. At the bottom, I look up, and the ceiling is falling in, the old beams spiderwebbed with cracks, flames racing along them like fuse lines.

The last thing I see is the front door, wide open, light flooding through. I crawl toward it, fingers digging into the burning carpet, and for a second I think I'll make it.

But I don't.

The beams come down with a thunderclap. Everything goes white.

I wake up screaming, legs kicking, the sheets twisted around me like a straitjacket. The world snaps from fire to darkness, and for a second I don't know where I am. There's a shadow at the edge of the bed, moving fast, and I flinch away, thinking the nightmare followed me out.

Then Lucas is there, hands on my shoulders, voice low and steady. "Hey. Hey, it's okay. You're here, Soph. You're safe."

I can't stop shaking. I'm soaked in sweat, hair plastered to my forehead, the taste of smoke still raw at the back of my throat. My mouth works, trying to form words, but all that comes out is a noise somewhere between a sob and a gasp.

Lucas wraps his arms around me, pulling me against his chest. His heartbeat is a metronome, slow and unhurried, and I latch onto it like a lifeline.

"It was the house," I manage, voice shredded. "It was burning and I— I couldn't get out."

He strokes my hair, thumb rubbing slow circles behind my ear. "You did. You're here, remember? You made it."

I bury my face in his shirt. I want to be stoic, to swallow the panic and put it back in its box, but for the first time in years I just let it happen. The tears come hot and silent, soaking through cotton and skin. Lucas doesn't try to shush me, doesn't do anything but hold on and ride it out with me.

My hands are shaking so badly I have to clutch at his bicep to steady myself. He murmurs nonsense words—"You're okay, I got you, I'm not going anywhere"—until the tremors start to ease.

It feels endless, but it's only a few minutes before the sobs taper off, replaced by that hollow, wrung-out feeling you get after a really good cry. My chest hurts. My throat is raw.

He kisses the top of my head, lips lingering like he's trying to memorize the taste of my hair. "You want to talk about it?" he asks, voice barely more than a whisper.

I shake my head. "Not yet."

He nods, like that's all the answer he needs.

For a long time, we just sit there. The only light in the room is from the street lamp outside, painting soft stripes across the ceiling. His shirt is soaked where I cried, but he doesn't care. He just rocks us both, slow and gentle.

When I can finally breathe again, I look up. His face is lined with worry, but also something else—pride, maybe, or relief.

"I'm sorry," I say, and the words sting more than I expect.

He brushes a strand of hair off my face, gentle. "You don't have to be."

I believe him, for once. I let myself believe it.

He pulls back just far enough to cup my face in his hands, thumbs tracing the wet tracks on my cheeks. He kisses my eyelids, one after the other, then down to the corner of my mouth. Each touch is soft, almost reverent.

"I love you," he says. "Even when you're a mess."

I laugh, but it breaks on the way out. "Especially then?"

"Especially then," he says, and I know he means it.

He's still holding my face when he kisses me for real—slow, deliberate, like he's got all the time in the world. His hands are warm on my skin, steady and sure. I open my mouth for him, let him in, and the panic that's been coiled in my stomach for weeks starts to unwind.

I pull him closer, wrapping my arms around his neck. He shifts, easing me onto my back, then slides next to me so we're face to face on the pillow. I study his eyes, the little flecks of gold at the edges, the way they crinkle when he smiles.

He runs his hand down my arm, finds my hand, laces our fingers together. My pulse is still frantic, but it's not fear anymore. It's need.

He must see something in my face, because his eyes go soft. "You okay?" he asks.

I nod. "Yeah. I just... I need—" I stop, not sure how to say it.

He understands anyway. "You need me."

"Yeah," I say, voice thin, but true.

He presses his forehead to mine, breath warm on my cheek. "You got me."

His hands are on me, everywhere at once—my hair, my neck, the curve of my hip. He moves slowly, carefully, checking in with every touch, like he's afraid I'll break. I don't want careful. I want to feel something that isn't fear.

I tug at his shirt, pulling it over his head. He helps, then returns the favor, unbuttoning the old fire department tee I stole from him and tossing it on the floor. He kisses every inch of exposed skin—my collarbone, the scar on my shoulder, the hollow just above my ribs.

When his mouth moves lower, I arch into him, greedy for contact. He laughs against my skin, the sound low and rough.

"Still want me to go slow?" he teases, mouth at my stomach.

I shake my head. "I want you to make it real."

He grins, then kisses his way up to my lips. "As you wish," he says.

We fit together like we're built for it, bodies slotting in all the right places. He moves inside me, slow at first, then deeper, each thrust pushing out the air, the memory, the panic.

I cling to him, nails digging into his back, and when I come, it's with a violence that surprises us both. I cry out, loud enough to echo off the walls, but it's not fear anymore—it's release.

He follows a second later, shuddering, holding me so tight I think he might never let go.

We stay tangled together, sticky with sweat and tears and everything we don't say. He strokes my hair until my breathing slows, then pulls the blanket up around us both.

After a while, I start to drift. The nightmare lingers at the edges, but it can't reach me now.

Lucas kisses the top of my head again, whispers, "You're safe," until I believe it.

For the first time in years, I sleep through the night.

When I wake, he's still there.

And I know, in my bones, that this time, I made it out.

7

Hot Spot

SOPHIE

I FIND THE BOX AT MIDNIGHT, JUST AS MY PHONE DIES AND the street outside goes black in a rolling brownout that takes the whole block with it. There's no ceremony—just me in threadbare sweats, hair pulled up, sweating through a third mug of insomnia coffee and pawing at the lowest shelf in the coat closet like a raccoon with a grudge. The box is lighter than I expect, but when I pull it out, the bottom sags and a dust-shrouded avalanche of old photos, newsprint, and one scorched ballcap floods across the entryway.

The lid is marked in my dad's handwriting, black Sharpie faded to a kind of ghost gray: "GRANT—PERSONAL / ARCHIVE." The way the G hooks down and then up again, an arrow pointing nowhere. If I squint I can almost see the hand that wrote it, big and bony, skin a shade too pink from a life of burns and scrapes. I half expect the next thing I touch to bite back.

I drag the whole mess to the living room and kneel on the rug, light from the window casting stripes over everything. The house is dead quiet. Even the fridge is on strike. For a few minutes I just sift, pulling out photos in no order, laying them side by side until the carpet looks like a yearbook of things I never wanted to remember.

My dad's senior portrait—grin too big for his face, tie askew. Next to it, a Polaroid of the Willow Creek firehouse, pre-renovation, when the bay doors were still red, and the flag hung limp all summer. Clippings about his medals and citations, a laminated card with the local suicide hotline, yellowed at the corners. His old badge, shiny even after all these years, the edges smoothed down to a weaponless dullness. I run my thumb over the numbers, then set it aside.

It takes an hour to get through the top layer. Underneath, I find the real relics: a patched turnout sleeve he kept for luck, a folder of union grievance forms (most never sent), and, at the very bottom, a pile of faxes stapled together at random intervals. The paper is so brittle it nearly splits when I try to flatten it, and it's water-damaged, rings of blue and purple bleeding out from the margins.

I'm about to call it for the night when I see the edge of something silver, wedged between two stacks of old department rosters. At first, I think it's a dog tag, but when I fish it out, it's a backup drive—one of those cheap, plastic rectangles you get for free at conferences. No label, no hint of what might be on it. I turn it over in my hand, weighing the possibilities: nothing, or everything.

The laptop's battery is shot, so I have to dig for the charger, untangle it from a nest of unused cords. When I finally plug the drive in, the screen lights up with a folder called "WCFD – REQ / CONF," and inside, a mess of document scans, photos, and audio files, all with names like "Station_Closure_Rpt.pdf" or "WCFD_CASE_832.wav." Most of it is the kind of digital detritus that gets left behind when someone cleans out a desk in a hurry. But there's one file, dated exactly one week before my father died, named only with the time stamp: "03-14-2009-1127.wav."

I click it.

At first, nothing. Then a burst of static, the sound of someone fumbling with a phone and a loud, shaky breath. The voice is a woman's, aged but still sharp, and she's trying to keep it low: "Chief, I don't know how else to say this. They're watching. I saw the transfer forms myself. If you try to move forward, it won't end well for you or for your daughter." The words come out in a rush, clipped by fear or the need to get it said before something interrupts. "I can't talk on this line. You need to get rid of anything that connects you. If you're thinking they don't know, it's already too late."

There's a noise—maybe the bang of a door, maybe just a bad splice—and then the call cuts out. Ten seconds of silence, and that's it. The file ends.

I replay it, over and over, each time listening for some trace of my father in the background, for a cough or a yes or any sign that he was even on the line. But it's just the woman, voice shaking, and the warning.

On the fifth listen, I realize what nags at me: the accent. Midwestern, but with an undercurrent of something else, something clipped and precise. I let the voice roll around my head until it starts to sound familiar.

Dispatcher. From the old station. Marlene, maybe, or Maryellen. I make a note, then another. The more I listen, the more I hear—the drag on certain syllables, the way she says "you need to get rid of anything." The certainty, and the fear.

My hands are sweating. I wipe them on my thighs, then take a photo of the screen and send it to myself, just in case. The urge to call Lucas is immediate, but I make myself listen two more times before I do it.

The phone rings twice before he picks up, his voice groggy but alert. "Sophie? Everything all right?"

"I need you to hear something," I say, and I don't recognize the steadiness in my own voice. "Now."

He doesn't argue. I play him the message, holding the phone speaker to the laptop and turning up the volume. When it ends, there's a long, deep silence.

"You know who it is?" he asks.

"I think so. I'm going to find out. But Lucas—she knew. She warned him, and he still—"

"He wanted to protect you," Lucas says, quiet.

The words hit harder than any truth in the message.

I sit on the floor, surrounded by photos and rosters and the crumbling ghosts of my father's life, and for the first time in months, I'm not afraid.

I'm furious.

"We're going to finish this," I say.

Lucas just says, "Damn right," and tells me to lock the door and get some sleep.

I don't. Not for a long time.

Instead, I play the message again, and again, letting the voice etch itself into memory.

Somewhere, under all that fear, is a clue.

And I'm not going to stop until I find it.

By the time Lucas shows up, the sun has barely cleared the roof, turning the living room into a harsh wash of geometry and regret. He's still in his uniform—navy polo, badge clipped and slightly askew, dark pants streaked with whatever passes for dirt in an arson evidence lab. He doesn't knock. Just opens the door with the key I forgot to return and stands in the entry, surveying the mess of last night.

I don't bother to stand. I'm cross-legged on the rug, photos fanned around me, backup drive plugged into the laptop like an IV drip.

"Still haven't slept?" Lucas says.

"Did you?" I counter, and his half-smile is all the answer I need.

He sets his bag down and goes straight for the coffee, pouring a mug so full it sloshes over his fingers. He doesn't flinch at the burn, just wipes his hand on his shirt and crouches beside me.

"Let me hear it again," he says, voice stripped down to the skeleton.

I play the message. I watch his face, how the tension starts at the corner of his jaw and works its way up to the scalp, how his breathing evens out, then slows. He's hearing something I can't —something in the tone, or the pauses, or the things left unsaid. When it ends, he says nothing for a long time.

Then: "Play it once more. From the top."

This time he closes his eyes, head down, hands steepled in front of his mouth. The voice comes through the tinny laptop speakers, even more desperate in daylight: "Chief, I don't know how else to say this. They're watching. I saw the transfer forms myself. If you try to move forward, it won't end well for you or for your daughter."

Lucas is stone. But when the message cuts out, he exhales like he's been holding his breath for a month.

"Holy shit," he says. "That's Marlene. Has to be."

He runs a hand through his hair, as if pulling on a loose thread might unravel the whole case. "Marlene Winters. Dispatcher. She worked at WCFD for twenty-seven years. Retired right after your dad's funeral, moved to Michigan. Said it was for her health, but—" He shakes his head. "She was scared. Everyone knew it, but nobody talked about it."

I open my mouth, then close it again. I know the name. The voice fits.

"You think she knows what happened?" I ask, not really expecting an answer.

Lucas shrugs, but there's heat under it. "If anyone did, it was her. She was the last one to talk to your dad before he went home that night. I remember because she called me. Asked if I'd heard from him. She sounded... not like herself."

I watch him, weighing every word. "You never said."

He winces. "You had enough on your plate. And I thought it was just—grief. For both of us." He picks up a photo, flips it over, then sets it down gently. "If she left a trace, it's on that drive. Or she took it with her."

I spend the next hour digging. Google, social, the county's own weird little legacy employee directory. Marlene's profile is a graveyard: no posts in years, every photo either a grandkid or a casserole, the most recent update a GoFundMe for "complicated heart surgery." But there's a mailing address in the fund's details—a town up north, population less than a thousand, the kind of place where every street is a variant of Main.

I write it on a sticky note, slap it to the side of the screen. Lucas reads it, lips moving.

"You think she'll talk?" he asks.

"If she doesn't, I'll make her," I say, surprising even myself.

The words hang in the air. Lucas just studies me, like he's reading a damage report.

"I'm coming with you," he says.

I shake my head, and he narrows his eyes in that way he does when he's trying not to fight.

"It's my father," I say. "I need to do this alone."

He opens his mouth, but I cut him off. "You can back me up from here. If I'm not back by midnight, you burn it all down."

Lucas looks at the laptop, the badge, the riot of photos. "I mean it, Soph. If it feels wrong—if you think for a second she's setting you up—"

"I know," I say. "You'll come running."

He reaches over and covers my hand with his. "You got this?"

I squeeze his fingers, just once. "I got this."

Packing for a three-hour drive is easy when you plan for the worst. I load up a duffel with clothes, a phone charger, two burner phones, and an emergency kit I've kept in the trunk since the water tower incident. On a whim, I grab my dad's badge from the living room, slip it into my pocket. For luck, or armor, or maybe just to feel him close.

Before I go, I check my dad's old journals for any mention of Marlene. The entries are as dry as always—lists, dates, cryptic one-liners. But in the log for March 7, I find a notation: "MW called. Panic. Said: Not safe. More tomorrow." The last entry before his death.

I photograph the page, heart thudding. It's enough.

As I shoulder the bag, Lucas stands in the doorway, arms folded, blocking the exit.

"You sure about this?" he asks. "It doesn't have to be your fight alone."

I step in close, nearly chest to chest. "I need to know. I need to end it."

He nods, but his jaw is set. "I'll be waiting."

For a second, neither of us moves. The unsaid things between us—fear, hope, everything—spool out until I can barely breathe.

Then I lean up, kiss him hard, and walk out before I lose my nerve.

In the car, I roll down the window and let the cold wake me up. I tap the address into the GPS, watch the route populate, three hours of back roads and speed traps and too much time to think.

As I pull away from the curb, I look in the rearview. Lucas stands on the porch, silhouetted by the empty sun, hands shoved deep in his pockets. He doesn't wave.

He just watches, like he's willing me to come back in one piece.

I drive.

The town falls away behind me, replaced by an endless stretch of fields and interstate, horizon shimmering with heat and memory.

Three hours to the truth.

Three hours to the next fire.

The last fifteen miles are nothing but strip malls, used car lots, and subdivisions that never filled in. My stomach sours as I pull off the highway, the GPS recalculating through a labyrinth of county roads and identical cul-de-sacs. Each street is named after a different kind of tree, but every block looks the same—ranch houses, mailboxes with team decals, winter lawns the color of dirty snow.

Marlene Winters lives in a tan bungalow that squats on the end of a dead-end, sandwiched between two lots full of dormant rose bushes and the slow-rolling crawl of neighborhood-watch SUVs. Her porch is swept clean, but the paint on the steps is peeling in neat, curling ribbons, and the front door is covered in a spread of faded stickers: "PROUD TO SUPPORT LOCAL FIREFIGHTERS," "THIS HOME PROTECTED BY COMMUNITY," and a sun-bleached yellow ribbon that droops in the wind like an old bandage.

I park across the street and sit for a minute, letting the engine tick down and my pulse catch up. Through the windshield, I spot movement—curtain twitch at the right window, then a slow, practiced lowering of a set of blinds. I grip the steering wheel, tell myself that nobody who's scared enough to watch the street for visitors is looking to ambush the first one who shows up.

Still, I slip the phone into my jacket pocket, hit record, and pull my dad's badge from the console. I don't know if it's a shield or a curse, but either way, I want it close.

The sidewalk crunches under my boots. As I cross the lawn, a little old dog with white fur and mean eyes barks three times, then bolts back inside through a dog door. I count the steps to the porch. At six, the front door opens two inches, then stops.

"Yes?" The voice is sharp, wary, and a little hoarse.

"Ms. Winters?" I keep my tone soft, hands in clear view. "I'm Sophie Grant."

She hesitates, then opens the door the rest of the way. Her hair is silver at the scalp, cut short and tight around her head like she's still prepping for a job that might call her back at any moment. Her eyes are the same cold blue as the lake in January. She wears an oversized Green Bay sweatshirt and what might be pajama pants, but her feet are bare on the threshold.

"I know who you are," Marlene says, and there's no friendliness in it.

I stand my ground. "I'd like to talk. Five minutes, that's all."

She looks me up and down, then at the street, then back to me. "What for?"

I try for the truth. "Because you called my dad a week before he died. Because you're the last one who did."

For a second, her face shutters. Then she snorts, dry and dismissive. "That was years ago."

"It's not over for me," I say.

She shakes her head, starts to close the door.

I slide my hand into my pocket and pull out the phone. "Please. I just want you to listen to something."

She hesitates again. I see the calculation—the risk, the old habit of weighing threat versus reward. She doesn't open the door wider, but she doesn't shut it, either.

I play the message. At the sound of her own voice, Marlene goes rigid. She bites her lip, eyes darting down the block, then gestures me inside with a sharp flick of her chin.

"Not here," she says. "Someone could be watching."

I step into the entryway. The smell is a punch of lavender, coffee, and the damp, iron-rich tang of boiled tap water. The place is small, dark even with all the blinds up, every surface crowded with framed photos—grandkids in soccer uniforms, old men in turnout gear, the faded sepia of wedding days and barbecues. There are two recliners in the living room, both covered in identical blue plaid blankets. She gestures at one, then walks past into the kitchen.

I sit. My knees bounce with every tick of the wall clock.

She comes back carrying two mugs, sets one on the end table and hands me the other. The tea inside is black, no sugar, so hot it burns my tongue.

Marlene sits down, tucks her feet under herself, and stares at the floor.

"You came all this way for a dead man's secrets," she says, voice flat.

I hold the mug in both hands, waiting.

She picks up her own cup, but her hands tremble so much she puts it straight down again.

"I tried to warn him," she says. "I did. But he wouldn't listen.

Or maybe he did, and that's what killed him." Her eyes are glassy, but she doesn't blink.

"I need you to tell me," I say, quietly.

Marlene glances at the front door, then at the window again. "They're still out there, you know. The ones who did it. They don't forget."

"I don't care," I say. "I just want the truth."

For a second, I see the old dispatcher—the woman who once ran a dozen radios, called the shots on disasters, and held the town's fate in her headset every shift. Her back straightens. Her hands fold in her lap.

"It wasn't just your father," she starts. "There were others. All over the state. The gear—the detectors, the collection kits, even the software—they were supposed to be locked, inventoried. But someone was moving it. Little bits at a time, always signed off, always a reason. Then the fires started getting cleaner. Not random, not like the old days. These were surgical. No evidence left, nothing for the state to pin on anybody."

She wipes her mouth, and I see her bite the inside of her cheek hard.

"Your dad noticed. He started tracking the serial numbers, making notes. When he came to me, he said he thought it was a ring, maybe even higher. I laughed. Told him he was paranoid. But then I saw the forms myself—transfer requests, inventory logs that made no sense. Some of it was so obvious I couldn't believe it."

She looks up, eyes shiny.

"That's when I called him. I told him to back off, to let it go. He said he would, for you. Said it was better to take the hit himself than put you in the line of fire."

My throat is so tight I can barely breathe.

"Do you know who was behind it?" I ask.

She nods, slow. "I got a name, once. Just the last name. Bennett."

A cold sweat rips down my back. "Troy Bennett?"

Marlene's face twists. "He was the one moving the equipment. But I think he was just a middleman—he covered for the real operators, the ones in charge. Your dad got too close, and then he—" She stops, shakes her head. "They said a heart attack during the house fire, but I know. I know what a heart attack looks like, and that wasn't it."

The words are a lead weight. I sip the tea just to keep from shaking.

"Why didn't you go to the police?" I ask, and the question sounds childish even as I say it.

She laughs, but there's no humor. "You think the cops weren't in on it? If you're lucky, half the state's clean. The rest just do what they're told."

She leans forward, voice lowering. "Your father had a notebook. He kept it in his desk at the station, the old rolltop. All the names, dates, everything he found. If you can find it, you have the proof."

I nod, the gears turning.

Marlene goes to the window, peels back the curtain, and looks out. For a second, she's so tense I think she might bolt.

"They'll come after you if you go public," she says. "They don't care if you're the last Grant left."

I stand, heart pounding. "Let them try."

Marlene laughs again, and this time it's almost relief. "You're just like him," she says.

I want to say thank you, but it doesn't feel like a compliment.

Instead, I walk to the door, open it, and step out into the thin, cold sun. I cross the yard, get in the car, and sit for a minute, head against the steering wheel.

The truth is worse than I thought.

But at least I have it now.

As I pull away from the curb, I see Marlene standing behind the glass, her eyes following me all the way down the block.

It's only when I hit the main road that I let myself cry.

I let the tears fall, hot and fast, until the pain is less than the need to finish what my father started.

The next town over, I pull off at a gas station, scrub my face with the rough brown paper towels, and call Lucas.

He answers on the first ring. "You okay?"

I nod, even though he can't see it. "I'm coming home."

He's silent, but I can hear the pride and fear and everything else in the way he breathes out.

"I'll be waiting," he says.

I drive.

There are still hours to go, and the world feels emptier, but I know where I'm going now.

And I know what comes next.

By the time I make it back, the sun has long since set. The porch light is on, and there's a second car in the driveway, Lucas's old Tacoma, still dusty with soot from whatever scene he last responded to. The neighborhood is dead quiet except for a dog barking somewhere down the street—the kind of sound that never stops, just echoes forever.

Lucas sits on the top step, elbows on knees, hands clasped like he's holding back a tide. He stands the second he sees my headlights, relief plain on his face, but when I get out, he doesn't move to hug me. He knows better than to rush me. He just waits.

"Hey," I say, voice flat.

"Hey," he echoes, softer. "You made good time."

I shrug, because the words are buried under all the new knowledge crowding my head.

He holds the door for me, follows me inside. My house smells like it always does—a mixture of cheap candles and whatever's left of the last meal I cooked. But tonight, I can't stand the scent. I open two windows and set my bag down by the door.

Lucas watches me make a lap of the kitchen, then the living room, then back to the kitchen. I can feel his questions, but he keeps them holstered.

I pour a glass of water, then start talking. I tell him everything. Marlene, the bungalow, her hands shaking on the mug. The tea, the paranoia, the way every word seemed to cost her a year of her life. I tell him about the firefighter ribbon on her curtains, the way she kept checking the locks, how she was so afraid, but somehow also relieved to finally get it out.

Lucas listens, nodding, sometimes making a low sound in the back of his throat. When I get to the part about Bennett, his jaw tightens, and when I say my father's name, he reaches out and lays a hand on the table, palm up. I rest my hand on his, the touch light but anchoring.

"She said there's a notebook," I finish, voice gone hoarse. "A record of everything my dad found. Names, dates, the works."

"Do you know where it is?" he asks.

I shake my head. "Just that it's hidden in the old station's rolltop desk."

"But everything burned in the fire; do you think it somehow survived?" "I don't know, but if there's a chance, we have to check," I shrug.

Lucas is silent for a moment. Then: "We can get it. We'll go in tonight, if you want."

There's no bravado in it, just a simple certainty.

I look at him, really look, and the exhaustion hits me all at once —body, brain, every cell. I want to sleep for a year, but even more than that, I want something I can't name, something hot and alive and real.

"Not tonight," I say. "I need—"

He stands, crosses the room, and wraps his arms around me from behind. He doesn't squeeze, just lets me rest my weight against him. I can feel his chest rise and fall, slow and steady, and the roughness of his stubble against my temple.

He doesn't say anything, but I hear it anyway: You're not alone.

It undoes me.

I twist in his arms, bury my face in his neck. My hands fumble at his waist, desperate for purchase, and I pull him in for a kiss that's less about want and more about needing to be held together.

He kisses back, slow at first, then with a heat that builds until it scorches. I guide his hands to my hips, then my back, then under my shirt. I want him to know it's okay to take, but only if I'm the one to give.

We move to the bedroom, shoes and jackets left in a trail behind us. I push him down on the bed, straddle him, and kiss him until my lips ache. He lets me set the pace, lets me decide what happens, and it's that—more than the friction or the urgency—that makes me start to feel whole again.

I take off his shirt, fingers shaking, and trace the scars on his chest like I'm reading Braille. He does the same to me, but slower, reverent, like every inch of my skin is a miracle he can't quite believe.

"Don't hold back," he says.

And I don't.

We fit together the way people do when they've spent years denying it—clumsy, desperate, teeth and tongue and hands everywhere at once. I dig my nails into his shoulders, mark him as mine, and he groans, the sound raw and almost broken.

I lean down to him, and he kisses down my neck and chest as I sit back up. His mouth traces down my stomach, moving slowly enough to drive me crazy. I reach down between us and grasp him firmly, positioning him at my entrance. I pause for a moment, then lower myself onto him as deep as he can go.

We fuck like we're trying to erase the last twenty-four hours, the last ten years, all the fear and grief and anger. It hurts, a little, but I like it. I want to feel it tomorrow, want to have a reason to remember tonight.

I come hard, twice, the second time biting his shoulder so I don't scream.

Afterward, we collapse together, sweaty and shaking, limbs tangled in the sheets. For a long time, neither of us speaks.

Then, quietly, Lucas says, "What do you want to do?"

I think about it. Really think.

"I want to finish what my dad started," I say. "I want to take Bennett down, and anyone else who helped him."

Lucas nods. "I'll back you. Whatever it takes."

I believe him. And for the first time, it's enough.

We lie there, the world outside dark and silent, and I let myself believe we can win.

In the morning, we'll go for the notebook.

In the morning, I'll testify.

Tonight, I let myself be held.

Tonight, I let myself heal.

And when I finally fall asleep, I dream—not of fire, but of water.

Of being saved.

Of coming up for air, and finding myself alive.

8

Smoke Ring

SOPHIE

THE DAY STARTS WITH THE SMELL OF BURNING TOAST AND the thud of something heavy against the side of the house. I'm still bleary-eyed, hair in a failed ponytail, bare feet cold on the kitchen linoleum. The percolator gurgles its last, and I pour the coffee black, using both hands to steady the mug. There's a dull ache in my ribs—a souvenir from last night, or maybe just the memory of being wanted, a feeling so new it still sits in my skin like a splinter.

The day just seems to vanish around me; my mind drifts, overwhelmed with thoughts about recent events, information to sort through, and old feelings resurfacing. Before I know it, hours have passed, and the only clue to how long I've been sitting is the stiffness in my joints.

As dusk falls, I glance out the window and notice the orange porch light reflected in my car's windshield. Then, my eyes catch a tire—or rather, the empty space where it once was. The rubber is torn in three deliberate gashes, each one seemingly a signature left by someone.

I set down the mug and go outside, gravel biting at the soles of my feet. There's frost on the grass, but the tire is dry—slashed after dawn, when I was already awake, close enough that I should have heard something. I squat, knees cracking, and run my fingers along the edge. The cut is too clean for a pocketknife, too shallow for a box cutter. Utility blade, maybe. Whoever did it was quick and careful.

The other tires are untouched. I check them anyway, giving each a squeeze like I'm testing for a pulse. Only the front left, the one closest to the house. Message received.

I don't call Lucas, not yet. He's probably still asleep, or if not, he's already at the station prepping for the evidence sweep we're supposed to do together. Instead, I go back inside, grab the spare from the trunk, and dig out the ancient jack my dad kept for emergencies. The socket wrench is worn to a shine, handle taped with electrician's blue, a chunk missing from the head where my dad once threw it across the driveway at a neighbor's yappy dog. I smile, just a little, at the memory.

The lug nuts are on tight. I brace my foot against the wrench and lean in, putting my whole body into it. The metal gives with a screech that sets my teeth on edge. I loosen them, one by one, sweat beading on my forehead. The air is crisp and still, but every so often I catch the echo of footsteps—maybe a runner, maybe just the neighborhood settling into itself. Or maybe nothing at all.

I have the wheel off and the spare halfway on when the world goes dark.

It's not the sun going behind a cloud. It's not even the winter blackout we get every February when the grid can't handle all the space heaters and hope. This is immediate, total, a light switch thrown somewhere deep in the ground.

I stand, heart thumping. The house is black, every window a mirror. No streetlights. No glow from the gas station on the corner. Even the neighbor's Christmas inflatables sag, unlit and obscene, on their patchy lawn.

I wipe my hands on my jeans and walk back inside, leaving the wheel propped against the porch. The door makes its usual squeak, but the familiar is a stranger in the dark. My phone's in my pocket, so I switch on the flashlight, using the edge of the beam to map the living room: couch, coffee table, the stack of folders I left on the armrest last night. I check the hallway, the bathroom, the bedroom. Every switch is dead. I try the outlets with a spare charger—nothing.

I check the breaker box in the basement. The air down there is heavy, and I catch a faint, sour whiff—copper and burnt insulation. The breaker is untouched, every switch still toggled to on. I flick the main, then the individual circuits, but the house stays dead.

It means someone cut the line from outside.

Now I call Lucas.

He answers on the second ring, voice sharp with adrenaline. "What's wrong?"

"Power's out," I say. "Just mine. But the breaker's fine."

He's quiet for a beat, then: "Stay inside. Lock the doors. I'm on my way."

I want to argue, but the silence on the line tells me it's not a request.

I check the back door, then the windows, then the front again. Every lock is set, but it feels like a ritual—an act of hope rather than a guarantee.

I go to the kitchen and check my supplies: three bottles of water, half a loaf of bread, a can of chili with a dent so deep it's probably botulism by now. My hand shakes as I light a candle, the kind with a fake vanilla scent that reminds me of grade school birthday parties and fire safety talks.

I sit at the kitchen table and wait.

It's less than ten minutes before Lucas is at the door, moving with a caution that's all muscle memory. He sweeps the porch with his flashlight, then the foyer, then every room in the house. He says nothing at first, just walks the perimeter, scanning windows and floorboards.

When he finally speaks, his voice is low. "Someone was here. Fresh boot prints in the mud behind the garage. They cut the power at the pole—wire snips, not even insulated. Could have fried themselves, but didn't."

I feel the words settle on my skin, heavier than I expect.

Lucas stands in the middle of the kitchen, arms crossed, scanning for any sign of weakness. He looks at me, then the table, then at the old ceramic sugar bowl my dad used to fill with sand to stub out cigarettes. He lifts it, turns it over. There's a folded scrap of paper underneath, thin as a receipt.

He slides it across the table. I read it upside down.

YOU'RE NOT SAFE, SOPHIE.

No punctuation. Block print, all caps, the letters spaced too evenly to be casual.

I sit hard, the chair biting into the back of my thighs. My hands start to tremble, so I shove them under my legs.

Lucas reads the fear on my face, but he doesn't call it out. Instead, he gets on one knee and checks under the table, running his fingers along the crossbeam.

He freezes, then swears under his breath.

There's a wire—thin, copper, looped through the table leg and trailing toward the vent at the far end of the kitchen.

"Stay back," Lucas says, and I do.

He follows the wire to the vent, unscrews the grate with his pocket knife, and pulls out a black cylinder the size of a marker. A listening device.

He holds it up, rotating it in the light. "State-issue, but modified. Whoever did this, they have access."

I can't breathe for a second.

Lucas goes to the living room, checks behind the TV, the couch, the lamp. In the hall closet, he runs a hand along the top shelf and pulls out a second device, this one taped to the inside of a shoebox.

"Two bugs. One for voice, one for movement," he mutters. "They're watching and listening."

I nod, too numb to say anything.

He tears up the welcome mat, then the floorboard under it, revealing a tangle of copper wire snaking toward the foundation. He follows it to the porch, where he finds the cut power line—spliced, stripped, and tied off with electrical tape, the ends fused together in a way that says I'm not just going to listen to you, I'm going to make you afraid to even breathe.

Lucas stands and turns to me, his face gone hard.

"I'm not letting you stay here," he says. "Not like this."

I shake my head. "I'm not running. If they want me, let them come."

He slams his fist on the table, loud enough to rattle the sugar bowl. "You don't get it, Soph. This isn't just intimidation anymore. They want you silent."

I stand, matching him glare for glare. "Let them try. I won't be the one hiding in the dark."

We stare each other down, both of us too stubborn to blink.

The silence is broken by the chirp of my phone—a text, then another, then a call.

I glance at the screen. Unknown number, local area code.

I answer, voice steady.

"Hello?"

The line is clear, no static, no lag. "This is Channel 5. We'd like to speak to you about your father's legacy—and the recent developments in your investigation."

I don't respond right away. Lucas is at my side, listening in.

The voice continues. "We understand you're testifying tomorrow. We want to give you a chance to speak before anyone else gets to tell your story. Are you willing?"

I look at Lucas, then at the table, at the bugs and the wires and the shadows that have started to fill the corners of my house. My heart is still pounding, but now it's from something like anger.

"Yeah," I say. "I'm ready."

"Great," the voice says. "We'll send a car."

I hang up, set the phone on the table, and meet Lucas's eyes.

"They want my truth," I say, voice flat. "They're going to get it."

He doesn't say anything, just reaches out and takes my hand. His grip is tight, grounding.

We sit like that, side by side, while the last of the candle burns down.

Let them come, I think. I'll light the match myself.

The studio is colder than a meat locker, and the air smells like a cross between burnt plastic and rental blazer. They seat me on a stool, clip a mic to my collar, and tell me to "look natural," as if that's ever been an option. The lights are a thousand watts each, trained on my face until every pore and scar casts a shadow. The makeup girl dabs at my forehead, then my jaw, then gives up entirely. She hands me a tissue and tells me to "hold steady."

I ball the tissue in my palm and lock my hands in my lap. My legs bounce. I try to focus on the script in my head—what not to say, which details to leave out, how to dodge questions that could get someone killed. I want to check my phone, but they already took it, "studio protocol." I want to check the exits, but I already did that twice.

The host is a local guy, all teeth and winter tan, wearing a tie so red it looks like a warning sign. He sits across from me on a matching stool, legs crossed at the knee, hands folded on a stack of blue index cards. He introduces himself as "Greg," but the earpiece and the staccato hand gestures say he's just the face, not the brains.

The camera rolls. The countdown hits zero, and suddenly we're live.

Greg opens with a softball: "You're the daughter of a decorated fire chief, and now you're at the center of the biggest corruption scandal this county's ever seen. How does that feel?"

I wait a beat, let the silence stretch. "Like an alarm I can't turn off," I say. "You don't get used to it. You just learn to move with it."

He grins, a flash of teeth, and flips to the next card. "You've made some serious accusations. Misuse of equipment, cover-ups, even murder. Do you have proof?"

My father's badge is in my jacket pocket, thumbed smooth by a thousand worries. I picture it. "I have what he left me," I say. "Notes, files, names. Enough to scare the people who want this buried."

He leans in, earnest. "Why come forward now?"

I glance past the lights, past the cameras, to where Lucas stands just outside the circle of glare. He's in civvies, but the posture's pure cop. Arms folded, feet planted, eyes never still. He's got a line of sight on every exit, every staffer, even the maintenance guy pretending to adjust a vent above the stage.

I meet his gaze, just for a second, and feel the heat of his support, his faith, his fear.

I look back at Greg. "Because every time I stay silent, someone else gets hurt. And I'm tired of counting the bodies."

He nods, feigning empathy, then pivots to the cards. "What do you want the people of Willow Creek to know? What do you want to tell the families who lost so much?"

My hands stop shaking.

"My father believed that corruption thrives in darkness," I say, letting the words slow and settle. "The truth doesn't burn. It survives. Even if you torch every record, every home, every goddamn firehouse in the county, the truth waits in the ashes."

Greg blinks, then recovers, plowing ahead. "Some say you're putting yourself in danger by speaking out."

I give him the flattest smile I can. "Maybe. But it's not the fire that scares me. It's letting them win."

The rest of the interview blurs—talk of whistleblowers, legal threats, the county's official response. I keep my answers clipped and clean, refusing to give an inch. Every time he tries to spin it, I yank the wheel back. Off-camera, Lucas's jaw works a steady grind. He's tracking everyone in the studio, not just me. His body language is code: stay alert, don't relax, this is just another hazard zone.

When the segment finally ends, the techs unplug my mic and usher me out with fake smiles and quick handshakes. Greg leans in, voice pitched for my ears only: "You're brave, you know. Not everyone comes in here ready for a fight."

I shake his hand. "You should see me with a hose."

He laughs, but it doesn't reach his eyes.

Lucas meets me at the edge of the stage, fingers ghosting my elbow as we head for the parking lot. Outside, the lot is nearly empty—just our car, a camera crew packing up, and the thick hush that comes after a fire's been doused.

"You okay?" he asks.

I check the sky, the horizon, the rooflines. "I think so."

He opens the door for me, then circles the car, scanning the lot. He never relaxes, not even now.

As he drives, I stare at the city lights streaking past the window, and the feeling that the whole world is watching me through glass.

We make it back to my place just after nine. The power's still out, so we light the living room with candles and Lucas's tactical flashlight. It's weirdly cozy, like the blackout is a snow day instead of a siege.

We sit at the kitchen table, laptop open, Lucas's phone acting as a hotspot. Within minutes, the interview is everywhere—shared by local teachers, old classmates, even a couple of national accounts. The view count climbs by the hundreds, then thousands. Comments pour in: some kind, most brutal, all of them proof that what I said is out in the world now, unerasable.

I scroll, heart racing, as people argue over whether I'm a hero or a fraud. I don't care. I watch the numbers climb and feel a strange pride. My words are alive, burning their way through the noise.

Lucas sits next to me, one hand on his mug, the other drumming a silent beat on the table. He's watching me, not the screen.

"You did good," he says.

"Yeah?" I glance at him, looking for a crack in the armor.

He nods, serious. "You got through. More than you know."

I smile, tight-lipped, and go back to scrolling. The glow from the laptop lights his face, and for a moment he looks tired—exhausted in a way I've never seen, like he's been carrying me through the fire and finally hit the end of the hose.

He pushes the laptop aside and pulls me in, arms snug around my shoulders.

I let myself relax, just for a second. The house is quiet, and the only light is the cold blue of the screen.

But after a minute, I notice his eyes, tracking the windows, always looking for the next threat.

He doesn't say it, but I hear him anyway: Stay ready. Don't let them catch you off guard.

I nod, and he kisses the top of my head.

We sit like that for a long time, watching the world react, waiting for what comes next.

Outside, the street is dark and empty.

Inside, we are a flame waiting for oxygen.

We pull up to the park just before midnight, the streets slick with black ice and completely deserted. Lucas drives with one hand, the other tapping a quick rhythm on my thigh as we enter the dimly lit lot. At the corner taco truck, we grab two foil-wrapped burritos and a bag of fries—our makeshift feast for one last stop before heading home.

The park's wrought-iron gate stands half-open. We slip through it and find a single picnic table under a flickering lamp. Frost clings to the wooden benches; the air smells of pine needles and warm salsa. Lucas sets our takeout on the table, peels back the foil, then leans across and snags a fry. I snort at the grease drip on his lip.

Before I can tease him, his hand slides from the edge of the table to my hip. He presses me back against the bench's cold wood; my burrito box rattled to the ground. His mouth finds mine, rough and demanding, and the bench's frost bit through my jeans. I hook my fingers in his jacket and pull him closer, laughter mixing with moans in the hush of the park.

His hands hunt under my sweater, fingertips like ice against my skin. I arch into him. He whispers against my mouth, "You still think you can handle this out in the open?"

"Only one way to find out," I dare, and flip us so he is pinned between me and the table.

My nails score across his shirt as he hisses low in pleasure. He catches my wrists, pins them above my head on the tabletop's edge, then meets me thrust for thrust. The sound of us echoed off the empty playground, the slap of our bodies drowning out the distant hum of traffic.

I bite his shoulder to stifle a scream, legs wrapping tight around his waist. His jeans grind into me, and I come so hard the world spins white. He tensed, buried his face in my neck, and emptied himself inside me with a ragged groan.

When the tremors fade, we sag to the ground against the bench legs, heartbeats settling in our ears. After a long minute, Lucas cracks a grin and brushes a fry crumb from my chin.

"Best midnight snack ever," he murmurs.

I smile, leaning back against him. "Don't ever underestimate late-night tacos—and me."

We sit there in the cold, wrapped in our own warmth, breathing each other in until the park falls completely silent again.

He touches my hand, lacing our fingers together. “You know what you said on TV? About the truth surviving?”

I nod.

He squeezes my hand, not looking at me. “It got to people. It got to me.”

I look at him, and the fear that’s been lodged in my chest for months loosens, just a little. “I meant it,” I say. “Even if nobody listens. Even if we get burned.”

He leans in, kisses me slowly. “I’m listening,” he says.

I rest my head on his shoulder and let myself believe him, just for this moment.

We're about to leave the park when I see it—a flash of movement through the pines, just beyond the picnic area. Not a person, but a shape, quick and purposeful, gone before I can process.

I tense, fingers freezing around my coffee cup.

"What is it?" Lucas whispers, already on his feet.

I point toward the tree line, heart pounding. "Thought I saw something."

He moves across the frost-covered grass, silent as a cat, and slips between the first row of pines. The branches sway in his wake. Nothing. No sound, no footsteps. He checks the path, then peers deeper into the woods, his breath making ghost clouds in the night air.

"Nobody there," he says, but I hear the lie in his voice.

We hurry to the parking lot, the air biting colder than before, and climb into the truck. He locks the doors, then checks the rearview, eyes scanning for headlights or movement between the trees.

My phone buzzes—a new notification. Another clip of the interview, this one posted by a national account. I watch the numbers spike: ten thousand, twenty, fifty, the story spreading like a controlled burn with no hope of containment.

Lucas drives us home in silence, his hand never leaving the gearshift, every muscle tensed for the next hit.

I scroll the comments, the DMs, the news articles with my face front and center. I feel exposed, but I don't care. My story is out there now. Nobody can take it back.

We pull up to my house. The power is still out, but the porch is bathed in the blue wash of the neighbor's generator. As we walk to the door, I glance behind us, searching the darkness for a hint of the shadow from the park.

It's not there.

But I know it will be, soon.

Inside, we collapse onto the couch, tangled together, and let exhaustion pull us under.

Before I drift off, I set my phone on the windowsill, screen facing out. A small act of defiance.

Let them come, I think.

We're ready to burn.

9

Fireline Redemption

LUCAS

THE HEADQUARTERS CONFERENCE ROOM IS PURE intimidation—oak walls, high windows, the kind of boardroom table that could double as a runway for private jets. The coffee is burned, the pastries untouched, and I'm the only one in uniform. The rest wear suits: navy, gray, a single maroon that makes the guy look like he bled out at his own desk. There's a skyline view of Willow Creek that makes the town look smaller than it ever felt from the street.

Chief Kelly presides from the head of the table, his hands folded like he's waiting to pray. He doesn't acknowledge me at first, lets me stew while the admin types murmur and a city lawyer checks her phone. It's all posturing, the kind that makes you want to break something just to see if anyone has the guts to react.

I grip the plastic pen they gave me so hard the clip cracks. The folder in front of me is labeled "Transfer and Advancement Opportunity"—all caps, no flourish. I know what's in it before I look: a permanent desk job, six figures, and a seat on the kind of committee that spends a year debating how many dogs can fit in a firehouse. My name is typed at the top, like they're already writing my obituary.

Chief Kelly clears his throat, which is how you know he's about to say something that matters. "Hayes. You've been through more than most. The review panel's impressed—your service in the Rowe case, your work on the tower. The department could use your discipline, your... consistency." He lets the word dangle, as if he means stubbornness but is too polite to say it.

The woman to his left—a Deputy Commissioner from the State —tilts her head, studying me like I'm a bug she's not sure whether to squash or mount for display. "This is a real opportunity, Lucas," she says, voice syrupy. "Director of Field Operations. You'd set the standards for the next decade."

What she doesn't say: the brass ring is only brass. It would mean no more field work, no more real action. Just paperwork, policy, and the steady, suffocating pressure of other people's expectations.

I don't look at the form. Instead, I look out the window, count the roofs I've dragged a hose across, the alleys I've run with an axe or a body in my arms. I can see the old firehouse from here

—or at least the skeleton of what's left. I think of Sophie, of the way her hands shook the night she found her father's badge, and how she still signed on for every second of pain that followed.

Chief Kelly leans in, voice low. "It's a big ask, I know. But you've earned the next step. We need people like you up here, making the calls, not just answering them."

I picture myself in this room, day after day, until the walls close in and the window is just a memory of oxygen.

I uncap the pen, the tip digging into the paper as I sign. I add a line through my name and, in the margin, write: "Respectfully decline." I slide the folder back across the table.

The room goes quiet. The Deputy's lips purse; someone at the far end coughs into his fist.

"Are you sure?" Kelly asks, the words flat, but his eyes are sharp.

"I am," I say. "There's work to do in Willow Creek. People there still think the department's a joke, or worse. I want to fix that. Build the new house from scratch, with a team that hasn't spent their whole life cutting corners." My voice is even, but my jaw aches from how tight I'm clenching.

A few of the suits look at each other—one shrugs, another rolls her eyes like she's just seen a kid drop his ice cream on the sidewalk.

Chief Kelly nods, almost like he expected this. "You'll have your chance," he says. "But if you change your mind—"

"I won't," I say, and stand.

The table hums with surprise, a flicker of respect from the maroon jacket, a scowl from the Deputy. I walk out, uniform too tight across my chest, but breathing easier with every step.

By the time I hit the street, the wind's cut through the last of my nerves. I stand in front of the building, watching the sun hit the empty frame of the old firehouse. There's nothing left to burn.

I walk back to where I belong, each footfall steady, the weight of the decision already feeling less like a burden and more like something I could, eventually, be proud of.

I text Sophie: "Still here. Still us."

Her reply: "You're a stubborn bastard. I like it."

So do I.

SOPHIE

They gutted the firehouse down to studs, ripped up every inch of tile and linoleum and stained gear mat, but the old bones still show. The sun slices through a grid of brand-new windows, the kind of energy-efficient glass that makes a grant writer weep, and lands on the concrete floor in gold pools. The air smells like sawdust and ambition. Above us, workers bicker in Spanish as they anchor a duct run with rivets that echo through the shell.

Lucas walks ahead, hard hat just a shade too bright, hands jammed in his jacket pockets. He doesn't look back to see if I'm keeping up. He knows I am. Every footstep lands on the memory of what this place used to be, and every step forward is a test to see if I'll flinch.

The main bay is empty, all the trucks gone, the gear racks replaced by temporary plywood tables crowded with blueprints, thermoses, and battered laptops. Lucas pauses at the edge of the space and waits for me to catch up.

"Not bad, right?" he says. The pride in his voice is small, almost embarrassed.

"It's better than the old place," I say, and mean it. The old house had a damp rot under the tile and a mildew stench that nothing could mask. This place still vibrates with its own trauma, but at least it's honest.

He leads me down the hall, the sound of boots and power tools fading behind us. We reach the corner office, which isn't finished but already feels different—quiet, bright, a slab of sunlight resting on the drywall where a door will go. The view is full-on town square: the library, the battered statue of some local hero, a sprawl of kids' bikes tangled around a tree.

Lucas pulls something from under his jacket, wrapped in a shop rag. He sets it on the floor and peels away the cloth.

It's a plaque, bronze, already tarnished at the edges. The words are sharp and simple.

CAPTAIN MICHAEL GRANT

1957-2009

"LEAVE IT BETTER THAN YOU FOUND IT"

For a second, the rest of the world goes silent.

I crouch beside it, press my thumb against the raised letters. They're cold, even in the sun. I don't say anything because the alternative is to say everything, and that would mean never stopping.

Lucas stands awkwardly in the doorway, a hand at the back of his neck. "We want to put this here. In the outreach office." He hesitates, searching for the next line. "I want you to run it."

I let the words settle, my thumb still caught in the valley of my father's name.

"Outreach?" I say, because I need him to keep talking, not me.

He nods, gaining momentum. "Fire prevention, first response training, advocacy. We can use the space for school visits, seniors, at-risk stuff. You'd be the face, Soph. The new chief likes the idea." A pause. "I like the idea."

The lump in my throat is half grief, half relief. I manage to stand, dust off my knees, and pick up the plaque. The weight is satisfying, as if it might anchor the whole building.

"I'll do it," I say. "But only if I get to pick the paint color."

He grins, the line of it splitting the tension in two. "Deal. But no lavender. I've seen what it does to grown men."

We spend the next hour with the blueprints, spread across a folding table in the empty bay. The construction crew is on lunch, so the only sound is our pencils scratching at copies and the rumble of an ancient radio trying to pick up classic rock. We circle wall placements, argue over where the shelving should go, debate the merits of tile versus linoleum for the outreach room.

We lean over the plans, shoulders touching. He marks something with a highlighter, and I bump his elbow, just to see if he'll lose his train of thought. He doesn't. He never does.

"You know you could still take the Director job," I say, keeping my tone light.

He snorts. "And leave you here to terrorize the next generation of kindergartners? Not a chance."

I like that he's not bullshitting. I like that the man who nearly died in this building is still willing to show up, even if it means starting over at the bottom.

We get lost in the details—accent walls, window film, the best place to mount a wall-sized whiteboard. I forget, for a while, what it's like to want to run. I forget that the only reason this job exists is because my father died.

It's only when Lucas's phone buzzes that the spell breaks.

He checks the notification, face going sharp.

"Trial's set," he says. "Caleb's up in two months. Pleading not guilty."

I nod. "Of course he is."

We let the news sink in. The radio drifts through a static-fuzzed "More Than a Feeling." Lucas sets his phone down and rests his hand on the table, close enough to mine that the hairs on my arm rise.

"You want to be there?" he asks.

"Yeah," I say. "I want to see the look on his face when he realizes it's over."

Lucas nods, like that's exactly what he expected.

He taps the plans with a finger. "Let's get this right, okay? No more corners cut, no more secrets."

We work until the sun fades and the bay is dark. We're both covered in dust and pencil marks and the kind of fatigue that feels earned.

On the way out, I prop the plaque on a windowsill. The light catches the name, and for a moment, it feels like my dad's here, watching to make sure we don't fuck it up.

As we leave, Lucas's hand finds the small of my back, steady and sure.

This time, I don't flinch.

The jail is fifteen minutes out of town, but the drive takes forty with the roadwork and the convoy of livestock trucks all bent on going exactly the speed limit. The sign at the entrance says "Willow Creek Correctional Facility," but the locals just call it "the box." It sits in a field of mud and battered grass, ringed with a double fence and enough razor wire to keep the whole town from ever leaving.

Lucas parks by the visitor entrance. He offers to wait inside, but I see the nerves in his fingers—three taps on the steering wheel, then one on the gearshift, then back again. I tell him I'll be fine, that this is just a formality, and if I'm not out in thirty minutes, he should call the cavalry.

The intake process is slow and boring, which I guess is the point. A bored deputy scans my ID, walks me through a metal detector, and hands me a visitor badge with my name spelled wrong. The walls are painted off-white and have that spattered texture that makes everything look like it's covered in the residue of old secrets. The visiting room is just as I remember from the last time I had to ID a suspect: thick glass, a row of plastic chairs, and a table bolted to the floor.

Troy Bennett sits at the far end, hands folded neatly in front of him, elbows just inside the painted rectangle that marks where he's allowed to exist. His hair is shorter, almost military now, and the orange jumpsuit is pristine—no stains, no frayed edges. The chain on his cuffs is short enough to make sure he can't stand up without looking ridiculous.

He doesn't look up as I approach. He stares at a speck of dust on the table and waits.

I sit. The chair is built for someone half my height. I cross my legs and wait until he breaks the silence.

"Ms. Grant," he says, finally. The voice is softer than I remember, but the cadence is all cop: each word weighed, measured, never wasted.

"Detective," I reply.

He smirks. "Not anymore, not in here."

"I guess not." I smile, just enough to be rude.

He shifts, and the chain rattles. "You didn't have to come here. Could have just sent a letter."

I lean forward, elbows on the table, hands folded to match his. "I wanted to see if you'd say the same things to my face."

He considers this, head cocked to the side, like a crow sizing up a dead thing. "Most people come here to ask for forgiveness, or to rub it in."

"I'm not most people." I scan his face, looking for a crack. "I want to know why."

He blinks, then shakes his head slow, as if he's disappointed in my lack of imagination. "You know why. You've always known why."

I let the silence expand, the way Dr. Riley taught me. It works. He fills it.

"Your father was the last honest man in the county," Bennett says. "But he had a blind spot, and that's what killed him. Loyalty. It's a poison." His smile is thin. "Did you know he tried to take the whole thing on himself? He was going to fall on his sword, let everyone else walk away clean."

I don't react. "You're not him. You never were."

The smile vanishes. "No. I did what needed doing. I played the game. You think anyone here cares about the truth?" He jerks his head toward the ceiling, the walls, the invisible audience behind the glass.

"They care now," I say. "The investigation is public. There's nowhere left to hide."

He snorts, a humorless sound. "You think this is over? You haven't put out the last flame yet." The words are rehearsed, but there's something desperate at the edge.

I file that away, but don't show it. "Then tell me what comes next. Help me end it."

He leans back, the chair creaking. "You already know. You're smarter than your father, but you make the same mistakes."

I set my jaw, determined not to let him see he's gotten to me. "You're going away for a long time, Bennett. And when you do, I'll make sure everyone remembers what you did. No more hiding behind badges."

He shrugs, the gesture loose and indifferent. "Everyone's got something to hide. Even you."

"Not anymore," I say, and stand.

He watches me go, and the last thing I see is his smile—small, cold, and utterly alone.

Lucas is waiting just inside the door, arms folded. His jaw is set, but he's careful not to crowd me.

"You good?" he asks.

"Yeah," I say. "He's just noise now."

He walks me to the car, and when we're on the road, he finally speaks. "I don't like you going in there alone."

I glance at him, then at the long line of sunset on the horizon. "I wasn't alone."

He smiles, but it's the tired kind, the kind that says he knows I'll never let him shield me from anything.

"He said there's more coming. More fires, more secrets." I say it like it's nothing, but my voice comes out strained.

Lucas's hand finds mine on the console. "Let them come," he says, echoing the words I'd once thrown at him like a challenge.

We drive home with the windows cracked, the cold air keeping us sharp, awake. I watch the world blur by, the horizon edged with the promise of night.

Whatever's left, we'll face it.

Together.

10

Rekindled

SOPHIE

MOVING IN TOGETHER IS SUPPOSED TO BE A ROMANTIC milestone, the kind that gets its own set of matching wine glasses and a staged photo for the fridge. In reality, it's a hellmouth of cardboard, sweat, and passive-aggressive negotiations about which ancient crockpot gets to live under the counter and which is condemned to the garage. Our new house—a brick duplex with fake shutters and a lawn so flat it looks ironed—smells like paint, dust, and the last tenants' cologne.

I'm standing in the middle of the living room, surrounded by box towers labeled with my handwriting or Lucas's, surveying the territory like a general about to declare martial law. Sunlight slices through the east window, highlighting the streaks on the glass and turning the heap of moving blankets into a theatrical set piece. The couch is mine—a plaid monstrosity with mysterious stains and springs that attack the unsuspecting. The bookshelf is his, steel-framed and industrial, each shelf already allocated by subject and subcategory.

Lucas is in the entryway, taping off a patch of baseboard that "needs another coat." He moves with his usual methodical grace, every gesture purposeful, every tool returned to its exact place when he's done. He's already unpacked two boxes of firefighting manuals and is organizing them by publisher date and "personal relevance." I watch as he flips through one, lips moving like he's taking inventory of every paragraph.

The difference in our methods is as stark as the difference in our histories: he wants order, a promise that things will stay where he puts them. I want proof that I was here, that my family's debris matters, even if only as evidence. So I go for the photos. Out comes the battered shoebox, out tumble the snapshots—Mom in her garden, Dad in his dress uniform, my cousin and I at the county fair, faces sticky with funnel cake. I scatter them across the mantle, the bookshelf, and wedge one into the corner of the bathroom mirror. I want the house to feel lived in, even if it's only by ghosts.

"Where do you want this?" Lucas holds up a framed shot from my high school graduation. I'm in cap and gown, grinning like an idiot. Dad stands next to me, one hand on my shoulder, the other balled into a fist in his pocket. You can't see the anger in his eyes, only the way his jaw locks when he's holding back disappointment.

I take the frame, trace the edge with my thumb. "Somewhere you'll have to look at it every day. So, kitchen?"

He shrugs, sets it on the counter. "You got it."

There's a lull, the kind of silence that's not quite comfortable, not quite awkward. I break it by cranking up the stereo—old punk, Dad's favorite, the kind of music that makes paint dry faster and spackle cure hard as concrete. Lucas winces at the volume, but he lets it go.

We work through the boxes, the piles of stuff that survived the purges and fires and goodbyes. My mother's ceramic mixing bowls, each with a crack running down the side like a roadmap of every argument we ever had. Lucas's Army duffel, its contents folded with a care that borders on religious. The overlap is minimal, which is good: there's only so much of each other's past we can fit into a space this small.

In the kitchen, I find the plates—a mismatched set, half mine and half his, the colors clashing in a way I kind of love. I start stacking them in the cabinet, but my hands pause on the edge of a chipped saucer. It's from Dad's old house, the one that went up in smoke. The blue around the rim is faded almost white.

Lucas comes up behind me, sets down a box labeled "utensils—

USEFUL." He waits, patient, the way he always does when I'm drifting.

"You all right?" he asks.

I nod, but the motion feels shaky. "Just thinking."

He leans against the counter, arms folded, and watches me finish stacking the dishes. I keep my back to him until the last plate's in place, then turn, hands flat on the Formica. He's studying me, eyes soft, waiting for whatever I want to say.

"I don't want this to just be...survival," I say, surprising myself with how fast it comes out. "I want to actually build something here. Not just patch holes and hope they hold."

He considers that, then nods. "What does building look like, for you?"

I chew on the words. "I want to start a fire ed program. For the town. For the schools. In Dad's name, maybe. Not just as a memorial, but...so people remember what he was trying to do. What he actually died for."

Lucas doesn't smile, not really, but something in his face opens.

He moves closer, sets his hand over mine. "Then we build it. You know I'm in."

I let the silence stretch, then shake my head, half-laughing. "You say that now, but you haven't seen me try to teach a room full of five-year-olds about stop, drop, and roll."

"I've seen you wrangle a whole town through a three-alarm. You'll be fine." His voice is gentle, the kind of gentle that doesn't sound like pity. It's support, plain and solid as brick.

I look around the kitchen—the paint is still fresh enough to give off a chemical sting, the light bulb over the sink flickers when the wind hits the house just right. The table is an old one, scratched with initials from at least three different owners. It's ugly, but it's sturdy, and I kind of love it already.

"Do you want to paint this room?" I ask.

Lucas shrugs. "I was going to ask you the same thing. I figured you'd pick some wild color."

I grab a post-it, jot down "Sunflower" and slap it to the fridge. "Compromise: we each pick a wall. I get yellow, you get whatever industrial shade you want."

He grins. "Deal."

THE REST OF THE DAY IS A BLUR OF UNPACKING, rearranging, occasionally stopping to argue over whether the blender goes under the sink or in the pantry. Lucas insists on labeling every box before he opens it, reading the contents like it's a classified briefing. I just tear into things, half the time forgetting what I even packed. At one point, I find a box labeled "Christmas?" and it's just filled with tangled string lights and the creepy ceramic Santa my mom hated. I plug it in; the eyes light up red, and I set it in the window as a challenge to the neighborhood.

We break for pizza around dusk. There's nowhere to sit except the floor, so we use a moving blanket as a picnic mat. Lucas cracks open a beer, hands it to me, then takes one for himself. The silence is comfortable now, filled with the sound of the house settling and the street outside winding down.

"So," he says, picking at the crust. "When do you want to start on the fire ed thing?"

I shrug. "Whenever. There's no funding, but I figure if I show up at the school with enough handouts, they'll let me talk to the kids."

He nods, thoughtful. "I can help with curriculum. And get you in with the city. They love a pilot program."

I raise my beer. "To pilot programs."

He clinks bottles, then wipes the foam from his lip with the back of his hand. "You ever think about what comes after?"

I tilt my head. "After what?"

He shrugs, like he's trying to play it casual, but the set of his jaw says he means it. "After all this. After the town calms down, after the fire ed is up and running. What do you want for yourself?"

I have no answer. For so long, my only goal was to outlive the next disaster. The idea of wanting something that wasn't just survival feels...dangerous. But also exhilarating.

"Ask me again tomorrow," I say, and he laughs, deep and real.

We finish the pizza, then get back to work. At one point, he's hauling a box up the stairs and the whole thing comes apart—books, socks, a set of cheap steak knives, and my dad's old badge, which slides across the landing and lands at my feet. I pick it up, dust it off, and tuck it in the junk drawer for safekeeping.

Lucas sees me do it, but he doesn't say anything. He just puts a hand on my shoulder and squeezes.

The night comes on fast, and by the time we collapse into bed, every muscle in my body aches. The sheets are scratchy, the mattress too soft, but it's the best sleep I've had in years.

In the morning, the house smells like coffee and fresh paint. I pad downstairs, find Lucas already in the kitchen, reading the news on his phone and eating a bowl of oatmeal. He looks up, grins, and gestures to the new plaque he's already hung on the wall:

"LEAVE IT BETTER THAN YOU FOUND IT."

I shake my head, but I'm smiling.

I grab a mug, pour the coffee, and join him at the table. Sunlight floods the kitchen, turning the yellow post-it on the fridge to gold.

This time, I let myself believe it: we could actually build something here.

Maybe even something that lasts.

The kitchen table is buried, and I mean buried, in the detritus of good intentions: legal pads with corners chewed, stacks of post-it notes in colors that should not coexist, at least three empty coffee mugs, and a flock of fire safety brochures that came in a box so big I had to drag it inside with a strap and a prayer. Somewhere under the flyers is my laptop, open to a spreadsheet that mocks my attempts at organization with its blank columns and blinking cursor.

Lucas sits across from me, pen spinning in his hand like a tiny, lethal baton. His phone is on speaker, and the voice on the other end is a Town Council rep who I'm pretty sure once voted against fire prevention funding because he thought "kids should learn to fear consequences." Lucas's voice is patient, measured, almost soothing. Mine is two decibels louder than I mean it to be, because I keep forgetting that in this house I'm allowed to take up space.

"Absolutely, we'll have a full curriculum draft ready for review by Monday," Lucas says. "No, we're not planning to use open flame. Yes, we know the school board still has a restraining order against pyrotechnics." He pauses, then gives me a look that says, See? I told you they'd be worried about that.

I scowl, but it's fake. "Let me know if you want me to talk to him," I mouth.

Lucas holds up a finger. "We'll send the packet. Thanks so much, Dave." He disconnects, then sets the phone down with a soft click. "You owe me a beer," he says, grinning.

"You don't even like beer."

"I like being right. That's close enough."

I grab a handful of colored markers and start sketching a poster, trying to remember what actual children respond to. (Bright colors? Cartoon flames with friendly faces?) In the process, I get orange Sharpie on my wrist and a smear of blue under my thumbnail. I don't bother wiping it off. Instead, I attack the phone tree, dialing through the list of volunteers, each conversation a little easier than the last. Maybe it's the caffeine, maybe it's the way Lucas nods at my side of the conversation like I'm the world's best negotiator, but for the first time in weeks, I don't stutter when I ask for help.

"Hi, this is Sophie Grant, I'm organizing the fire education day next month... Yes, that Grant... No, I'm not running for office... We'd love to have you—really? Three dozen cupcakes? That's amazing. Thank you so much."

Every call is a new surprise. People remember my dad, remember the old firehouse, the way he used to dress up in the sad foam mascot suit for Safety Days. The word spreads, and soon the emails start rolling in: "My son's Cub Scout troop wants to help." "The Lions Club can donate banners." "Do you need anyone to drive the fire truck for the parade?"

By the end of the week, we have more volunteers than slots and an inbox stuffed with offers from every business in town—everyone who ever owed my father a favor, and a few who just want their logo on the back of the event t-shirts.

I print out the first run of flyers and spread them on the table. Lucas reads each one, checks for typos, and stacks them with military precision.

"You know," he says, "if this keeps up, we're going to have to find a bigger venue."

I look at him, marker cap between my teeth. "Is that a humblebrag?"

He leans forward, voice pitched low. "I'm proud of you."

The words hit harder than they should. I make a joke of it, flicking a wadded post-it at his forehead. "Wait until the first kindergartener torches his own eyebrows off. Then we'll see how proud you are."

He snorts. "You want me to make dinner?"

"God, yes."

He stands, grabs the takeout menu from the fridge, and starts dialing. I sit back and look at the table—a mess, but a mess with purpose.

Two nights later, we have a dry run with the volunteers. The new community center smells like wet paint and burnt popcorn from the movie night before. I set up stations: "Crawl Low and Go," "Fire Extinguisher Demo," "Safe Escape Plan," and, for the brave, a "Meet the Firefighter" selfie booth. Lucas runs the extinguisher station, demonstrating proper technique with the same focus he brought to his old job, but with kids instead of chaos.

The volunteers are a mix of retired fire personnel, high school seniors, and parents who are suspiciously well-versed in crowd control. I assign jobs, tweak the schedule, and try not to micromanage. When I notice the former captain of the Ladies' Auxiliary gently correcting one of my banners, I just nod and let her do it better.

By the end of the night, my feet hurt and my throat is raw, but I can't stop smiling. Lucas finds me by the supply closet, a smear of charcoal on his cheek and a length of caution tape draped around his shoulders like a sash.

"You look like you fought a fire and lost," I say.

He grins. "Kids wanted to see the suit. One of them hit me with a marshmallow shooter."

I laugh, louder than I mean to. It echoes off the cinderblock.

Lucas's eyes go soft. "You did good, Soph."

The morning of the event, I wake up to the sound of the town itself. Car horns, a garbage truck, the thump of someone's bass two streets over. I roll over and see Lucas, already up, tacking a handwritten "Welcome!" sign to the front door.

We drive to the community center in convoy: Lucas, me, two fire trucks, a police car on escort, and a parade of minivans filled with every kid in Willow Creek. The parking lot is a controlled disaster, but nobody's mad. Even the parents look excited, their skepticism replaced with something close to pride.

Inside, the place is alive. Kids in plastic fire hats swarm the stations. Parents crowd around the "Home Hazards" table, swapping horror stories. Lucas mans the big red engine, letting kids take turns at the siren. Every time I look over, he's crouched to kid-level, making jokes and fielding questions with the patience of a saint.

I drift from table to table, checking in, making small talk, fixing what breaks. At one point, the former Ladies' Auxiliary captain pulls me aside and hands me a plate of cookies shaped like flames. "Your father would have loved this," she says, squeezing my arm just tight enough to hurt.

The words settle into me, heavy and hot. I nod, unable to answer.

After the closing speech—brief, mostly thank-yous—I step outside, blinking in the sharp spring sunlight. The crowd noise fades, replaced by the buzz of a world that suddenly feels open.

I walk to the edge of the lot, where the grass gives way to an ugly patch of mud. I let myself breathe for the first time all day.

A moment later, Lucas finds me. He stands beside me, close but not touching, hands shoved in his pockets.

"You okay?" he asks.

I nod, but tears are stinging behind my eyes, so I keep looking straight ahead.

He waits, giving me space.

"They actually showed up," I say, voice barely more than a whisper.

"They showed up for you," he says.

I shake my head, wipe my nose with the back of my hand. "For Dad, maybe. For the idea of him."

He leans in, voice warm. "For both of you. They see you, Sophie."

I let the tears come, just a little. Lucas puts his arm around my waist, pulls me in. We watch the crowd together, the town that once called us trouble and now calls us...something else. Something better.

The sun is bright, the air smells like mud and hope.

I let myself believe, for once, that we're part of it. That we belong.

And that maybe, just maybe, the best is still ahead.

The community center smells like a strange cocktail of cinnamon buns, hand sanitizer, and the bitter, institutional tang of fresh latex paint. The walls are splashed with color—fire safety posters in crayon and marker, a banner that reads "Fire Prevention Saves Lives" flanked by clip-art flames, and a photo collage someone made of my father in every known variant of firehouse mustache.

It's a full house. There are kids everywhere, most with plastic helmets or some piece of turnout gear that dwarfs their bodies. The parents hover at the tables, gathering pamphlets or trying to convince their youngest to return the fire truck-shaped stress ball. There's an energy to the air, a current of nervous excitement that I feel in my bones, right down to the ache that lives between my shoulder blades.

I hover at the edge of the activity, one hand wrapped tight around a travel mug of burnt coffee. I should be circulating, shaking hands, doing the glad-handing thing, but my nerves are still raw from the morning news spot and the five different reporters who called before breakfast. Every time I take a step toward the crowd, I can feel the old panic squeeze my lungs. I focus instead on Lucas, who is in his natural element at the "Put Out the Fire!" demo. He's ringmaster for a cluster of middle schoolers, all of whom are laser-focused on his instructions.

He holds up a miniature fire extinguisher, flips it end over end, and gives a quick safety spiel. Then he hands it off to a kid who can barely keep the nozzle steady. The kid nails the target anyway—red confetti bursts from the fake candle, and the crowd erupts into shrieks and applause. Lucas catches my eye across the room, and the look he gives me is part pride, part dare.

You got this, his face says.

I take a shaky breath and square my shoulders.

The schedule says my turn at the podium is in three minutes, but the volunteers are ahead of the game. The program director, a woman with the posture of a ballerina and the voice of a drill sergeant, motions me forward with a bright, expectant smile. I fish the notecards from my pocket—creased, sweaty, hopelessly out of order—and force myself to move through the crowd.

The podium is small and unsteady, the kind that wobbles if you breathe too hard. The microphone whines as they adjust it down to my height. I blink out into the sea of faces, see at least three former high school classmates, the mayor in a cheap suit, and—dead center—Lucas, arms folded, mouth tipped up in a not-quite smile.

I start with the script. "Thank you all for coming," I say, and the room settles instantly. "When I first thought about putting this together, I wasn't sure anyone would show up. It's a Saturday, and it's March Madness, and..." I glance at the mascot costume parked in the corner, currently inhabited by a volunteer with questionable stamina, "...we don't have a bounce house, so I'm grateful to see so many of you here anyway."

A ripple of laughter, real and genuine.

I look down at my notes, but my eyes blur the ink. "Some of you knew my dad," I say. "He was the guy who'd show up to your house if you burned a turkey or locked yourself out of your car, but he was also the guy who believed that the best way to fight a fire was to keep it from starting in the first place. I used to think that was corny. But now—after everything—I get it."

I put the cards aside. My hands shake. I anchor them to the edges of the podium.

"I spent a lot of my life running from the past. From what happened to him, to me, to all of us. But today, standing here, I realize that we're not supposed to run. We're supposed to rebuild. That's what this is. A chance to start over."

There's a hush, the kind that makes every cough sound like a cannon.

I look at Lucas. He gives a tiny nod, like a green light I didn't know I was waiting for.

"There's something else," I say, voice thin but steady. I reach into my jacket and pull out an envelope—the battered kind you find wedged in the back of a drawer, yellowed at the edge, the paper gone soft as cloth. I slide the letter free, careful not to tear it.

"My dad left me something," I say. "A letter. I found it after... well. I found it. And I'd like to read it, if that's okay."

A few heads nod, solemn. Someone in the back sniffles.

I unfold the letter, hands trembling.

"'Dear Soph,'" I read, the words strange and familiar all at once. "'I know you don't want a speech, but this is the only way I can say what I need to. Life is going to burn you. People will let you down. Sometimes you'll think you don't have anything left to give. But you're stronger than you know. You're the smartest, bravest person I've ever met. You'll do things I never had the guts to try. Don't let the world tell you you're too much, or not enough. You're exactly what this place needs. You are the fire they never expected.'"

I stop. My mouth is dry. I look up, and I can't see anything except the blur of faces. The applause is a wall of sound, loud and rolling, and for a second, I just stand there, letting it crash over me.

When I step down, Lucas is waiting. He doesn't say anything, just puts his arm around my shoulders and pulls me into a side hug that's more steadying than anything I could have asked for. The line of people waiting to talk to me is endless. Old men with trembling hands, kids clutching plastic helmets, parents with voices thick from crying. They tell me stories about my father, about fires he put out and lives he touched. They hug me, clap me on the back, say things like, "You're making him proud."

The event is a hit. The firehouse mascot makes it to the last hour without fainting, the kids collect enough stickers to wallpaper their bedrooms, and the parents leave with a new respect for smoke detectors. Lucas spends the entire afternoon running the "hands-on demo" and only sets off the building's actual alarm once.

We go home exhausted, each of us limping in a different way. The house is warm and alive, and I collapse onto the couch while Lucas digs a pint of ice cream out of the freezer. He flops next to me, flicks on a terrible action movie, and lets the noise fill up all the leftover spaces inside us.

I turn to him, spoon halfway to my mouth. "Did you mean it? Before? That you're proud of me?"

He sets his bowl down, wipes the corner of his mouth. "Every word."

I reach out, take his hand in mine, and thread our fingers together.

"I want to do more," I say. "Not just the program, but...more. A life. A legacy. Maybe even a family, someday."

He squeezes my hand, gentle and strong. "All of it," he says, his voice low and certain. "Whatever you want. We'll build it together."

That night, I wake to moonlight slanting across the bed, painting the sheets in stripes of silver and blue. Lucas is already awake, propped on an elbow, watching me with a look that's half desire, half awe.

He reaches for me, and I go to him, straddling his lap with my knees on either side of his hips. The air between us is thick with everything we haven't said, every dream we're afraid to speak aloud. I cup his face in both hands and kiss him slow, a kind of promise.

He grins, then tugs my shirt over my head, hands warm on my skin. I push him back into the mattress, pinning his wrists above his head. He lets me, eyes locked on mine, breathing ragged.

I lean down, mouth at his ear. "I want it all, Lucas. I want to be someone who leaves things better than she found them. I want you—every part of you. Forever, if you can stand it."

He groans, low and desperate, and I feel him hard and wanting between my thighs. "You drive me crazy," he says.

"That's the plan," I whisper, and roll my hips against him, slow and deliberate.

He breaks his hands free, slides them up my spine, and holds me as if I might disappear. I move above him, slow at first, savoring every gasp and shiver. He meets me, thrust for thrust, and the world shrinks to just the two of us—our bodies, our sweat, the sound of his name on my lips.

When I come, it's with a force that leaves me shaking. He follows, gripping my hips so tight I know I'll have marks tomorrow.

After, we lie tangled together, chests heaving, skin slick. He pulls me into the curve of his body and buries his face in my hair.

"I love you," he says. "God, I love you."

I laugh, breathless, and kiss the hollow of his throat. "I love you, too."

We stay like that, drifting, the moon our only witness.

In the morning, there are still boxes to unpack, flyers to file, and a thousand small things that make up a life. But for now, there's coffee, and the quiet knowledge that we are exactly where we're supposed to be.

I look at Lucas, his hair sticking up, his face unguarded in the soft morning light.

"We did good," I say.

He nods, serious. "We're just getting started."

This is our beginning.

And I can't wait to see what we make of it.

11

Fault Line

LUCAS

There are days when the firehouse feels like a sanctuary, and days when it's just a waiting room for the next disaster. Today is neither. Today is a holding cell, fluorescent lights, old coffee, and paperwork that won't stop breeding. I'm at my desk working through a stack of vendor invoices when the station line rings, shrill enough to punch through the din of construction next door.

I let it go three, four rings before I answer, hoping it's just a vendor with another backorder. But the number on the display is downtown. Internal Affairs.

"Hayes," I say, pen hovering over a requisition form.

The voice on the other end is clipped, unfamiliar. "Captain, this is Janice Walsh, Office of Legal Review. I'm calling about the Bennett case."

"Go ahead," I say, bracing myself for another round of follow-up forms, another request for the same incident summaries I've already bled dry.

"There's been a development," she says. "The defense has retained external counsel. High-profile. They're seeking an immediate evidentiary review ahead of the upcoming parole hearing."

It takes a second for the words to land. When they do, my mouth goes dry.

"Who's the lawyer?" I ask.

She hesitates, which tells me everything.

"Caleb's family hired Grayson & Fogg," she says. "Lead is Daniel Fogg. You know the name?"

"Yeah," I say. Everyone in this business knows the name. Daniel Fogg: the grave robber of convictions, king of loopholes and technicalities, a man who's made his fortune flipping slam-dunk sentences with a smirk and a single precedent.

I can feel my pulse in my teeth.

Walsh continues: "They're citing new evidence. Alleged mishandling of arson scene records, possible bias in witness statements. You're named in the supporting documents."

I grip the phone tighter, feel the plastic groan in my hand.

"What's the chance they'll win?" I ask, flat.

"Right now? Too close to call," she says. "If you want my advice: get your story straight. It's about to get ugly."

She hangs up before I can respond.

The office feels smaller than before. My hands won't stop shaking. I try to refocus on the invoice, but all I see is Fogg's name, the echo of "mishandling" repeating like a siren.

By the time I get home, it's past six. The front door is painted the same sunflower yellow Sophie insisted on, bright even in dusk. Inside, the house smells like dinner I'm too late for—

garlic, some kind of roasted root vegetable, and the high note of burnt cheese.

Sophie's at the kitchen island, grading a stack of fire safety pamphlets with a red pen, her glasses perched low and her hair in a messy knot. She looks up when I come in, studies my face the way a medic checks a wound.

"You're late," she says. "You okay?"

I drop my keys in the bowl, try for a shrug, but my shoulders are welded to my ears.

"Long day," I say. "You got a minute?"

Her eyes narrow. She pushes the stack of pamphlets aside, making room. "For you? Always."

I sit across from her, hands folded tight. The kitchen feels too bright, like an interrogation room. Sophie waits, not patient, exactly, but giving me room to find the words.

"Got a call from IA," I start. "They're reviewing the Bennett case. Defense hired a celebrity lawyer. They want to put everything on trial again—evidence, witness statements, even the old department records."

I try to sound casual, but the words are glass in my mouth.

Sophie's face goes stone still. She leans forward, elbows on the counter, voice a scalpel.

"Who's the lawyer?"

"Daniel Fogg."

She doesn't gasp, but her jaw sets hard enough to crack. I watch her hands—how she curls them into fists, the way she taps her wedding band once, twice against the Formica. For a long second, neither of us speaks.

Then she slams her coffee mug down on the counter, so hard coffee sloshes over the rim.

"They can't do this," she says. Her voice is sharp, the old edge in it, the one she uses when a town hall meeting goes sideways or someone tries to cheat the system.

I want to tell her it'll be okay, but I can't.

She stands abruptly, wipes her hands on her jeans, and grabs her laptop from the charger. She disappears down the hallway, returns with three binders—red, green, blue—all labeled in her precise block print: "WCFD INCIDENTS," "LEGAL PRECEDENT," "GRANT ARCHIVE." She opens the laptop, starts typing before it even fully boots. She's already searching for a crack in Fogg's reputation, a place to wedge the crowbar of fact.

I watch her work: the way her eyes flick back and forth, the way she brings up old PDFs and court records with the speed of muscle memory. She clicks, highlights, bookmarks. Every motion is measured and deliberate, a woman in full command of her war.

I want to help. I want to do something besides sit here and let her fight for me.

But she's faster than I am, and smarter.

"Do you want coffee?" I ask, just to break the momentum.

She shakes her head, eyes locked on the screen. "This isn't about coffee, Lucas. This is about them trying to erase everything we built. Everything your team did. Everything my father died for." Her voice cracks, just for a second. Then she closes the gap, double clicks, and the steel returns.

She starts stacking papers—court filings, hearing notices, department logs—until the kitchen is more file room than home. I realize I've never seen her like this: so focused, so angry, so alive.

I stand, round the island, put my hand on her shoulder. She flinches, just a little, then relaxes into my grip.

"You don't have to do this alone," I say, low.

She doesn't look at me, but her hand covers mine, squeezes once.

"Neither do you," she replies.

I stay beside her, watching as she builds a fortress of facts between us and the rest of the world.

She'll find the hole in their argument. She always does.

And when she does, I'll be ready to burn it down with her.

SOPHIE

The world narrows to a tunnel of paper and blue light. I lose track of time, maybe even lose myself, somewhere between the third refill of coffee and the second spiral-bound notebook I fill with scribbled notes. I work in increments: one hearing transcript, one database query, one untangling of the past for every hour that passes. By midnight, the dining room looks like the aftermath of a document grenade.

Lucas hovers at the edge of my world. He brings coffee, sometimes snacks, rarely words. He sits at the head of the table, flipping through incident logs with the same tension he brings to waiting for a call. His phone buzzes every ten minutes: updates from the station, from Legal, from people he pretends not to care about but can't stop tracking. He paces. He opens and closes the fridge. He rubs his jaw like he's trying to erase the stubble. I don't mind; his orbit is grounding.

I am method. I am pattern recognition. I am the sum of every obsessive impulse I ever called a flaw. When I feel the first migraine ping at the base of my skull, I tie my hair tighter, adjust my glasses, and tell myself I can sort it all if I just keep digging.

By 2:47 a.m., I'm onto something. It's subtle, a thread of missing paperwork in a year nobody wanted to remember. I print out the incident reports and line them up by date, a parade of half-legible scrawl across the kitchen island. The town's arson problem wasn't new, but there was a spike—summer of 2008, a period so bad the local paper called it the "Black July." I remember because my dad stopped coming home for dinner that entire month. And Lucas, back then, was just a new transfer, barely out of the academy.

I scan the names on the bottom of each report. "L. HAYES," again and again, always the secondary officer, sometimes the only signature.

There are gaps. Big ones.

I pull a sharpie, start a timeline on the butcher paper I saved from a hardware run. Every incident, every responder, every deviation from protocol. It takes an hour, but a shape starts to form: a string of missing reports, every one in Lucas's rookie year, every one signed off by then-captain Bennett.

I call up the personnel records, crosscheck dates. A sinking feeling presses into my stomach.

The clincher comes at 4:06. I find a digital file, flagged in the old archive system as "ENTRY BY L. HAYES / 07-15-2012—MISSING." The system isn't supposed to show you what isn't there, but sometimes the audit logs leave ghosts. My finger traces the line of text. I look up at Lucas, who is staring into the distance, lost in thought.

"These are all supposed to have your signature," I say, voice just above a whisper.

Lucas stops mid-sip, his mug suspended in the air, arm bent like he's bracing for an explosion.

I slide the printouts across the table. "There's a pattern," I say. "Bennett was running a paper trail. But he needed you to sign off—because he knew the auditors would believe you."

Lucas's face drains of color. He sets the mug down, the click of ceramic on wood loud in the hush of the house.

He stares at the page, at the line with his own name, and I see a thousand memories flashing behind his eyes.

"I remember that summer," he says, voice barely there. "Bennett always made me sign the reports. Wouldn't let me write them, just sign off. I figured it was some bullshit rookie hazing. I didn't know—" He breaks off, jaw set so hard the muscle jumps.

I push the evidence toward him, gentle but insistent. "You were just a kid, Lucas. You didn't light the match."

He shakes his head, once, but the guilt is already in him, eating at the places trauma likes to nest. He flips through the stack, each page a gut punch.

"I didn't know what he was using them for," Lucas says, softer than before. "He'd say, 'Just sign here. It's all protocol.' If I ever hesitated, he'd say it was about discipline. Chain of command."

I reach across the table, lay my hand over his. "You didn't know. But now you do."

The words hang in the air. He closes his eyes, breathes slow.

I watch him, the man who never ran from a fire, frozen by the realization he might have fueled one, if only on paper.

I get up, walk behind him, and wrap my arms around his shoulders. I feel the tremor running through him.

"You're not him," I say, right into his hair.

He nods, but I can tell he's not convinced.

"Should I keep looking?" I ask.

He takes a moment. Then: "Yes. If there's more, we need to know."

I keep at it, Lucas beside me, both of us chasing ghosts through town archives and old news clippings. At dawn, we have a full timeline, every forged report and every missing signature, all of them pointing to a system that was rigged from the start.

Lucas finally speaks, voice low. "If these come up in court, I'll be on the hook. They'll say I was complicit."

I slide the last report into the stack and look him dead in the eye. "You're not the villain here. You're the witness."

He laughs, sharp and sad. "Let's see if anyone else believes that."

But I do. I always have.

We sit in the silence of the new day, each of us holding the weight of what we've found. The kitchen is a mess. My hair is a disaster. His face is shadowed with more worry than sleep.

But we're still here.

And we know what we're fighting.

LUCAS

After the sun rises, everything feels heavier. I sit on the couch in the living room, elbows on my knees, hands knotted tight against my skull. The stack of paper from the kitchen migrated with us—timeline, audit log, every little slice of the past that's now a ticking bomb. I stare at the mess, wishing I could un-know it. Wishing I could go back and rewrite the story where I didn't sign away my future for the sake of protocol.

Sophie stands in the doorway, arms crossed. Her face is impossible to read: part cop, part comfort, all hers.

"If these missing reports come to light during the hearing," I say, voice so raw it's a stranger's, "they'll say I was complicit. They'll say I helped. My testimony won't mean anything."

She comes forward, steps quiet on the creaking floor. She kneels down in front of me, pries my hands apart, and holds them between hers. Her skin is warm, fingers wrapped so tight it almost hurts.

"You were a kid," she says, voice absolute. "You didn't light the match."

I shake my head. "Doesn't matter. I should have known. I should have seen it coming."

She moves closer, so her knees touch mine, her face inches away. "You couldn't have known. That's what people like Bennett count on. They count on good men being too scared to question orders."

She doesn't blink. She holds my gaze, refuses to look away.

"I'm not a good man," I say. It's not self-pity, just the ugly truth, cracked open for inspection.

She lets out a breath. "You're the best man I know. And you're not running from this, so don't start now."

Her grip tightens. She's shaking, just a little, but her voice never wavers. "You want to quit? You want to roll over and let Fogg win? Go ahead. But you know what happens if you do."

I do. I've lived that future every night for the last decade.

I look away, can't stand her conviction.

She stands, pulling me up with her. The weight of her hand anchors me, even as everything else threatens to float away. She guides me to the window, the one that looks out on the back yard and the street lamp still flickering from last night's storm.

Outside, the world is dark, puddles gleaming on the sidewalk. My reflection in the glass is ghostly—shoulders hunched, face pale, eyes hollow. I barely recognize myself.

Sophie comes up behind me, slides her arms around my waist, presses her cheek against my back. The pressure is grounding. For a minute, we just stand there, watching the rain, the window cold against my forehead.

"You're not your mistakes," she says, a whisper against my skin.

I want to believe her. I really do.

She pulls me in, holds me so tight my ribs ache. I bury my face in her neck, breathe in the smell of her—coffee, vanilla, a trace of smoke from a lifetime spent in the aftermath.

I'm shaking, but she never lets go. Her hands move up, into my hair, cradling the back of my head.

"You're good," she says again, and this time it sinks in, just a little.

I want to ask how she can be so sure. I want to ask what she sees that I can't.

But her mouth finds mine, and her tongue is insistent, and all the questions burn away.

She walks me backward, out of the living room, down the hall, toward the only place in the house where the lights are still off. The world narrows to her touch, her breath, the way she never lets me go.

The house is silent, but her footsteps are loud in my ears. She pushes me gently onto the edge of the bed, follows me down, straddles my lap and pins my hands above my head. Her hair falls around us, a dark curtain.

She leans down, kisses the hollow of my throat, the scar on my collarbone. She's mapping me, cell by cell, trying to overwrite the shame with her own heat.

"Let me," she says, and her voice is pure need.

I nod. She smiles, a little sad, a little wicked, and starts to undress me, slow and deliberate.

I let her.

I let myself be seen.

I let myself believe, just for now, that I can still do good.

The only light in the bedroom is the moon, spilling through the half-open window and painting everything in blue. I sit on the edge of the bed, chest bare, every scar and old burn picked out in ghostly silver. Sophie stands in the doorway for a second, watching me, her arms folded across her chest like she's holding herself together. Then she lets the robe slide off her shoulders and comes to me.

She climbs onto the mattress, knees on either side of my hips, her hands warm and steady as she finds my face. Her thumbs brush my cheekbones, my jaw, the furrow in my brow. She kisses each spot in turn, like she's erasing my old history, rewriting it cell by cell.

She works the rest of my clothes off—slow, deliberate, never breaking eye contact. Her hands find my ribs, the new bruises, the faded lines of old surgeries. She runs her fingertips over each one like she's reading a secret code. My breath stutters, but she just smiles, soft and unafraid.

"You're not your mistakes," she whispers, and for once I almost believe it.

She kisses me, slow and deep. The kind of kiss that makes you forget what day it is, or how you ended up in this life, or what's waiting on the other side of morning. I pull her closer, greedy for every inch of skin.

She shoves me back onto the pillows, follows me down, her hair tumbling loose and cool around our faces. She straddles me, palms flat on my chest, and pins me there like a butterfly under glass.

Her hips move, a slow, grinding rhythm that starts to unspool me. Every time I reach for her, she grabs my hands and pins them above my head. She's smiling, but it's not playful. It's an act of will, of protection.

She kisses my neck, bites down just enough to leave a mark, then whispers: "You're good, Lucas. You're mine. You always have been."

I shudder, not from cold but from the ache in my chest. I want to say thank you, or I love you, or don't stop, but the words tangle up and catch in my throat.

She starts to move faster, her breath growing ragged. I watch the muscles of her arms tense, the curve of her back in the low light. When I try to sit up, she pushes me back, kisses me again, harder, until I melt into the sheets.

Her hands find my hips, dig in, anchor me. Her head falls forward, hair curtaining our faces. "Let it go," she says, and the words break me open.

I do. I let the guilt go, let the shame go, just for now. I let her take over.

She rocks her hips, faster and faster, until we're both panting, both shaking. She leans down, her mouth at my ear: "I need you, Lucas. I need you here."

She bites my shoulder, hard, as she comes. The sound she makes is low, desperate, hungry. It tears through me, leaves nothing behind but heat and want.

I follow, clinging to her as if I might fall apart otherwise. I grip her hips, bury my face in her neck, and let it all out—the fear, the anger, the love I'm still learning how to carry.

After, she collapses on top of me, her skin slick and warm, our heartbeats wild and tangled. We lie like that for a long time, the only sound our breathing and the night wind outside the window.

She rolls off, curls up at my side. Her head rests on my chest, her hand splayed over my heart like she's checking to make sure it's still beating.

For the first time in hours, my hands are steady.

We drift, not quite asleep. The world outside is all storm and dark, but in here it's just us.

I stare at the ceiling, tracing the cracks in the paint, counting them like I might count the number of times I've been given a second chance.

After a long while, I find my voice. "I'll do it," I say, not loud, but enough that she hears.

She lifts her head, eyes searching my face. "Do what?"

"I'll testify. About everything. Even if it buries me."

She studies me for a heartbeat, then nods. "We'll face it together."

I turn, pull her close. "Yeah?"

She smiles, the kind of smile that used to get her out of detention, the kind that's all teeth and dare.

"Yeah," she says. She kisses me, a promise more than anything else.

We stay like that, tangled and bruised and a little bit saved.

The moon moves across the bed, and I listen to the sound of her breathing.

I tell myself, over and over, that I can do this.

That I'm not my mistakes.

That I'm good, if only for her.

In the morning, the sun will rise, the fight will start all over.

But tonight, we are whole.

Tonight, we are enough.

12

Wild Fire

LUCAS

Courtrooms are nothing like TV, unless you count the way the seats are too close, the air is always at least five degrees too cold, and everyone's pretending they haven't already decided how it ends. My dress uniform is starched so stiff it could walk in without me. I try not to sweat through it, but my palms are clammy and every time I shift in my seat I hear the crinkle of fabric. I spot Sophie in the gallery before I spot anyone else. She's wedged between two reporters, knuckles white on the bench rail. There's a look in her eyes—half pride, half fear—that does more to wreck me than all the years of hazing and hellfire combined.

They call me up, and I walk the aisle slow. There's a weird gravity to it, like every step is through deep mud, and I can feel a hundred pairs of eyes peeling me open. The prosecutor's a woman with ice-blonde hair and an expression like she's just caught me trying to break into her house. The defense attorney, Fogg, leans back in his chair, all lazy confidence. Caleb is at the end of the table, cuffs barely visible under the sleeves of a department suit he probably stole from evidence. He looks at me with dead-cold eyes, lips curled up in a sneer.

The bailiff reads the oath. I raise my right hand and swear, hoping it'll be enough to outweigh all the times I looked the other way.

The prosecutor wastes no time.

"Please state your name and occupation for the record."

"Lucas Hayes. I'm a Captain with the Willow Creek Fire Department."

She runs me through the paces—how long I've served, my credentials, the nature of my relationship to both Grant and Bennett. She says Sophie's name like a trap, waiting for me to trip into it.

"She's my girlfriend," I say, and someone in the back row clicks their tongue. I wonder if it's a reporter or just some sadist who came for blood.

The prosecutor pivots, sharp as a snakebite. "Captain Hayes, you previously submitted a sworn statement regarding the incidents in question. Today, you indicated you wish to supplement or amend your original testimony. Is that correct?"

My mouth goes dry, but I nod. "Yes, ma'am."

"Would you please explain to the court what you're amending, and why?"

I take a breath, feel the starch pull at my ribs, and look out at the sea of faces. I make sure to find Sophie's, just for a second, before I answer.

"There's something I left out of my original statement," I say. "About the reports I signed for Bennett, and what I knew about the arson evidence."

The gallery murmurs. The judge raps his gavel and the room stills, but I can feel the anticipation coil tighter.

"Go on," the prosecutor urges.

I force my eyes to Bennett's, but he doesn't even blink. The bastard's hands are folded in front of him, like he's about to bless the food.

"In 2012," I say, "there was a string of fires—the ones they later called the 'Black July' blazes. I was a rookie, brand new to Willow Creek. Bennett was my captain. I thought he walked on water."

That gets a laugh somewhere behind me, and the judge scowls.

"Every time there was an incident, he'd have me sign off on the reports. Sometimes, he'd say the paperwork had to be redone, or that my signature didn't match the official file, and he'd walk the corrected sheet into Records himself. I thought it was just rookie hazing, or maybe just his way of teaching me about chain of command."

I swallow. My hands are shaking, so I clamp them together in my lap.

"I didn't realize what he was doing until later. That he was covering up evidence—missing accelerant traces, bad witness statements, even failing to report missing gear. Every time I asked, he said not to worry, that he'd 'take care of it.' He told me it was about protecting the department. And I believed him."

The prosecutor lets the silence stretch, then: "And did you ever personally alter any evidence, Captain Hayes?"

My heart stutters. "No," I say, maybe too quick. "But I did sign off on reports I knew were incomplete, or didn't match my recollection of the incident."

She nods, gentle. "Why are you coming forward now?"

I look straight at her. "Because it's the right thing to do. And because I couldn't live with the lie anymore."

She gives me a tiny, grateful smile. "Nothing further," she says, but she's not the one I'm afraid of.

Fogg is up, slow and easy, like he's got all the time in the world. He approaches the stand, one eyebrow cocked in perpetual skepticism.

"Captain Hayes," he says, "you say you were a rookie at the time. How old were you, exactly?"

"Twenty."

He smirks, as if to say: still a child. "And you admit, under oath, that you knowingly signed off on reports you believed to be false or misleading?"

I hesitate, just long enough for him to pounce.

"Is that a yes, Captain?"

"Yes."

"And yet you expect this court to believe that you only realized the extent of Captain Bennett's wrongdoing years later? You, an officer with exemplary training and record?"

I force myself to stay calm. "I was new to the department. I trusted my captain."

Fogg's lips twitch. "You trusted your captain so much, you never once questioned why he needed to 'fix' your paperwork?"

"I questioned it," I say. "But he said it was standard procedure."

"So you were complicit," Fogg says, voice rising. "You were not only a participant, but an enabler."

I feel the sweat bead on my neck. "I was manipulated, same as anyone else under his command."

Fogg slams a hand on the rail. "But you are an officer of the law, Captain Hayes. You expect us to believe you had no idea you were facilitating a cover-up?"

I feel myself flush, hot and ashamed. I look at Sophie, whose hands are pressed so tight to the bench the skin's gone white. She gives me the smallest nod, and I find my voice again.

"People like Bennett," I say, "they know how to use trust. They know how to make you believe it's all for the greater good. I wanted to fit in. I wanted to do my job. But I never, ever wanted to help a murderer walk free."

Fogg opens his mouth, but the judge waves him off. "That's enough, Mr. Fogg. We'll leave the closing arguments for later."

Fogg bows his head, but his eyes are daggers.

I step down, my knees jelly, and walk back to my seat. As I pass the gallery, Sophie's hand reaches out. Our fingers brush, just a second, but it's enough to let me breathe again. Her touch says: I see you. I know what it cost.

The judge calls a recess. The courtroom explodes into noise—reporters shouting, lawyers barking, the murmur of a town realizing the truth has just burned down every safe story it ever believed.

I sit, head in my hands, and wait for the smoke to clear.

The sound that wakes me is sharp enough to crack a tooth. I'm out of bed before I'm conscious, Sophie right behind me, her body pressed so close to my back that I feel her heartbeat. The clock says it's just after three, the time of night when even the nightmares take a break.

There's another crash, this time followed by the scatter of pebbles on tile. Sophie slides past me, opens her bedside drawer, and pulls out the flare gun we keep for emergencies—our kind of emergencies, anyway. She checks the load with the same fluidity she uses to tie her hair, then nods to me. I grab my phone, dial the station's overnight line, and whisper: "Possible 10-62 at my address. Need assistance."

The dispatcher answers with a click, the rest of her sentence lost in the static. I hang up, slip the phone in my pocket, and follow Sophie down the hall.

The house is silent except for the wheeze of the old fridge and the faint shudder in the walls from last night's storm. The moonlight is enough to see by, but Sophie kills the switch anyway, the darkness amplifying every noise. We move in tandem, two shadows skimming the perimeter. I know every creak of the boards, but tonight they all sound wrong, like someone's testing which ones will hold.

Sophie reaches the end of the hall, signals with a flat hand: stop. She listens, head tilted, then points toward the back door. There's movement, a silhouette flickering against the frosted glass, hunched and clumsy. She glances at me, and I give her the go.

She moves like a cat, barefoot and silent, then lifts the flare gun and shouts, "Back the fuck off!" The intruder freezes. I see the gleam of a tool in his hand—crowbar, maybe, or a tire iron.

He doesn't run. Instead, he jams the tool at the lock, splintering wood. Sophie fires. The flare erupts, bright and angry, slamming into the door frame. The light is nuclear, filling the kitchen with a pulse of red so strong it paints the room in blood. The figure ducks, arms flailing, then bolts for the yard. He's fast, but not fast enough—he catches the edge of the window and tears loose a strip of fabric, leaves it behind like a snake shedding skin.

The smell of sulfur and burning plastic chokes the air. Sophie stands, breathing hard, the flare gun still aimed at the door in case he comes back.

I check the lock, then scan the yard. The bastard's gone, but he left a trail—boot prints in the mud, a chunk of shirt dangling from the broken pane.

Sophie lowers the gun, hands shaking just a little. She doesn't notice the cut on her palm, where she must've caught glass when she braced against the counter.

"Bandages in the drawer," I say, voice low.

She nods, still running hot on adrenaline, and starts tearing the kitchen apart for first aid. I call the station again, get a real human this time, and relay the details.

As I talk, I pick up the scrap of cloth. Even before I turn it over, I know what it is: the sleeve of a fire department uniform. The same blue as Caleb's, the cuff patched where he once burned it on a rookie prank gone sideways.

Sophie sees it, and her mouth goes tight. "It was him," she says. "It had to be."

I nod. "You sure he's not just trying to scare us off?"

She snorts, bitter. "He's not smart enough for subtlety."

We clean up what we can. I wedge a broom handle into the door for leverage, tape a towel over the broken glass. Sophie bandages her hand, then helps me sweep the rest of the kitchen. The whole time, we don't say a word about how close it was, or what might've happened if she hadn't acted first.

When the cops show up, it's two patrol guys I don't know well, both of them green and overeager. They take our statements, poke around the yard, and mutter something about "upping patrols." It's clear they don't expect much—if the bad guy's not dead or bleeding, the night's just another unsolved.

After they leave, Sophie and I sit at the table, the flare gun and the scrap of cloth between us. She pours us both a shot of bourbon, no words, just the sound of the liquid hitting glass.

"He won't stop," I say, staring at the fabric. "Not until one more blaze takes you down."

Sophie's eyes narrow, jaw set hard as iron. "Let him try. We've already survived worse."

We touch our glasses together, the sound sharp as a warning.

Outside, the town is dark and quiet again, but we know it's just a lull.

Inside, the kitchen is scarred but standing, lit by the faint red glow still smoldering in the window.

We clean up, lock the doors, and get ready for morning.

SOPHIE

The light of morning is a different kind of brutal—a cold wash that strips away the drama of the night and leaves nothing but the raw aftermath. I wake to the sound of crows, their calls echoing off the eaves, and for a second I forget why my heart is pounding so hard. Then I see the line of blood across my palm, the way Lucas sleeps with one arm thrown toward me, fingers flexed like he's reaching for the flare gun even in dreams.

Downstairs, the kitchen is a ruin. The towel I taped over the window has turned brown with smoke, and the floor is a mosaic of glass shards, each piece catching the sunrise like a warning. The only sign of last night's fight—besides the mess—is the thin strip of blue cloth I pinned to the fridge, a trophy or a curse.

Lucas finds me standing in the doorway, coffee in hand, bare feet pressed flat against the wood. He comes up behind me, slides his arms around my waist, and rests his chin on my shoulder.

"Did you sleep?" he asks.

"A little. You?"

He grunts, the answer obvious.

We stand there, both looking out at the yard where the flare burned a patch of grass to a crisp. There's something weirdly peaceful about the scene: the sky gone gold, the world pretending nothing happened, even as the scent of burned plastic and fear lingers in the air.

"They'll be back," I say, voice barely above a whisper.

Lucas nods. "Probably with friends."

He squeezes my hips, gentle but grounding, and I lean into his chest. I think about the trial, the headlines, the years we spent running from our own fire. I think about the town, about the kids in plastic helmets, about the future that's supposed to belong to us if we can just make it through one more day.

"The wildfire of truth has been unleashed," I say, quoting something I heard on the news once, but it feels true.

He laughs, soft. "And though it may consume everything in its path, we'll rise from the ashes stronger together."

I tilt my head back, let him kiss my cheek, my temple, the curve of my jaw. He's always warm, always steady, even when the world is coming apart.

We spend the morning cleaning up. The cuts on my hand sting, but I ignore them. Lucas hammers the board over the window with the precision of a man who knows it won't hold forever, but will damn well hold for now. We eat breakfast standing up, plates balanced on the edge of the sink. Every time we brush against each other, he finds a way to touch me—shoulder, arm, back of the neck—like he's reminding both of us that we're still here.

When it's time to go, I pull my hair back, fix my makeup, and lace up the boots that survived two house fires and a flood. Lucas slides into his dress blues, buttons every button, and smooths the badge with a thumb.

At the door, I hesitate. He catches my hand, holds it tight.

"We got this," he says.

I believe him.

We step outside together, the sun at our backs, the glass on the sidewalk shining like so many tiny stars. The air is cold and sharp, but I don't feel it. Not with him beside me.

The day will bring more testimony, more danger, more chances for everything to burn down around us.

But for now, there is this: his hand in mine, our shadows crossing the lawn, and the knowledge that even if the world tries to break us, we'll light our own way out.

13

Emberfall

SOPHIE

THERE'S A SILENCE IN THE COURTROOM THAT'S NOT JUST the hush of bodies crowded together, not just the absence of noise. It's the absence of breath. Even the air holds its lungs, waiting for a ruling that will either cauterize or reopen every wound this town's ever suffered. I sit front row, hands folded so tight my knuckles ache. My nails cut crescents into my palms, but I don't let go. My suit is the only one I own that fits; it still smells faintly of smoke and the lavender sachet I shoved in the pockets last night.

The judge's bench is ten feet high, maybe more, but the man behind it looks smaller in person—gray-haired, glasses perched on the tip of his nose, the kind of face that used to scare me when I was five and Dad dragged me along to City Council. Now I see him for what he is: a man exhausted by the weight of decisions, a man who would rather be anywhere else.

Troy Bennett sits across the aisle, back straight, orange jumpsuit so new it still has the creases. He's shaved for the occasion, and the stubble that once made him seem more human is gone, replaced by that cold cop stare. His eyes flick across the room, tallying friend from foe, and when they land on me, he holds the look just a beat too long.

Lucas is a shadow at the back wall, arms folded, legs braced wide. He's not in uniform; today he's just a man, not a symbol. But his gaze is a laser, and the only thing keeping me from running out the door.

The judge shuffles his papers, adjusts his glasses, and finally looks up. "This court finds the defendant, Troy Bennett, guilty of arson, conspiracy, and aggravated manslaughter, murder, and attempted murder." The words drop like stones into water, sending ripples through the room: a cough here, a mutter there, a low gasp from the gallery.

He continues, voice flat and steady. "Sentencing is as follows: life without the possibility of parole."

A woman two rows back lets out a sob. I don't turn. I keep my eyes locked on the judge, because if I look at anything else, I'll unravel.

"Ms. Grant," the judge says. "Would you like to make a statement?"

I'd practiced this. In front of the bathroom mirror, in the car, once in the canned goods aisle at Safeway, when I thought no one was watching. Still, my knees go liquid as I stand. My hands leave damp prints on the fabric of my skirt. I walk to the podium, the clack of my heels punctuating every step.

The bailiff hands me a sheet of paper. My own handwriting looks foreign—each letter squared off, as if written by a stranger.

I clear my throat. My voice starts small, then builds.

"My name is Sophie Grant," I say. "I am the daughter of Captain Michael Grant, and I am here because I survived."

I pause, let the words fill the space. My eyes dart to Lucas, who gives me a single, slow nod.

"For years, I thought justice was a story that ended in fire. That if you just exposed the truth, it would burn away everything bad. But it doesn't." My voice is steadier now. "Justice doesn't always look like fire. Sometimes, it looks like survival."

I look directly at Troy, his eyes flat and cold as lake ice.

"My father once told me, 'If you want to change the world, you have to be willing to survive it first.' I believe that now. I believe he was right. I believe everyone in this room has lost something they can never get back. And I hope this ruling is the first step in making sure no one else loses a damn thing to men like Troy Bennett."

I fold the paper and set it on the podium. My hands are steady. "Thank you."

The judge nods. "Thank you, Ms. Grant. We appreciate your candor and your strength."

As I turn to walk back, I see movement in the gallery. An old woman dabs her eyes with a wrinkled tissue, her hands shaking. A man in a suit—one of the town's lawyers, maybe—gives a little exhale, like he's been underwater for months. A reporter, one I recognize from Channel 5, sets her notepad down and just watches me, eyes shining. For the first time in a year, I don't feel like a suspect. I feel like a person again.

Bailiffs move to cuff Troy. He doesn't fight, but he doesn't go gentle, either. As they lead him past my row, he turns. "You think this fixes anything?" His voice is just for me.

I meet his stare, flat and unblinking. "It fixes enough."

His jaw twitches. For the first time, I see the crack in him—a hairline fracture, but enough.

The courtroom empties in a flurry of suits and uniforms. Lucas waits at the back, not moving until the last of the crowd has filtered out. When I reach him, he pulls me into a hug so tight it knocks the air from my chest. I let myself melt, just for a second.

"You were perfect," he whispers.

I shake my head, but his hands are anchors at my waist. "It's over," I say.

"For now," he says, but the words aren't bitter. They're a warning, and a promise.

Outside the courthouse, the world is blinding. News vans choke the curb, their dish antennas aimed skyward like sunflowers. I flinch from the flashbulbs, but Lucas shields me, one arm at my back, the other up to block the cameras.

"Sophie! Over here!" shouts a woman in a red blazer, and

suddenly the press is all around, microphones shoved so close I can smell the gum on their breath.

I answer the questions the same as always. "Yes, I'm relieved. Yes, I believe justice was served. No, I don't have further comment."

Lucas steers me through the crowd. At the edge of the sidewalk, the fire marshal waits. His uniform is pressed, his hair combed with military precision. He smiles, but it doesn't reach his eyes.

"Hayes," he says. "A word?"

Lucas glances at me, then steps aside.

The marshal's voice is low, but not private. "The Department's offering reinstatement. Chief wants you to run the new arson unit. Full benefits. Even a bump in grade."

Lucas doesn't answer. His eyes find mine, and for a second, the world shrinks to just us.

I nod, barely.

He turns back to the marshal. "With respect, sir—my place is here." He reaches for my hand, laces his fingers through mine. "I'm not here for rank. I'm here for her."

The words hang in the air, heavier than any badge.

A ripple of reaction runs through the small crowd—some applause, a few camera shutters, a collective intake of breath as the narrative changes in real time.

The marshal nods, a faint smile ghosting his lips. "Understood." He holds out a hand. Lucas shakes it, firm and final.

As the crowd disperses, I feel the weight in my chest loosen. Every step away from the courthouse is a step toward something lighter, something that might even be hope.

We walk together, hand in hand, the sun cutting new lines of shadow across the sidewalk. The world isn't fixed, not by a long shot. But for the first time in forever, I believe it can be rebuilt.

Lucas squeezes my hand, and I squeeze back.

We survived.

We survived, and that's enough.

For now.

The first thing I notice is the quiet.

We walk home, the courthouse shrinking behind us, and for once it isn't the threat of sirens or the pop of distant glass that rides my nerves—it's the absence. The world has gone hushed, as if the entire town of Willow Creek is afraid to exhale too soon, lest it call down another firestorm. Lucas's hand is in mine, his thumb tracing the back of my knuckles, and every so often I look down just to make sure we're still connected.

The sky is that late-winter blue, the kind that looks painted on by someone with more optimism than sense. Sunlight angles sharp and long across the street, glinting off parked cars and the gloss of rain puddles, making the sidewalk shimmer. Our shadows—his taller, mine a stutter of movement as I limp slightly from the old injury—stretch ahead of us like warnings or invitations, depending on your perspective.

We pass the corner store where we first met. Back then, he'd been a year ahead of me, already in cadet blues, buying Gatorade and protein bars with the seriousness of a man about to be deployed. I was just a girl in cutoff shorts, trailing after my dad's shopping list. The store is different now: new awning, new sign, even the old graffiti sandblasted away and replaced with a mural of the town's water tower. I point it out, and Lucas grins, squeezing my hand.

"Remember when you bet me fifty bucks I couldn't eat a whole bag of ghost pepper chips?" he asks.

"You did it," I say. "And then you puked behind the dumpster."

He laughs, softly. "Worth it."

I walk a little slower than usual, not because I'm tired, but because I want to remember how this feels. To be on the street in daylight, not ducking the shadows or scanning every car for threat. People glance at us—some familiar faces, some strangers—but no one stares too long. There's a weird respect in the way they look away, as if to say: You made it. You can have this day.

We turn down the block toward home, and I catch a glimpse of the new firehouse, all glass and steel, its construction almost finished. The old station is a burnt husk on the other side of town, but this one stands clean and hopeful, like a scar turned to something better.

Lucas slows as we approach our house. The paint is still bright, the lawn muddy but clear of debris. For a second, we just stand at the gate, looking at it.

"You want to go in?" he asks.

I nod, but I don't move. "I just... I didn't think I'd ever see this place again. Not really."

He lets me take my time. The lock is stiff, but my hand is steady as I turn it. Inside, the kitchen smells like the sourdough starter I left out, the air warm from the timer that Lucas set before we left. I run my fingers along the counter, every inch familiar, every groove and chip a tiny declaration of ownership.

He follows me to the living room, where the boxes we never unpacked from the last move still line the wall. It doesn't matter. The furniture is ugly, the curtains don't match, but the place is ours.

We collapse onto the couch, not speaking for a while. My head rests on his shoulder, the side that isn't still bruised from the last fight. I listen to his heartbeat, slow and regular, and let myself believe that maybe it will always be there.

Eventually, hunger gets the better of us. Lucas heats leftovers and serves them on mismatched plates. We eat at the counter, legs dangling, and talk about nothing—how the new neighbor's dog barks at every delivery truck, how the basement smells like paint. Normal things.

When the dishes are done, he looks at me with that intensity that used to scare me but now just feels like home.

"You okay?" he asks.

I nod. "For the first time in... I don't know. Maybe ever."

That night, we spread a blanket on the backyard grass. The air is cold, but clear, and the stars have come out in defiance of the town's old reputation for gray. Lucas brings two mugs of hot cider, sets them down, and lies beside me, our shoulders touching.

There's a stillness here that I didn't know I needed. We stare up at the sky, the moon so bright it casts our shadows even now. He reaches over and takes my hand, pulling it to his chest, holding it there like a promise.

After a while, he turns to face me, his eyes dark and bright at once.

"I ever tell you about the first fire I worked?" he says.

I shake my head, but I already know the story. I want to hear him tell it.

"It was a barn," he says. "Middle of summer, hay stacked to the rafters. The whole thing was a furnace by the time we got there. I remember the sound—like a train. We couldn't save much, but there was this kid's bike, melted half to hell, but still standing in the yard. I pulled it out, and the kid came running, bare feet, screaming with relief. His mom just hugged me and cried."

He pauses. "I think that's when I knew. That it wasn't about putting out fires. It was about what you could save."

He rolls onto his side, propped on one elbow. He looks at my face, at the scar on my temple, at the way my hair falls in a tangled mess.

"What about you?" he asks.

I think. "I always thought it was about control. That if I could just plan, just be ready, nothing would ever hurt again. But the fires come anyway. They always do. All you can do is decide what matters enough to risk saving."

He nods, and for a minute we just lie there, the air steaming from our breath.

I reach out, brush a strand of hair from his forehead, and trace the edge of the scar above his eyebrow. "You ever think about what comes next?" I ask.

He doesn't answer right away. He rolls over, closer, and his hand finds my waist. The touch is gentle, but electric.

"I think I want to find out," he says. "With you."

We kiss, slow at first, then with more heat. The blanket is rough under my back, the air cold on my skin, but his body is fire, his hands mapping every inch as if learning me for the first time. He pulls away just enough to look at me, his eyes soft.

"Okay?" he asks.

"Always," I whisper.

He undresses me with reverence, every movement deliberate, every button and zipper an act of devotion. He kisses the scar on my shoulder, the burn on my thigh, the faint stretch marks on my stomach. When he enters me, it's a slow, aching press, and I wrap my arms around his neck, needing to be as close as humanly possible.

We move together, unhurried, savoring every sensation. The grass is cold, but we are not. The stars above us burn, but not as bright as what's between us. I arch into him, and he groans, the sound raw and perfect.

When we finish, I am shaking. He holds me, both arms wrapped tight, and we breathe together, our hearts racing and slowing in tandem.

For a long time, neither of us says anything.

Then, in the darkness, I find his hand and squeeze it.

"We made it through the fire," I say, voice rough.

He pulls me close, burying his face in my hair. "And we'll keep burning bright together."

We fall asleep on the blanket, the chill held at bay by the tangle of our bodies. In my dream, I see our house, the lights on, laughter inside. It isn't perfect, but it's safe. In the morning, we will have to face the world again—the bills, the news, the old ghosts.

But right now, I have everything I ever wanted.

And nothing, not even the memory of fire, can take it away.

I wake up with a crick in my neck and the sense that someone, somewhere, has hit the reset button on the universe. Lucas is already up, fussing around the kitchen. I hear the sputter of the percolator, the thud of a fridge door, the scrape of his spoon in the sugar jar. I close my eyes for a second, savoring the sound—our sound, the proof that we are still here.

When I finally drag myself upright, he's waiting for me with coffee already poured, the table set for two. There's even a plate of toast, the edges burnt just the way I like, because I always forget the timer.

We eat in companionable silence. The sun is barely up, but the kitchen is bright with possibility. I flip through the news on my phone, skipping past the trial recaps and the op-eds about Willow Creek's "Hero Daughter." I don't care about any of it.

What I care about is the envelope on the windowsill, cream-colored and heavy, with my name written in careful script. No return address. No postage. Just my name, Sophie Grant.

I pick it up, turn it over in my hands.

"Fan mail?" Lucas asks, smiling crooked.

I roll my eyes. "Probably just another subpoena."

But when I open it, the paper is soft, the ink a shaky blue. The letter begins: "Dear Ms. Grant, You don't know me, but I watched your testimony. I lost my son in a fire. For years, I blamed myself. Your words helped me realize I'm not alone. Thank you for surviving, so the rest of us could too."

I have to stop, because my throat is full of sand. I blink hard, once, then again.

Lucas comes over, puts his hands on my shoulders. He doesn't say anything, just lets me finish.

The letter goes on, page after page. A life lived in small-town shadows, the pain of loss, the slow work of forgiveness. At the end: "If you ever start that foundation, or the outreach program you mentioned, let me know. I want to help."

I set the letter down, smoothing the paper so it doesn't curl. I stare at it, not really seeing, until Lucas pulls out the chair beside me and sits, his hand still on my back.

"People are listening," he says. "You did that."

I don't know what to say. I just nod.

He nudges my chin up, makes me look him in the eye. "So what's next?"

I think. Then, for the first time in my life, I know.

"We start with survivor support," I say. "A real network. Not just for fire, but for any disaster. Nobody should have to go through it alone."

He grins, proud and a little awed. "You're going to need a home office."

I snort. "The spare room. I'll get on it today."

He shakes his head, then kisses my temple. "You're amazing."

I lean into his touch, letting it soak in. "You make it easier."

By noon, we've made a list—resources to gather, people to call, foundations to research. I post a single message online: "If you need someone, reach out. I'll listen." Within an hour, there are forty replies. By nightfall, my inbox is a living thing.

Lucas brings me a glass of wine and sits on the floor while I type, his back to the wall, his hands busy repairing a picture frame I knocked over last week.

"You regret it?" I ask, eyes on the screen. "Turning down the chief's job?"

He considers. "Every now and then. But mostly? No. I wanted a different kind of legacy."

I close the laptop, stretch my arms overhead. "We're not heroes, you know."

He stands, crosses the room, and pulls me up by the hand. "No," he agrees. "We're just stubborn."

He kisses me, slow and sweet.

"You ready for bed?" he asks.

I nod. "Yeah. But can we leave the letter on the nightstand?"

He smiles, brushing hair from my face. "It'll be the first thing we see in the morning."

We climb under the covers, limbs tangled, and listen to the wind. The world is still messy, still unpredictable. But it's ours.

As I drift off, I think about the words in that letter, about all the people I'll never meet but might help anyway. I think about Dad, about the way he always believed you should leave things better than you found them.

I think maybe, just maybe, I'm on my way.

Outside, the night is full of silent witnesses.

Inside, we dream of things that last.

And in the morning, we'll start again.

14

Fireproof

SOPHIE

PACKING IS A BLOOD SPORT IN OUR HOUSE. EVEN ON A good day, it devolves into a low-grade standoff over sock colors, what qualifies as "weather appropriate," and how many chargers two people really need for a single weekend. The bedroom is a minefield of open suitcases, balled T-shirts, travel-sized deodorants, and the hair dryer Lucas claims he "doesn't need" but always ends up borrowing. He's at the dresser now, folding and refolding the same set of dark blue Henleys with the grim determination of a man prepping for a mission, not a vacation.

I sit on the edge of the bed, surrounded by half-packed gym bags and a duffel with a broken zipper. I'm supposed to be focused on shoes, but I keep getting distracted by the way Lucas moves—shoulders tight, face set, every muscle broadcasting the kind of tension that belongs to bomb techs and groomsmen, not firefighters used to seeing each other naked on the regular.

I hold up a pair of shorts. "Are you really planning to hike in these?"

He grunts, not looking up. "Those are for emergencies."

"In case we get stranded at the pool?"

He gives a crooked smile. "You joke, but it's happened before."

The joke lands, but it doesn't stick. I watch as he methodically checks his suitcase zipper, then checks it again, then—oh my god—unzips and rezips it for a third time. It's like living with a robot programmed for anxiety.

I throw my hands up, dramatic. "You know, if you keep pacing, you'll burn a hole through the carpet. I won't get our deposit back."

He slows, but only a little. "Just want to make sure I've got everything."

I walk over and wrap my arms around his waist from behind, nestling my face between his shoulder blades. "You're packed for three days, not a Mars mission. What's actually going on?"

He stiffens, and for a split second, I think he might just snap in half. But then he sighs, the air hissing out of him like steam from a pressure valve. He turns in my arms, and I can see his face—every line of it mapped by years of holding back.

"I just want this to go right," he says, and it sounds like he means it on about ten levels I can't even name.

I reach up, brushing a thumb across his stubbled jaw. "Hey. You could forget the entire suitcase and I'd still have a great time. Especially if you forgot underwear."

He tries to laugh, but his hands are busy—one fidgeting with the end of the zipper pull, the other digging in his jeans pocket like he's searching for the secret to cold fusion.

It happens so fast I almost miss it. One minute, he's fussing over the duffel bag; the next, he drops to one knee, and a little velvet box appears in his hand like a magic trick. The world screeches to a halt. The only sound is my own heartbeat, thudding like a warning.

He opens the box. Inside, nestled on white silk, is a fire-opal ring set in gold. It catches the late light slanting through the blinds, the stone pulsing orange-red, shot through with all the colors of a second sunrise.

Lucas's hands tremble just a little. "I know it's not traditional," he says, voice thick. "But I wanted something that felt like you."

I stare. There's a whole speech in his eyes, some deep, careful thing about how we both got burned by our families and our town and our own worst mistakes, and how we rebuilt anyway. He opens his mouth, and what comes out is:

"You're the only fire I never want to put out."

I try for a joke. "That's the sappiest thing you've ever said."

But my voice breaks, and the tears are already happening, and before he can finish whatever line he's practiced, I say, "Yes. God, yes."

He grins, all teeth and relief, and I throw my arms around his neck. The momentum knocks us both onto the carpet, the little ring box popping out of his hand and skittering under the dresser. We both scramble for it, bumping heads, laughing, the kind of laugh that has nothing to do with jokes and everything to do with being alive.

He catches the box first and pops it open again. "Let's try this one more time," he says. He slides the ring onto my finger, and the opal flashes in the shadowed light, the gold band snug against my skin.

I look down, and it's the most beautiful thing I've ever seen. Not just the ring, but the way it looks on my hand—like it's been there forever, like it belongs.

Lucas tugs me close, burying his face in my neck. His breath is hot and shaky against my skin. "Is it weird that I'm more nervous about this than running into a burning building?"

I thread my fingers through his hair. "Not weird. You've never had to convince a burning building to marry you."

He laughs again, and the sound is steadier now. He pulls me onto his lap, my legs straddling his hips. The proposal, such as it was, has gone gloriously off-script, but I wouldn't trade it for anything.

He kisses me, slow at first, then hungry. His mouth tastes like toothpaste and the last traces of bitter coffee, and I let him push me backward onto the comforter, the world narrowing to the heat of his hands and the way his body molds to mine. My new ring presses cool against the back of his neck, a perfect circle—soft, sharp, a promise.

We lie there for a long minute, just breathing together, hearts racing, bodies tangled in the mess of half-packed luggage and emotion.

I hold my hand up, let the ring catch the light again. "Do you want to call your sister or should I?"

He groans, burying his face in the pillow. "God, let's wait until we get through the weekend."

I grin. "Deal. But I get to tell my mom. She'll lose her mind."

He props himself on one elbow, brushing my hair off my face. "She's already called dibs on hosting the rehearsal dinner."

I snort. "You're not even officially engaged for thirty seconds and you're already thinking about seating charts?"

He kisses the tip of my nose. "I'm just trying to plan for every possibility."

"That's my job," I say, but he's already rolling me under him, laughing, the tension gone from his muscles for the first time in weeks.

Later, as we finally get back to packing, I catch him watching me in the mirror, his expression unreadable.

"What?" I ask, tugging a hoodie over my head.

He just shakes his head, wonderstruck. "Nothing. Just making sure this is real."

I flash him the ring, flipping him off in the process. "Pretty damn real."

He laughs, and this time it's pure joy.

The future is still a minefield. The trial is still looming, the threat of fire always just one spark away. But for now, we have this: two suitcases, one ring, and the promise that, together, we can survive anything.

We're halfway through a victory lap of toast—orange juice in mismatched mugs, because neither of us trusts ourselves around real glass—when Lucas's phone rings. The name on the screen is all caps, FIREHOUSE, and he lets it go three buzzes before answering. I can tell from the way he glances at me—

quick, apologetic—that whatever's coming, it's not a routine check-in.

He takes the call, turns away. His voice is calm, but I see the way his knuckles blanch, his posture collapsing in on itself. The color drains from his face, and I swear I watch every line in his body turn to steel as he listens, silent, to whoever is on the other end.

He hangs up. His mouth opens and shuts, but nothing comes out. I set my juice down, the mug clinking just a little too loud on the kitchen island.

"Lucas," I say, and my voice is already fraying at the edges.

He runs both hands through his hair, then tries for a smile and fails. "Babe, you might want to sit down."

I'm already sitting, but I brace my hands on the countertop, ready for a hit.

He hits the speaker and redials. The voice on the other end is familiar—Dispatcher Henson, who once baked me a birthday cake shaped like a fire truck and who never, ever calls unless there's a reason.

"Hayes, you there?"

"Yeah. Sophie's here, too. Go ahead."

There's a pause. A paper shuffle. Henson's voice loses the usual gruffness. "You two need to stay put until further notice. Caleb's out. Faked a seizure during hospital transfer. He's been missing for three hours."

I feel it, the old instinct to run, to start packing bags and checking windows. But I don't move. Not yet.

"Any leads?" Lucas asks.

"He left a message," Henson says. "In the ER. Scrawled it on the wall in... well. In blood, we think. 'YOU WILL BURN LIKE THE REST.' I think it was meant for you both."

Silence. I hear the hum of the hospital on the line, the clatter of phones, the background chaos of panic held barely in check.

"PD's increasing patrols around your house," Henson continues. "Don't let anyone in. We're running everything, but—" she hesitates, and in that gap I feel the whole world narrow.

"Understood," Lucas says. "Text me any updates. We'll lock down."

The call ends. For a long minute, neither of us speaks.

Lucas stands in the center of the kitchen, lost. Then his training kicks in, and he moves—windows, doors, checking every latch and deadbolt. He checks his phone, makes two more calls, all the while narrating the steps in a flat, mechanical way that tells me he's terrified.

I watch him pace the length of the room. He's a live wire, every movement clipped, every word a little too loud. He calls his sister, then the chief, then back to Henson. He asks about the perimeter. He asks about traffic cams, about hospital security, about whether they checked the dumpsters and the rooftops.

I sit on the edge of the bed, hands in my lap. The ring on my finger is hot against my skin, as if it might burn a hole straight through to the bone.

For the first time in months, I don't know what to do. I just sit, still and silent, counting the seconds between Lucas's footfalls as he patrols the house.

When he finally returns, his voice is shot. He kneels in front of me, takes both my hands in his.

"I'm not letting anything happen to you," he says, like a vow. "Not now. Not ever."

I look down at our hands—his big, rough palms swallowing mine, the ring glinting between us like a tiny, furious sun. The fear is there, but so is something else. Something hard and alive.

I squeeze his hands. "We've survived every fire he set," I say. "We'll survive this one too."

He nods, jaw locked, eyes wet and shining.

"Promise?" he says.

I manage a smile, even as the terror climbs my throat. "Scout's honor."

He pulls me into his arms, and we just hold each other. The world is on fire again, but for the first time, I'm not running.

We'll stand our ground.

Let the bastard come.

The night is a slow burn. We lie side by side, backs sticky against the cool cotton sheets, every muscle alert. Neither of us says a word about the police cruiser idling outside or the gun on Lucas's side table, stripped and ready. The moon is obscene tonight—huge and high, throwing blue light through the window and making every shadow in our bedroom too sharp to ignore.

Lucas keeps one hand wrapped around my waist, thumb stroking the bare skin just above my waistband. It should be comforting, but it's more like a warning flare: he's keeping me close in case we have to move, in case the phone rings, in case the whole damn house goes up and we have to dive for the fire escape.

I shift, watching the way his chest rises and falls. He's pretending to sleep, but I know the rhythm of his body too well. Every inhale is a little too shallow, every exhale a little too loud. The cut on his lip—new from biting it earlier—looks black in the moonlight.

I want to say something. I want to promise him that everything will be fine, that we'll see the sun come up and this will all be just another story for the grandkids. But I can't. My mouth is dry, and my brain is spinning the same three words over and over: Caleb is out.

So I do the only thing I know how.

I roll over, facing him, and let my hand drift up his side. He stiffens, but doesn't pull away. I slip my fingers under the elastic of his boxers, just enough to make him flinch.

He opens his eyes, all ice and worry. "You okay?"

"No," I whisper, and then I sit up, peel my nightshirt over my head in one quick motion. The air hits my skin and I shiver, but it's not from cold. I straddle his hips, pinning him to the mattress, and let my hair fall around us like a blackout curtain.

He blinks, caught off guard. "Soph—"

"Don't let him steal this night," I say. "Not from us."

He grabs my wrists, gentle at first, then firmer, like he needs the anchor. I lean down and kiss him, deep, biting. He tastes like toothpaste and fear, and I want to scrub every trace of that bastard's threat off his tongue.

Lucas lets me take control, lets me move his arms above his head and pin them to the pillow. I use my thighs to hold him still. He's hard, the heat of him fierce against my thigh, but he waits for me—always waits for me, even when it nearly kills him.

I guide him inside, slow and deliberate, watching his face. The fear is still there, but it's joined by hunger, by that wild, reckless thing that used to get us both into trouble when we were kids. I ride him, using every muscle in my legs to set the rhythm, grinding down until the friction is sharp enough to hurt.

He moans, low and desperate. I slap a hand over his mouth, stifling the sound, and he groans louder. The bed creaks, the headboard tapping a slow metronome against the wall.

I move faster, letting the tension in my body break loose, letting every ounce of fear and anger and pure need flood into the space between us. He bucks up, matching my pace, eyes locked on mine like he's afraid I'll vanish if he looks away.

I bite his shoulder, hard, and he comes undone. His hands clench the sheets, his body arches, and I follow him over the edge, my vision white-hot with relief.

We collapse together, sweat cooling in the draft from the window. My hair sticks to his chest, and his hands find my hips, anchoring me in place.

Neither of us speaks for a long time.

Then, through the thin walls, I hear it: sirens, somewhere close. Lucas tenses, muscles locked and ready.

I put my hand on his chest, right over his heart, and whisper, "We're fireproof now."

He pulls me closer, lips to my hair, and we wait for dawn together, our bodies still joined, the ring on my finger flashing fire in the moonlight.

Let the world burn.

We'll face it as one.

15

Relight the Flame

THE MORNINGS USED TO HAVE A RHYTHM: LUCAS WOULD cook eggs or, if he was feeling generous, pancakes, and I'd fake complaints about his inability to make them the same way twice. Now, every day starts with the hollow clink of locks and the mechanical whir of security cams resetting. I wake to the sound of his boots on hardwood and the hush of his voice, already on the line with Henson or the chief or whoever's unlucky enough to draw perimeter duty.

By the time I make it downstairs, he's already done a sweep—windows, doors, even the crawlspace hatch under the stairs that no one but raccoons and very determined home invaders would ever find. He stands at the kitchen window, scanning the backyard, arms folded so tight the vein at his wrist bulges like it's trying to escape.

I pour myself coffee, hands shaking just enough to betray me. "Did you sleep?" I ask, not because I care about the answer but because it's what we do. Small talk, edge-of-the-knife edition.

Lucas's eyes don't leave the backyard. "A little. You?"

"I dreamt about fire alarms," I add two sugars, stir, and pretend the motion isn't just a way to burn off nerves.

He turns, finally, and I catch the new lines at the corners of his mouth. "You want eggs?"

"Toast is fine."

He starts the toaster, then stands directly in front of it, as if Caleb might slither up through the crumb tray and start trouble that way. I try to focus on the newspaper, but the print blurs and my mind keeps rerunning the footage of last night's attempted break-in. It's all in there: the sound of glass under my bare feet, the pulse of the flare, the way the silhouette ran—but not away. Just out of sight.

Lucas brings me a plate with two slices of toast, crusts unburnt. He places it in front of me like a bomb disposal tech with a suspicious package.

I make myself eat. The first bite is dry and tastes like dust.

"Security system's updated," he says. "If anything trips the perimeter, we'll know before he's within a hundred yards."

I nod, chewing, feeling the bread cement to the roof of my mouth. "And the window?"

"Reinforced glass arrives tomorrow." He looks down, fingers tapping the counter. "I got the impression Chief Kelly would rather pay for the upgrade himself than have us move somewhere safer."

"Safer than a bunker with you in it?"

He gives a flat smile. "Statistically, yes. Emotionally, I'm not so sure."

I reach for my coffee, hands steady now that they have something to do. "I'm going to shower. If you hear me scream, it's because you bought the hotel soap again."

"Ha ha," he says, but I catch him scanning the hallway as I walk away.

In the bathroom, I check every square inch before locking the door. The window is barely big enough for a cat, but I wedge a bottle of shampoo against the sill anyway. I keep my phone on the vanity, speaker on, so if something happens I can call for help mid-shampoo. This is how we live now—every routine bristling with contingency plans.

The shower helps. Hot water, the steam fogging the mirror, the way the pressure needles my scalp. For a few minutes I can almost forget. I close my eyes and let the water drown out everything. When I come out, Lucas is waiting in the hall, towel in hand.

He doesn't say anything, just holds it out. I take it, brush past him, and he follows me with his eyes the whole way to the bedroom.

I don't call him on it.

The house feels smaller every hour. I can hear the neighbor's dog three houses over, the hum of the fridge, even the scrape of branches on siding when the wind picks up. But what gets me isn't the big, obvious noises—it's the quiet. The way everything else seems to crouch, holding its breath, waiting for the next shoe to drop.

I sit on the edge of the bed and dress slowly, jeans and a hoodie, nothing fancy. Lucas has taken to keeping a jacket and boots at the foot of the stairs, ready to go at a moment's notice.

I notice the way the curtains are drawn tighter than usual. The way he's started pushing the armchair in front of the main door when he thinks I'm not looking.

He catches me staring at the window and says, "I set the cameras to motion capture. Anything bigger than a squirrel and we'll get a text."

I shrug, but inside I'm counting the seconds between the next alert and the time it would take for someone to get inside.

He sits next to me, close but not touching. "We could go somewhere, you know. Just until they catch him."

I shake my head. "He'd just follow."

Lucas nods, lips pressed to a thin line. He looks at my hands, at the way my thumb picks at the seam on my jeans.

"You're jumpy," he says.

I want to deny it, but I can't. "Every time a car door slams outside, I think it's him."

He doesn't say it out loud, but I know he feels the same.

He stands, paces the room, then stops in front of the dresser. The engagement ring box is still there, and for a second, he just looks at it, expression unreadable.

"I'll double-check the locks," he says, and leaves.

The day crawls. I try to do normal things—laundry, email, a half-assed attempt at reading. But every time I lose focus, my mind snaps back to the window, the door, the sound of footsteps that might be nothing or might be everything.

Lucas spends the morning cycling between the kitchen, the front hallway, and the home office. He carries his phone everywhere and answers every call on the first ring. Sometimes he stands in the middle of a room, just listening, as if waiting for the house to tell him what he's missed.

At noon, I find him in the laundry room, staring at the back door like he's trying to will it into disappearing. I touch his arm, light as a feather.

"You okay?"

He jolts, the reaction just a little too big. Then he composes himself and gives me the barest of smiles. "Yeah. Just thinking."

I nod, not pushing.

He looks down, rubs his hands together, then covers my hand with his. His fingers are rough, warm. "You know I'll keep you safe," he says.

"I know."

He doesn't let go. "I mean it. No matter what."

I squeeze back. "I know."

His face is so close, I can see the flecks of green in his eyes, the stubble along his jaw, the scar just above his eyebrow from the time a branch almost took his eye during a windstorm callout.

"I'm not leaving," I say, and it comes out more like a plea than a promise.

He shakes his head, voice low. "I don't want you to leave. I just want this to be over."

I lean into him, rest my head against his chest. The rhythm of his heartbeat steadies me more than any security system ever could.

Later, we try to distract ourselves with chores. Lucas runs the vacuum with ruthless efficiency, then moves on to re-caulking a window that never quite sealed right. I alphabetize the spice cabinet, even though neither of us cooks anything that requires more than salt and pepper.

The hours blur. I check my phone obsessively, even though I know there won't be any news until there is. I text my mother, brief and noncommittal. She texts back with a string of exclamation points and an offer to drive down and camp on our couch.

I don't answer right away.

Around three, the sky turns dark and heavy, the wind picking up. I watch the trees lean and sway, the neighbor's trash can rolling down the street. I almost miss the figure that appears at the edge of the yard, just inside the fence line.

My heart stops. I blink, and it's gone.

I stand, walk to the window, stare until my eyes water.

Lucas comes up behind me, peering over my shoulder. "See something?"

"Maybe," I say.

He opens the door, steps out onto the porch. I watch him scan the street, his hand never far from the heavy flashlight he keeps in his jacket pocket. He circles the yard, checks the gate, then comes back inside.

"Nobody out there," he says, and I want to believe him.

But I know what I saw.

By evening, we're both strung out. Lucas makes pasta, and we eat in silence, every clink of fork against plate a gunshot in the hush. He pours us each a beer, and we sip slow, savoring the illusion of normal.

After dinner, he drags a chair to the front window and sits, arms folded, eyes fixed on the street. I join him, perched on the armrest, my knee pressed against his shoulder.

We sit like that for a long time.

The sun goes down, the porch lights flicker on, and the neighborhood settles into the uneasy quiet of people who know something bad is in the air.

Lucas's phone buzzes. He checks it, then sighs. "False alarm at the high school. They thought they saw someone on the roof. Patrol's already swept it."

I nod. "Maybe he's not even here. Maybe he just wants us to think he is."

Lucas doesn't answer. His jaw flexes, and I know he's thinking the same thing I am: Caleb is here, or will be soon.

I look down at my hands, at the thin line of the engagement ring glinting on my finger. "Do you ever wish we could just start over?"

He looks at me, startled. "What do you mean?"

I think, then shake my head. "Nothing. Ignore me."

He takes my hand, laces his fingers through mine. "If you want to run, we'll run."

I look at him, really look, and I see it: the fear, the hope, the absolute certainty that he would die for me if it came to that.

"I don't want to run," I say. "I just want to feel safe in my own house again."

He squeezes my hand, gently. "We'll get there."

I hope he's right.

We go to bed early, exhaustion heavier than sleep. Lucas locks every door, checks every window, then lies beside me, arms around my waist. I nestle in, head tucked against his shoulder, and for a while, I almost believe we're untouchable.

In the dark, I whisper, "I can feel him watching."

Lucas's grip tightens, and for a long time, neither of us says a word.

We just listen to the wind, and the house settling, and the slow, steady beat of hearts refusing to break.

I wake with the taste of adrenaline on my tongue, a metallic tang that doesn't wash out with coffee or toothpaste. Lucas is already up, the sound of drawers and zippers filling the house with a nervous energy. I find him in the bedroom, suitcase open on the bed, moving so fast he's barely registering what he's packing.

He's all business, every motion deliberate. Socks, shirts, the first-aid kit from under the sink. He even checks the expiry date on the epi-pen before tossing it in. I watch from the doorway, arms crossed, feeling like a spectator in my own life.

"You're over-packing," I say, trying for levity, but my voice comes out flat.

Lucas doesn't even look up. "Not possible. We might have to go fast."

I step into the room, careful not to disturb the stacks of folded clothes lining the edge of the mattress. "I'm not leaving, Lucas."

He keeps going, rolling my favorite hoodie into a tight cylinder. "Just until they catch him. A week, two, tops."

"And what if he burns down the house while we're gone? Or comes after someone else?"

Lucas throws the hoodie into the suitcase, harder than necessary. "I'd rather have you alive and homeless than—" He stops, jaw tight, the words hanging in the air.

I move closer, plant myself between him and the suitcase. "We've fought for every inch of this, Lucas. Every fucking day. If we run now, what was the point?"

He meets my eyes, finally. His face is a battlefield—hope, fear, determination, all crammed into the space of a single, endless moment.

"My job is to keep you safe," he says, voice low. "I can't do that if you won't let me."

I gesture at the room—the cluttered dresser, the stack of library books, the faded Polaroids thumbtacked to the wall above the bed. "My job is to live. Here. With you."

He glances at the photos. There's one of us at the firehouse's pancake breakfast, both of us sticky with syrup and sunburn. Another from our first road trip, grinning in front of the world's ugliest concrete buffalo. The engagement ring box sits open on the dresser, the stone glinting in the morning light.

Lucas paces, back and forth, hands flexing at his sides. "You don't understand, Soph. He's obsessed. He's not going to stop."

I keep my voice steady. "I know. That's why we have to stay. If we hide, he wins. And I'm done giving him anything."

He looks at me, then at the ring box, then back. For a second, I think he might break. But instead, he slams the suitcase shut, the zipper screaming in protest.

"Fine," he says. "But if anything happens—"

"It won't," I interrupt. "We'll be ready."

He sits on the edge of the bed, head in his hands, elbows on knees. I sit beside him, close but not touching.

The silence is thick. I want to say something, to bridge the gap, but I don't know how.

So I just sit there, listening to the sound of his breathing, steady and stubborn.

He reaches for my hand. I let him hold it.

We stay like that, side by side, neither willing to move.

The suitcase sits on the floor, a silent reminder of the future we can't agree on.

Night comes slow, dragging its feet through every minute. We eat leftover pasta, then circle the house again, both of us pretending it's just habit. The silence between us is heavier now, shaped by the argument, but when Lucas reaches for my hand, I take it. His palm is callused and steady, a contradiction to the nerves thrumming beneath the skin.

By ten, neither of us has the energy to fake normal. We leave the dishes in the sink, the suitcase still on the floor, and climb under the sheets. Lucas lies flat on his back, eyes tracing cracks in the ceiling, while I curl on my side, watching the rise and fall of his chest.

The moonlight slips through the blinds, painting stripes across his body. I trace them with my eyes, then my fingers, starting at his shoulder and following the pattern down his arm.

"You're never this quiet," I say, voice low.

He huffs out a breath, more sigh than laugh. "I'm thinking."

"About what?"

"About how to keep you safe when you won't let me."

I don't answer. Instead, I slide closer, drape an arm across his chest, and tuck my head into the space between his jaw and collarbone. He smells like dish soap and sleep deprivation, and I anchor myself to the warmth of him.

For a while, we just breathe together. I listen to the sound of his heart, slow but not calm.

I run my fingertips over his cheek, brushing the new worry lines. "We've survived every fire he set," I remind him. "Even the ones we lit ourselves."

He pulls me in tighter, hand splayed across the small of my back. "Doesn't mean it won't hurt next time."

I press a kiss to his jaw. "We'll heal. We always do."

His arm tightens, a silent promise. "I hate that you're braver than me."

I snort. "Not braver. Just more stubborn."

He rolls onto his side, bringing us nose to nose. His eyes are dark and tired, but the look in them is all fight. He tucks a strand of hair behind my ear, fingertips lingering at the curve of my neck.

"If I lose you," he says, and the words stop there.

I kiss him, slow and deliberate. "You won't."

The need between us is sharp, edged with desperation. I tug his shirt up, press my hands to his ribs, feel the shudder as he exhales. He rolls over me, weight solid and familiar, and I let him take whatever comfort he needs.

We move like we're afraid of the world ending, and maybe it is. Our bodies know the drill: the bruised places, the scar on his thigh, the stubborn patch of skin above my hip that still stings when touched just so. He kisses the hollow of my throat, bites the place where my pulse hammers, and I arch into him, greedy for the heat, the friction, the proof that we're still alive.

He's always careful, even when he's wild. His hands find my wrists, pinning them above my head. I wrap my legs around his waist, meeting every movement with my own. We're tangled in the sheets, breathless and half-wrecked, and when he finally breaks, it's with my name on his lips.

After, we lie in a heap, sweat cooling, the world outside nothing but storm and darkness.

I let my fingers wander, tracing the lines of his face, memorizing the map of him. He closes his eyes, leans into the touch.

"Promise me something," he says, voice barely a whisper.

"Anything."

"If you ever have to run, don't look back."

I shake my head. "Not without you."

He pulls me close, kisses my forehead, and we drift in and out of sleep, always touching, always holding on.

It's the phone that wakes us. Not the ring, but the vibration, a low, insistent buzz on the nightstand. Lucas is up in an instant, all the softness gone from his body.

He answers on the first ring. "Hayes."

I sit up, sheets tangled around my waist. His face goes white as he listens, jaw clenching so tight I think he might break a tooth.

"Copy that," he says, and hangs up.

"What is it?" I ask, already knowing.

"Courthouse is on fire," he says. "Evidence room. It's a total loss."

I'm out of bed before he finishes, grabbing jeans and a sweatshirt. Lucas is already in his boots, pulling on a shirt.

We don't say anything as we dress. There's no need.

I catch my reflection in the mirror, hair wild, eyes fierce. The engagement ring glitters in the half-light, a flare against the chaos.

Lucas stands at the door, waiting. He looks at me, really looks, and I see the question there.

I slip the ring onto my finger, give him a nod. "He's back," I say, voice steady.

Lucas pulls me in, kisses me hard, then releases.

"This time," he says, "we end it for good."

We leave the house together, side by side, ready to meet the fire.

16

Ghosts to the Flame

SOPHIE

We walk the last two blocks in a silence that tastes like smoke. Neither of us says a word about what we saw at the courthouse—the warped beams, the spatter of blackened glass, the char on every surface where memory used to live. We don't talk about the way the squad cars cut through the night with their lights off, or the way the paramedics watched us with hollow eyes, as if we were already ghosts. It's barely past five in the morning when we let ourselves in through the kitchen door.

Inside, the house is a different planet. The air is thick with the staleness of hours unventilated, the overhead lights too sharp for the way my body wants to dissolve into the darkness. I kick off my shoes by the back mat, miss the edge, and trip over the pile of boots we never organize. Lucas just lets it happen. He's somewhere behind me, one hand on the door like he's expecting it to bark open again, the other rubbing circles into his left wrist, the spot where the burn scar puckers beneath his tattoo.

We don't turn on any more lights than we have to. I move through the kitchen by memory, palm on the counter, counting every step so I don't lose track of where the room ends and the night begins. Lucas follows, his footsteps a beat behind mine, as if he doesn't quite trust the floorboards to hold.

He steers us into the living room. The only illumination comes from the streetlamp outside, which paints a weak stripe across the carpet and onto the arm of the couch. I collapse into the cushions, my body folding in on itself. Lucas doesn't sit; he hovers, every muscle coiled, like a runner at the starting line with no finish in sight.

For a long time, there's just the soft ticking of the wall clock, the hum of the fridge. Then he kneels in front of me, knees on the threadbare rug, and pulls me forward until my cheek rests against his shoulder. His hands are shaking, but his arms around me are steel. I want to melt into him, to be erased from the edges inward.

He holds me like that for a long time. I listen to the sound of his breathing—steady, measured, nothing like my own. I memorize the prickle of his stubble, the scent of his shirt, the heat radiating off his chest where my forehead presses in. I could stay like this forever, but the world will not let us.

The answering machine blinks at us from the hallway console. Its red light is the only thing in the house brighter than Lucas's eyes. I see the message count: 1. It's always 1, these days. He doesn't let go of me when he stands; he just pulls me with him, like he's afraid if we break contact, one of us will vanish.

We walk the five steps together, my feet dragging, his stride careful and slow. He hits play.

The voice comes through the tinny speaker, low and almost friendly.

"Did you miss me?" it says, and I freeze. "Don't worry. You'll see me soon. Afterall, we're family. I will see you soon, Little So, So."

The silence that follows is the loudest sound I've ever heard.

My heart stops on the nickname. No one has called me that in years—not since Dad, and not even him after I turned sixteen and told him to cut it out. The words make my skin crawl and my scalp go hot. I stare at the blinking light, waiting for more, but the message ends there, a knife twist with no further explanation.

Lucas's arms close around me again, tighter this time. He pulls me back toward the living room, as if distance could shield us from what we just heard.

He sits on the couch and tugs me onto his lap. I want to resist, but my knees give out. His arms are the only thing holding me together. For a while, all I can do is count my breaths and hope he doesn't notice how shallow they are.

Finally, he tilts my face up to his.

"What does he mean, 'family'?" I ask. The words feel like gravel in my mouth. "Why would he say that?"

Lucas's eyes are molten, blue shot with something close to terror. "He's trying to mess with you. It's what he does. Caleb never knew how to play straight. He's probably talking about the fire unit. That's how they used to refer to themselves—brothers, sisters, family."

I shake my head. "No one ever called me that. Not even in the department. How does he know the nickname?"

He doesn't answer. His jaw is so tight it looks painful.

"Lucas," I say, voice thinner than I want. "What if he knows about Dad? About before?"

He crushes me to his chest, one hand splayed at the back of my neck. "I will not let him near you," he says. His voice is flat, absolute. "I promise you, Soph."

His hand cups my cheek, thumb stroking just below the line of my jaw. I try to read his expression, but all I see is fight—every inch of him braced for the kind of war we're never going to win. I want to be angry, or scared, or even just numb, but the only thing I feel is a wild, stupid need to keep him here, to keep this one small part of the world from burning down.

"I don't want to run," I say, my lips barely moving.

He pulls me in, rests his forehead against mine. "You won't have to."

We sit like that, locked together, listening to the city wake up around us. In a few hours, there will be reporters, questions, maybe even the old news van from Channel 5 parked at the end of the street. In a few hours, the world will expect us to stand up and start fighting again.

But for now, it's just us, the ticking clock, and the slow, certain knowledge that nothing will ever be safe again.

I close my eyes and let the seconds burn away.

Tomorrow, we start again.

Tonight, all that matters is that we made it home.

The night is a trench, and I'm crawling through it on my belly, breath by breath. I don't bother with the pretense of sleep. Lucas and I both know it's a lost cause, but we make a show of brushing our teeth, changing into threadbare cotton, folding ourselves under the covers like civilians in a peaceful world.

He lies on his back, one hand cradling his phone on the nightstand, the other hooked into mine. Our fingers interlock, and he strokes the web between my thumb and forefinger, back and forth, over and over. His body vibrates with the tension of a bomb technician, alert for any click or whisper that might mean the end.

I stare at the ceiling, tracing the path of the old water stain above our bed. My mind fixates on the message—on the way Caleb said my nickname, the slow deliberate drag of it. "Little So, So." It was just a sound, but it got under my skin in a way no threat ever had. The only person who ever used it after first grade was my father, and even then, only on the rarest of occasions—a birthday card, a whispered goodnight after a long shift, once in a scrawled note left by the fridge: "Don't let anyone tell you you're not enough, Little So, So." I'd buried that note in a box of old report cards the week after the fire. I don't remember seeing it since.

Lucas's breathing is steady but shallow. He's counting the seconds between sounds: the stretch and settle of the foundation, the distant rumble of a trash truck, the tap of rain beginning on the back porch. Every time the wind rattles the glass, my heart leaps into my throat. I try not to let it show, but Lucas always notices.

"You're shaking," he says, voice just a breath. "Come here."

I turn toward him, press my face into the hollow of his shoulder. He wraps an arm around me, pulling me in tight. His hand resumes its pattern, slow circles on my back, as if trying to rub out the message like chalk on pavement.

We lie like that for a long time. I wait for my brain to settle, for the replay to stop, but it never does. I see the tape over and over: the courthouse burning, the answering machine light, the way Lucas's face changed when he heard the message. He tried to hide it, but I saw the second he recognized something. He's protecting me from more than just Caleb, and I think I love him more for it, even if it means I'll never get the truth out of him without a fight.

Eventually, I whisper, "How does he know the name?"

Lucas's muscles tense, but his grip doesn't loosen. "Maybe he went through your dad's stuff. After the fire."

"He would have to know exactly what to look for."

"He's had years in the system, Soph. Plenty of time to learn."

I want to believe him, but I can't make the leap. "No one knew it. Not even the guys at the old station."

He sighs, breath hot against my temple. "Maybe he got lucky. Or maybe it's just a coincidence."

"It's not a coincidence," I say. The words taste like copper. "You saw what he did at the courthouse. He's not just after me. He's after you, too."

Lucas's hand tightens in mine. "He wants to scare us. It's all part of his game."

"He doesn't scare me," I lie, and Lucas doesn't call me on it. He just kisses the top of my head, and we go back to listening to the dark.

An hour passes, then two. The rain builds, soft at first, then hard enough to drum on the roof. I find myself focusing on the sound, on the regularity of it. It reminds me of the old firehouse, the way the water used to run down the metal gutters and pool by the garage door. Dad used to say the best nights for sleeping were stormy ones—"nature's white noise machine," he called it.

I wonder if he ever had nights like this, nights where sleep was a weapon he didn't trust. I try to remember if he ever paced, or lay awake in the dark, or stared at the ceiling the way I do now. If he did, he never let me see it. He always woke before me, already shaved and dressed, coffee mug in hand, smile just a little too wide.

My thoughts run wild, connecting old stories to new ones, as if somewhere in the past I might find the answer to what's coming for us now.

I drift for a while, not quite asleep, but not awake. In the liminal space, memory and dream blend: I see my childhood bedroom, the glow of my nightlight, Dad's silhouette in the doorway. I hear the nickname—Little So, So—and it echoes with something else, a shadow of another voice, deeper, sharper. I try to focus on it, but it slips away as soon as I get close.

I wake with a start, and Lucas's eyes are open, watching me.

He wipes a strand of hair from my cheek. “Nightmare?”

“Just weird dreams.” My mouth is dry. “You should try to sleep.”

He smiles, the kind that says he won’t. “You know I won’t.”

We lie like that, forehead to forehead, for what feels like a long time.

The house is quiet again. I let myself relax, just a little. Lucas’s hand moves to the small of my back, fingers spread, anchoring me.

“Do you remember,” I say, “the first night we spent together?”

He nods. “You asked me to tell you a story, so you could fall asleep.”

“What story did you pick?”

He thinks. “The one about the kid who was so afraid of the dark, he left the lights on every night, until the power went out. But he learned to see in the dark, and it wasn’t so bad after all.”

"That's right." I smile. "You're a terrible storyteller, but it worked."

He laughs, silent and deep. "You're a terrible sleeper, so we're even."

We fall quiet again.

This time, I reach for him. I put my hand on his chest, right over his heart. I can feel it hammering, even and strong, the pulse that means he's still here.

"Do you think," I whisper, "that Caleb's right? That we're family?"

Lucas doesn't answer right away. His eyes go distant. "Family isn't just blood," he says, eventually. "It's who you save, and who saves you."

The answer hurts, in a way I can't explain. I think about Dad, about the secrets he kept, about the way he never talked about the early years at Willow Creek. About the way every question about the past got deflected, or turned into a story about someone else. About the note, the nickname, the blank spaces in the story of who I am.

"What if there's something I'm missing?" I say, barely above a whisper.

"We'll figure it out," Lucas says. "We'll figure it out together."

I want to believe him.

I must drift again, because when I open my eyes, the sky outside is streaked with blue. The clock says it's just after six. The rain has stopped. The world is quiet, suspended between night and day.

Lucas is propped on one elbow, watching the window, the beginnings of sunrise reflected in his eyes. He looks older this morning, the lines on his face deeper, his stubble shading the sharp cut of his jaw.

I sit up, wrap the blanket around my shoulders, and lean against him.

He kisses my hair, and for a moment, we are just two people, huddled together against the dark.

"We should check the perimeter before the world wakes up," he says.

I nod.

He stands, stretches, and pulls on sweatpants and a hoodie. He hands me my own, waiting until I'm fully dressed before he opens the bedroom door.

We move through the house, side by side, checking locks, windows, the battery on the security panel. There's no sign of forced entry, no footprint, nothing out of place. The only evidence of the night before is the blinking light on the answering machine, reset to zero.

I look at Lucas, and he looks at me.

We survived the night, but something has changed. There's an edge to the air, a sense that the walls are closing in.

In the kitchen, I pour us both coffee. We sit at the table, steam rising, fingers laced together on the Formica.

"We're going to have to go back to the beginning," I say.

He nods. "Find out what started all this."

"And finish it."

He squeezes my hand.

Outside, the world is waking up—birds on the wires, the hiss of tires on wet pavement, the neighbor's garage door groaning open.

Inside, the fire in me is alive again, burning clean and bright.

We face each other across the coffee cups, a silent agreement between us.

No more running. No more hiding.

We're going to find the truth, whatever it costs.

And we're going to face it together.

17

Second Alarm

LUCAS

I WAKE TO THE TASTE OF BURNING PLASTIC AND THE SHARP claw of smoke in my throat. My brain takes a second to catch up. The air is thick, not just with dreams or sweat, but with something real—something that stings my eyes and grinds its way into my lungs.

I lurch up in bed. There's a pressure in my chest, a memory of every fire I've ever run toward or away from, and for a split second I think: Not this. Not now. Not here.

Beside me, Sophie is a dark shape, tangled in blankets, mouth open in the oblivion of deep sleep. I shake her shoulder, hard, and her eyelids flutter, then snap open, wild and uncomprehending.

"Up," I rasp. "Sophie, get up."

She inhales, coughs once—a deep, wracking sound—and sits bolt upright. The room is already filling, the smoke low at first, now rolling up from the floor, turning the lamp on her nightstand into a ghostly orb.

Sophie's hands go to her face. She blinks, tries to orient. Her voice is a raw whisper: "Is it—?"

I nod, already moving. She's beside me a half second later, grabbing jeans from the chair, pulling them on over bare legs. I yank on yesterday's T-shirt, feet jammed into untied boots, and scan the room for a light source. There's no flicker, no orange glow—just the steady, invasive creep of white smoke.

Sophie's already on her phone, thumb jabbing at the home security app, eyes flicking between the screen and the hall. She covers her mouth with her sleeve. "No alarms," she says, voice muffled. "System's green."

"That's not possible."

She doesn't answer. She's busy: hair yanked into a knot, arms shoved into her jacket, eyes sharp and clear despite the red rim at their edges. I watch the way she moves—efficient, precise, already shifting from victim to analyst.

We hit the hallway together. The air here is worse, visibility dropped to a few feet. Every surface—family photos, the chipped paint of the doorframe, the fake potted plant at the end of the hall—is smeared and distorted. The smoke is denser near the floor, but the ceiling's not much better.

I reach out, grab Sophie's wrist, and pull her close. We stay low, the way every training film tells you, and make our way toward the stairwell.

As we creep, Sophie keeps whispering: "No fire. No heat. Just smoke."

"Electrical?" I hazard.

She shakes her head. "No—no smell of plastic. No alarms, no heat signatures on the cams. Just this."

We hit the top of the stairs. The smoke is billowing up from below, but the wooden banister is cold to the touch. I run my palm along it, half expecting it to be slick with sweat, but it's dry, the finish just as rough as always.

Sophie grabs my shirt. "Listen," she says.

I do, straining past the roar in my ears, the hammer of my own pulse. There's a sound, faint at first, then louder: a low, mechanical hum, pulsing in regular intervals.

"Garage?" I ask.

She nods. "Or the front. Could be the vents."

We move, together, a single organism, training and terror welded into something that almost makes sense. The stairs creak under our weight. At the bottom, the kitchen is a wall of haze; I can barely see the fridge, much less the back door. The sound is louder now, a steady, predatory thrum.

We don't split up. Not after last time.

Past the kitchen, down the short hallway, we angle for the entryway. The smoke is thinner here—barely, but enough that I can make out the doormat, the old mail basket, the row of hooks with our coats. Sophie points at the front door. I see it, too: a thin seam of white fog curling inward from beneath, swirling in lazy eddies around the threshold.

She reaches for the doorknob. I clamp her shoulder.

"Check it," I whisper.

She drops to one knee, palms flat against the wood. She holds it there, a long beat, then looks up at me, confusion naked on her face.

"It's cold," she says. "No heat at all."

I grab the knob, turn it, and pull. The door sticks—swollen from the wet, like always—then gives with a pop. The outside air hits us with a fist of clarity, sharp and freezing, and we stagger onto the porch.

That's when I see it.

There, crouched on the top step, is a squat black box the size of a toolbox, the kind they use at haunted houses and bad wedding receptions. A length of ribbed hose runs from the machine, snakes up to the seam under the door, and pumps a steady, measured stream of synthetic smoke into the entryway.

Sophie stares, then lets out a sound halfway between a laugh and a sob.

"Fog machine," she says, incredulous. "He used a fucking fog machine."

I stand there, shivering, every nerve ending on fire, and try to process the whiplash from terror to... whatever this is. Not relief, exactly. Something angrier, something that tastes of humiliation and rage.

“He got in,” I say. “He set this up.”

Sophie’s already scanning the porch for other traps. “Or had someone else do it,” she mutters. “But yeah. It’s a message.”

I look at her, at the wild streak of soot on her cheek, the way her hair’s coming undone from the bun. She looks at me, lips pressed thin.

“We need to call it in,” I say, reaching for my phone with hands that can’t quite stop shaking.

She takes my hand, steadies it. “Wait. Look.”

She points to the machine: there’s a sticker on the side, a cheap label maker strip. On it, printed in block capitals, is a single word: “REMEMBER.”

My hands go numb. I fumble the phone anyway, punch in the station’s number, and wait for the dispatcher.

As I stand there, the first blue light is already painting the edges of the block, and the sun is barely up, and the whole neighborhood is probably watching from their windows.

I catch Sophie's eyes, and she's not scared. Not exactly. But she's something, and I recognize it.

She's ready.

So am I.

Let him come.

We're not going anywhere.

The front lawn is a circus of red and blue. Two patrol cars at the curb, one unmarked, hazard lights slicing through the predawn like a warning. The neighbors have started to cluster behind their curtains, some peering through half-opened doors, others standing in driveways with arms folded tight, trying to pretend they're not waiting for the next act.

An officer hands us rough wool blankets, the kind that itch even through two layers of clothing. We stand on the grass, coughing, not from the cold but from the ghost of smoke clinging to every fiber. Sophie holds her blanket around her like a cape, chin up, eyes tracking every movement of the uniforms as they swarm our porch.

I've never seen her look so furious and so empty at the same time.

The lead cop—a woman with a red ponytail and crow's feet deep enough to hold secrets—pulls us aside. "You called it in?"

I nod, voice raw. "Name's Hayes. Captain. Willow Creek Fire."

The cop glances at my badge, then at Sophie. "And you?"

"Grant," Sophie says, steady as a witness. "Same. Fire."

She writes it down, then gives us a once-over. "You two okay?"

"Fine," I lie.

Sophie answers, "We didn't see anyone. Didn't hear a thing. Just woke up to smoke."

The cop's pen skates over the form. "It's a hell of a prank for this hour," she says, not quite buying her own words. She motions to the other officers, who bag and tag the fog machine, take a dozen flash photos, and then start toward the house.

I watch as one cop bends to examine the hose snaked under the threshold, muttering to his partner. They take more photos, measure the distance from the door, do everything by the book. Sophie never looks away, eyes gone flat and strange.

When they're done, the cop with the crow's feet pulls us aside again. "We're going to check for prints, canvass the block, see if anyone caught anything on their doorbell cams. Might get lucky, but if the guy's even halfway smart—" She leaves the rest unsaid.

Sophie's voice cuts in. "You want us to walk you through the house?"

"Yeah," the cop says, "if you're up for it."

I can tell Sophie's been waiting for this. She drops her blanket, squares her shoulders, and strides toward the door. I follow, close, not touching her but close enough that if she started to fall, I could catch her before she hit the ground.

Inside, the smoke is already starting to thin, but the residue hangs over everything—soot on the counters, a smear of gray across the kitchen tiles, the hallway bathed in a light that's somehow both harsher and more muted than usual.

The cops move in a cluster, careful where they step. Sophie moves through them, eyes darting, hands hovering over surfaces but never quite making contact. She goes straight to the kitchen, scanning every inch.

That's where she sees it: the round, empty plastic where the smoke alarm used to live. The screws are still in the ceiling, but the unit itself is gone, wires dangling like nerves.

Sophie's face goes cold.

"Did you—?" the cop starts.

Sophie just shakes her head. "It was there last night. I tested it myself."

The cop pulls out a notepad, writes something down, then sends her partner to check the rest of the house.

We trail after. The second smoke detector—at the top of the stairs—is also missing, wires plucked clean, no sign of the plastic shell. The third, in the master bedroom, is there but dead: battery cover off, batteries gone.

Sophie kneels, inspects the fixture. She runs her finger over the lip, careful. There's a smear of black under her nail. Her hands don't shake, but when she stands, her knuckles are white.

The cop says, "Looks like someone disabled them before the smoke got bad."

Sophie nods, dead calm. "He came inside while we slept."

My stomach turns, a slow, molten roll that hits every rib on the way down.

I look at the bed—our bed, sheets still warm from where we'd tangled the night before—and the thought that someone stood here, in the dark, reaching up over us, makes me want to break something.

The cops keep at it, moving room by room. I watch Sophie, the way her posture never changes, the way her face never cracks. But her hand, when she brushes the back of her neck, is trembling.

She catches me watching and lifts her chin, daring me to say anything.

The officer finishes the sweep. "All entry points are locked. No signs of forced entry. Could have come in with a key, or picked it. You two keep any spare keys outside?"

I shake my head, still numb. "Never."

Sophie answers, "He's done it before. Picks locks like he's opening a can of soda."

The cop nods, not surprised. "If you have any old cameras, check the footage. Otherwise, you should maybe stay somewhere else tonight."

Sophie's voice is so flat it's almost a whisper. "No. We stay."

The cop glances at me. I answer for us both: "We're not running."

The cop gives us the kind of look you save for people who don't know when they're beat. She gathers her crew, then tells us they'll be in touch.

As the officers file out, Sophie stands in the hallway, looking up at the naked wires where the detector used to be. She traces them with her eyes, then runs her finger along the ceiling, as if trying to sense the memory of the device that was there.

She doesn't say a word.

When I touch her shoulder, she flinches, just a fraction, then leans back into my palm.

She whispers, so quiet I barely hear her: "Caleb."

The name is a curse. A promise. A wound.

I pull her in, hold her tight, and she finally lets her hands clutch my shirt, trembling like an aftershock.

This isn't a threat. It's a goddamn manifesto.

He's coming, and we're going to be ready.

No matter what.

We don't sleep. Not really. The house is a crypt, every breath of air heavy with the stink of burnt propylene glycol and what's left of our last shred of peace. The windows are open, but the breeze barely moves the air, just churns the residue around the living room where we sit, side by side, on the edge of the couch.

It's been hours since the last police cruiser rolled off the block, but neither of us has spoken more than a dozen words. I keep running the perimeter—windows, doors, even the crawlspace hatch. Every time I loop the house, I catch Sophie in the same place, cross-legged in the corner of the couch, her father's journal open on her lap. She doesn't read it, not really. She just flips pages, smooths them with her palm, then starts over.

I want to say something, to break the silence before it calcifies, but I don't have words for this kind of night.

The grandfather clock in the hallway ticks so loud it feels like a countdown. There's a mug of coffee on the table, cold and untouched. The only other sound is the scrape of my own boots as I pace between the window and the front door, counting the number of times I check the locks. I lose count around six.

At some point, Sophie closes the journal, not with a thud but with a soft, resigned click. She rests her chin on her knee, arms wrapped tight around her legs. In the thin blue light leaking from the street, she looks both ancient and unbreakable.

"He could have killed us," she says. Her voice is too steady. That scares me more than if she'd screamed.

I turn from the window. "But he didn't."

She looks up, eyes sharp as glass. "Because he didn't want to," she says. "He wants us afraid first."

I nod, because there's nothing else to do. "He's good at that."

Sophie tilts her head, thinking. "He always was. Even when we were kids. He could sense the weakest part of you and press until it cracked." Her mouth twists in something like a smile, but it doesn't make it to her eyes. "We thought he'd grown out of it. We thought the system would fix him."

I lean against the wall, arms folded. "We thought a lot of things."

A gust of wind rattles the porch chairs. For a second, I brace for the sound of footsteps, the click of a lighter, but it's just air and memory.

Sophie watches me, her gaze running over every inch like she's memorizing the blueprint of my face. "You're angry."

"Yeah."

"Not at me?"

I shake my head. "Never."

She lets out a breath, slow and measured. "You think we're bait."

I don't answer, but she reads it anyway.

"Let him come," she says, voice gaining force. "We'll be ready."

There's something in the way she says it that makes my chest tighten. Not the usual ache, but a sharp, kinetic thing. I want to reach for her, but I know better than to try and hold onto lightning.

Instead, I sit beside her, close enough to feel the warmth of her body. She sets the journal aside, then opens her hand and finds mine. Her fingers are ice cold, but her grip is iron.

"We don't run," she says. "Not from him. Not from anyone."

I nod. "We fight back."

She leans into my shoulder, just enough to let me know she's still here. I rest my chin on her hair, and together we listen to the hours crawl by.

At four, the world is blue and empty. Sophie has drifted to sleep, if you can call it that, her head on my lap, her hands curled into fists. I keep watch, counting the cars that slide past, the intervals between headlights, the minute sounds that, in any other life, would mean nothing at all.

I think about the name—Caleb—spoken in her voice, and how it sounded like a curse. I think about the way she traced the empty battery slot, the steadiness of her eyes when she looked at the wires. I think about all the ways she's been hurt, and all the ways I've failed to keep the fire away.

But mostly, I think about the way she refused to flinch, even when the air was poison and the night was a blade at our throats.

At six, the sky shifts from black to gray to the sickly yellow of morning. Sophie wakes on her own, sits up, rubs her face, and goes straight to the kitchen to make new coffee. I follow, not because I need caffeine but because I need to see her moving, alive, in the daylight.

She sets the mug in front of me, then perches on the edge of the table, hands tucked under her thighs.

"Next time," she says, "we don't wait for him. We go first."

There's a wildness in her I haven't seen since the old days, when she would bait the boys at the academy, or goad me into climbing the water tower at midnight. It's the look of someone who's got nothing left to lose, and everything left to prove.

I watch her, and I realize I love her more in this moment than in all the quiet ones before.

She stands, grabs her jacket from the chair, and shoulders into it. "I'm going to check the perimeter."

"Wait," I say, but she's already moving.

I follow her, out into the fresh, cold air. The street is empty, the houses asleep, the world scrubbed raw by what we survived. Sophie walks the length of the block, checking every fence, every gate, every possible angle of approach.

When she comes back, her face is flushed, her breath sharp in the morning air. "We'll get him," she says. "We'll end it."

I nod, because there's no arguing with her when she's like this.

We go back inside, close the door behind us, and the house no longer feels like a crypt.

It feels like a fortress.

And we're ready for the siege.

18

Final Burn

LUCAS

THE MORNING IS PALE AND HUNGOVER WHEN I SET OUT. The sky is washed out to almost white, a color that makes the town feel even smaller, even more exposed. Sophie's still at the house, double-checking the security system and watching the block like a wolf mother. I tell her I'm just going to run errands, pick up some hardware, but really I need to move, need to walk it off before I grind my teeth down to nubs.

The first stop is the station. Not my shift, but old habits don't die—they just mutate. I linger on the sidewalk, watching the door, thinking maybe I'll catch a glimpse of the new guy or see if the brass has posted anything about the courthouse. I hear voices inside. Laughter, loud and a little mean, the kind you hear in locker rooms and bars after last call.

I push the door and step in. The lobby's the same as always: old couches, department flag, the rack of glossy pamphlets about fire safety that nobody reads. I head for the break room, hoping to score a stale donut and a little news.

The moment I walk in, the conversation dies like a match in water. Three guys at the table—two I know, one a rookie with a baby face and hair so blond it looks like a joke. They stare at me for a second, then go back to their coffee, the silence sticky as pancake syrup.

I act casual. "Morning," I say, grabbing a mug from the rack and pouring sludge-thick coffee from the carafe.

The older guy, Malone, gives a noncommittal grunt. "Thought you were off today."

I shrug. "Just wanted to check in."

Rookie glances at the older guys, then takes his shot. "You hear about the courthouse?" he says. "Chief's still cleaning up, but they say it's a total loss. Evidence room, records, the whole shebang."

I nod. "Heard."

Malone snorts. "Supposed to be impossible to torch a place with that much fire suppression. But then, nobody told the arsonist."

The other guy, Sanchez, leans back. "Funny, though, how every time there's a fire like this, it comes back to that Grant girl."

I grip the mug tighter. "You mean Sophie?"

He smirks. "Yeah. Seems like trouble follows her around."

I take a sip, the coffee burning my tongue. I want to slam the mug down, but instead I ask, "Anyone know how Caleb even got out?"

They look at each other, each waiting for the other to spill. Finally, Malone says, "Rumor is he paid off the EMTs. Or maybe Bennett set it up before he got pinched."

Sanchez shakes his head. "Bennett wouldn't risk his pension for a kid like that."

"Hell he wouldn't," says Malone. "That kid was like a son to him."

The words hit me in the gut, a fast, cold punch. I put down my mug, careful not to crack the ceramic. "You guys ever work a call with Caleb?"

Rookie shakes his head, eyes wide. Malone looks away, suddenly interested in his donut. Sanchez grins, lazy and mean. "I saw him once, after a burn. Quiet kid. The scary ones always are."

I look at each of them, the air thick with something I don't want to name. "If you hear anything—anything real—let me know."

Sanchez holds my gaze. "Will do, Captain."

I nod and walk out, the door slamming a little too loud behind me.

I drive to the store. It's not the big chain—just a squat, low-slung grocery with a sign that says "Martin's" in faded red letters. I park in the corner, away from the vans and the pickups with fire department stickers in the back window.

Inside, the air is too cold and smells like bleach and freezer burn. I walk the aisles on autopilot, picking up milk, bread, batteries. I pass the dairy case, and I catch two women in conversation, their heads bowed close, whispering.

"—swear to god, I saw her with him last week. Right behind the dairy aisle."

"No way," the other says, eyes wide. "Isn't she with that firefighter?"

"Doesn't matter. They say she's the reason he started all this in the first place."

My blood goes cold. I grip the handle of the basket so tight my fingers throb.

The first woman looks up and sees me. She goes red, then snaps her mouth shut like a trap.

I walk past, keep my eyes forward. The whole time, I can feel their gaze on my back, like the heat you get from standing too close to a fire.

At the register, I unload my groceries in silence. The kid behind the counter barely looks at me, just scans and bags with the robotic efficiency of someone who wants to be anywhere else.

I pay in cash, thank the kid, and head out. Behind me, I hear one of the women say, "That's her boyfriend, you know." The other answers, "Poor bastard." I keep walking.

I make a last stop at the hardware. The bell over the door clangs, and the clerk looks up, eyes sharp behind thick glasses. He's the kind of man who's seen every kind of town drama and doesn't bother pretending he hasn't.

"Morning, Hayes," he says, nodding to me like he's known me forever.

"Morning," I reply. "Need some things for the house. Security upgrades."

He raises an eyebrow, but doesn't comment. I go straight to the aisle with the padlocks, take down four, then grab two sets of window reinforcements and a motion sensor kit. I add a heavy-duty flashlight for good measure.

At the counter, the clerk rings everything up, his fingers moving slow, deliberate. "Things okay at home?"

I keep my face blank. "Just taking precautions."

He nods, runs my card, and slides the bag across the counter. "You let us know if you need a hand. Half the town's rooting for you."

I thank him, meaning it more than I expected. He gives me a look—sympathy, maybe, or just the recognition that we both know how this ends.

I load everything into the back of the truck. The bag is heavier than it should be, the tools clinking together in a low, metallic warning.

As I turn to get in, I catch my reflection in the truck window. The lines in my face look deeper, the shadows under my eyes darker. I set my jaw, push back the dread, and drive home.

The rumors have a way of getting in, even when the locks are brand new.

But so do I.

Let them talk.

Let him come.

I'll be ready.

I'm halfway up the drive when I see the front door is unlocked. Not open—just that faint give, the way the latch fails to catch when someone comes in on autopilot. I put down the bags, thumb the knob, and step inside.

The living room is stripped to its bones. Furniture shoved to the edges. The carpet, a cheap rental beige, is littered with photographs—hundreds, maybe more, spread in a drifting spiral from the center of the floor. Sophie is cross-legged in the eye of the storm, hunched forward, hands moving without pattern through the paper mess.

She's so focused she doesn't hear me at first. I close the door soft, leave the bags against the wall. I see her shoulders shaking, the hitch in her breath that she tries to stifle, and something in me aches like a fresh bruise.

I kneel behind her, the photos crumpling under my jeans. She doesn't turn, but I wrap my arms around her anyway, pulling her back against my chest. She doesn't resist. She leans into me, clinging like she's cold, like I'm the only warmth left.

We sit there, breathing together. I watch her hands sift the photographs, some glossy, some matte, edges curled and corners soft. There are Polaroids in the pile—her as a toddler in a blue swimsuit, as a teenager scowling at the camera from behind a mess of tangled hair, as a woman in a firefighter's turnouts, soot on her cheek, grinning like a champ. There are pictures of her father, her mother, old friends I don't recognize, and a few of me and Sophie from back when everything felt possible.

She picks up a photo, stares at it. "I forgot this one," she says, voice so soft I almost miss it.

I look. It's a faded shot of her, maybe ten, sitting on a man's shoulders at a county fair. The man's face is obscured by a shadow, but I know from the set of his jaw that it's her dad. Sophie's face is all sunlight and gap-toothed pride.

I rest my chin on her shoulder. "He'd be proud of you," I say.

She laughs, a wet, shaky sound. "He'd tell me to stop crying. 'Crying doesn't fix the fire, kiddo.'"

I squeeze her tighter. "Sometimes it helps, though."

She lets the photo drift from her fingers, landing face-up on the rug.

"I'm scared, Lucas." Her voice cracks on the word.

I pull her in, shift so her back fits the curve of my chest, and tuck my chin into the warm, wild mess of her hair.

"It's okay," I say. "I am too."

We sit, tangled in a nest of old memories and new fear, and for a long minute, there's only the sound of our breathing and the slap of photos as she drops them, one by one.

I turn her gently in my lap so we're face to face. She doesn't fight it, just tucks her knees up and buries her head against my neck.

"I don't know why he's doing this," I whisper. "But I won't let him get close. I promise."

She shakes her head, pulls back so she can see my eyes. Her own are bloodshot, raw, but so goddamn alive it makes my chest tight.

"That's not what I'm scared of," she says.

"What, then?"

She's silent, searching my face, maybe looking for some trace of the boy I used to be, or the man she needs me to be now.

She bites her lip, then lets go. "I'm not scared he'll hurt me. I'm scared he'll hurt you."

The words gut me. I want to tell her it's fine, that I've been hurt before, that I can take it. But I know it's not the same, not this time.

I cup her face in both hands, wiping away the tracks of tears with my thumbs. "You're the bravest person I know," I tell her. "But you don't have to be. Not tonight."

She closes her eyes, leans into my palm. "You don't have to fix me, Lucas."

"I'm not trying to fix you. I just want to keep you safe."

She opens her eyes. The look she gives me is more powerful than any vow I could ever make. We sit, forehead to forehead, neither moving.

I feel every heartbeat in my chest, every shallow breath she takes. The past and the present crash together in the space between us—old wounds, old love, new terror.

The storm outside rattles the windows. The wind picks up, whistling through the gaps in the frame.

Sophie reaches up, touches my jaw, fingers trembling. "I need you," she says, so quietly I'm not sure I heard it right.

But I did.

I always have.

We stay like that, a mess of limbs and pictures and memory, for a long time. Her breathing slows. The trembling stops. My arms around her become less a shield and more a home.

She finally speaks. "If I don't make it—"

I cut her off. "Don't."

Her lips curl in a sad, fierce smile. "If I don't, you have to finish it. You have to put him down."

"I will," I say. It's a promise, a prayer, a curse.

We stay there, on the floor, the light from the window turning the photos gold and then gray as the day bleeds out.

When the sun finally sets, she moves first, standing with a groan. She reaches down and hauls me up, her hand tight in mine.

We don't need to say anything else.

The night ahead is dark and full of monsters, but we're not alone.

Not now.

Not ever.

She hauls me to my feet and we stand, inches apart, in the blue dusk of the living room. There's a moment where the world holds its breath—then she closes the gap and kisses me.

It starts soft, almost gentle, but neither of us is any good at holding back. Her hands climb my chest, anchor at my shoulders. I feel the tremor in her fingers, the suppressed voltage of everything she hasn't said. She parts her lips with a desperate kind of hunger, like she's hoping to swallow the ache right out of my bones.

I kiss her back. I put my hands on her waist, thumb catching the patch of bare skin where her shirt rides up. She tastes like salt and adrenaline, and when her breath stutters against my mouth, I feel something melt inside me. The heat ramps up, fast and reckless. She fumbles for the buttons on my shirt, pops two in the rush to get it off, and I hear one ping off the baseboard.

She doesn't care. She never has. I love that about her.

She breaks the kiss just long enough to get her hands under my shirt, palms flat against my ribs. I shiver at her touch, and she smirks—a wicked, wild thing—then bites my lower lip. It's not a tease. It's a warning. Or a dare.

"Bed," she says, voice hoarse.

I scoop her up, one arm under her knees, the other steady at her back. She wraps her arms around my neck. We crash through the hallway, banging shoulders and knees against the doorframe, and land on the bed in a tangle of limbs and laughter.

She's on top for once, straddling me, hair wild. She peels off her shirt, then reaches for my jeans, undoing them with deft, furious hands. I feel her body slide against mine, skin to skin, and the rush is like a backdraft—dangerous, overwhelming, impossible to resist.

She pins my hands above my head, kisses a line down my throat, then nips at the place where my pulse hammers. I groan, hips rising to meet her, but she holds me down. Her hair tickles my face, her breath hot at my ear.

"You're mine," she says, and it's not a question.

"Always," I answer, and mean it.

She releases my wrists, lets me flip us so I'm above her. I kiss down her collarbone, down her stomach, memorize every scar and freckle like I'm afraid she'll vanish if I don't. She runs her hands through my hair, tugs me closer, closer. We move together, urgent but not rough, not this time. This is need, pure and bright. This is the universe burning down and us refusing to be ashes.

She wraps her legs around me, heels digging into my back. "Don't stop," she whispers, over and over. I don't.

When I finally push into her, we both gasp. The sound is raw, sharp, a promise and a prayer. We find a rhythm, bodies matched, and every movement is a declaration: I am here, I am alive, I am not afraid.

She pulls me down for another kiss, messy and deep, and I lose myself in her completely.

When we come, it's like breaking through to the other side of a firestorm—everything white, everything clean. We hold on, shuddering, both of us crying, or maybe laughing. I can't tell, and it doesn't matter.

After, I collapse beside her. She rolls onto her side, hair sticking to her cheek. I pull her in, tuck her head under my chin, hold her like a life raft.

We stay that way for a long time. Her breathing slows, goes steady and sweet. My own heart finally stops pounding, but I don't let go.

She falls asleep first, arm slung across my chest, hand curled into the hollow above my heart. I listen to her dreams—the soft noises, the way her leg kicks when she chases something in her sleep. I don't sleep at all.

I lie there, staring at the ceiling, and think about what comes next.

I think about the look in her eyes when she said she was scared for me.

I think about the rumors, the whispers, the way the whole town is holding its breath for the next disaster.

I think about Caleb, and how he's always just one step behind us, or maybe ahead.

And I make myself a promise, silent and ironclad.

I won't let him win.

I won't let him take another piece of us.

Not now.

Not ever.

Dawn creeps in slow. The world outside is quiet, but I know it's just a lull before the next hit.

Sophie stirs, rubs her face against my chest, then opens her eyes and grins at me. "You didn't sleep," she says.

"Didn't need to."

She sits up, hair a mess, blanket slipping down her shoulder. She looks at me like she's seeing me for the first time, or maybe the last. "We should get ready," she says.

"Yeah." I get out of bed, pull on yesterday's jeans. The shirt is missing a button, but I don't care.

She watches me, then grabs my hand as I pass.

"Hey," she says. "We're gonna be okay."

I nod, squeeze her fingers. "I know."

I mean it.

I gather the hardware, the padlocks, the tools. I make a plan.

Today is the day.

Let him come.

Let him try.

We are fireproof now.

We are ready for the end.

19

Open Flame

SOPHIE

The morning is almost cruel in its perfection. Sunlight pours in through the kitchen's east windows, sharp as knives, painting a grid of gold across the scarred Formica. There's the smell of dark roast and burned toast and the sweeter, sour trace of last night's wine. Lucas sits across from me in a threadbare T-shirt, hair still wet from the shower, a permanent dimple in his cheek from how he always sleeps with his face mashed into his forearm. His eyes are blue and bright, and for the first time in months, he looks almost relaxed.

Between us, the table is crowded: two chipped mugs, a box of wedding magazines with bookmarks in half the pages, a lined notebook crammed with my chicken scratch. There are photos all over the fridge, magnets shaped like fruit holding up memories in wild disorder—Lucas as a kid, bucktoothed and sunburned, me at various ages, some of Dad, some of us together. On the counter by the stove, my stack of books leans into his, toppling sideways like the world's slowest collision.

He picks at a slice of toast, not eating, just tearing off bits and lining them up like chess pieces. His fingers are stained with grease from the tools he fiddled with all night, never able to sit still while the world kept turning.

"So," he says, smile crinkling the corners of his eyes. "I had an idea."

I look at him over the rim of my coffee. "Dangerous words, Captain."

He huffs a laugh. "Hear me out. What if—" He glances at the window, lowers his voice like we're being surveilled. "What if we ditch the whole wedding-palooza, and just do it small? Like, really small."

I set the mug down. "Define small."

He shrugs, a nervous little roll of the shoulders that reminds me of him at twenty, before all the scars. "You, me, your mom, my sister, a justice of the peace. Maybe a witness or two if the law insists."

I pretend to think about it, but the idea slips into my chest and makes a home there, warm and sudden. "You'd be okay with that?"

He leans forward, elbows on the table, hands folded. "More than okay. I'd prefer it. If I have to wear a suit, I want to be able to ditch the tie and not have it show up on someone's TikTok."

I bite the inside of my cheek. "I thought you wanted the reception. The dance, the food—"

"I want you," he says, cutting me off, voice low. "The rest is just... logistics."

I can feel the smile pulling at my mouth, but I make myself look at the wall, at the tangle of keys and sunglasses and unopened mail that says FINAL NOTICE in red. "You realize my mother will kill you."

He grins. "She can try. I'll bring her cake as a peace offering."

"You know, some people really want the whole thing. The flowers, the aisle, the first dance. We could at least do a cake."

He points a finger at me, triumphant. "Yes! This is the kind of compromise that will make our marriage indestructible."

The word sits between us for a second—marriage, whole and intact—and I let myself believe it, just for the time it takes to breathe in and out.

"Okay," I say. "Small. But I get to pick the cake."

He feigns outrage. "Not even a joint consultation?"

I shake my head, hair falling forward into my face. "You're just going to pick chocolate and call it a day. I want options."

He snorts, wipes a crumb off his mouth. "Wow, not even married and already you're a tyrant."

"Wouldn't want to startle you after the fact."

He laughs, and it's the kind of laugh that makes me think of road trips, the old stereo in his pickup, the way he used to rest his hand on my thigh at red lights like I was the only solid thing in the world. I find myself staring, trying to memorize the way the morning makes him look: the play of light across his jaw, the tiny scar at his temple, the way his eyes go soft when he thinks I'm not watching.

"Hey," he says, a little softer now. "You spaced out."

I jerk, then force a smile. "Just picturing the dress code. Do I have to wear white, or is that optional?"

He sits back, crosses his arms. "You could wear that sweatshirt with the weird cat print and I'd still say 'I do.'"

"Liar," I say, but it makes me laugh.

He moves his toast-chess piece, sets it down with finality. "Actually, I was thinking we could do it by the lake. Where your dad took you fishing."

The suggestion hits me sideways. There's an ache under my ribs, not quite sadness, not quite relief. "You'd want to?"

"Of course," he says. "It's a good place. Feels right."

I don't trust my voice, so I just nod. I look at the window, at the way the sun slices through the glass and lands on the battered linoleum. Every detail seems sharper today: the slightly crooked towel rack, the dust motes dancing in the air, the way Lucas's hands move when he talks. I want to hold it all in my head, just in case.

He nudges my foot with his under the table. "You okay?"

"Yeah," I lie. "Just tired."

He studies me, sees more than I wish he could. "We could take a day off. Just... do nothing."

I think of the list on the fridge, the hardware in the truck, the constant pulse of threat that sits in the back of my skull and refuses to fade. "Maybe tomorrow," I say.

He reaches across, takes my hand. His thumb draws a slow circle over my knuckle. "We're gonna make it," he says, not for the first time.

I nod, feeling the warmth of his hand, the steadiness of it. "I know."

We eat in silence for a while. He sketches out ideas for the ceremony on a napkin, stick figures in the margins, a cartoon cake with a question mark over it. I laugh when he draws a tiny me in a white dress holding a flare gun, but when he isn't looking, I fold the napkin and tuck it into my pocket.

When the last of the toast is gone, he stands and gathers the plates, stacking them with the precision of someone who needs to keep his hands busy. He starts rinsing them in the sink, sleeves rolled to the elbows. The muscles in his forearms flex with the movement, and I watch, aware of how strong he is, how gentle.

I linger at the table, not wanting to break the moment.

Lucas glances over his shoulder, smirk in place. "You gonna help, or just watch me do all the work?"

"Watching seems safer," I say.

He rolls his eyes. "Fine. But you get clean-up duty for dinner."

"Deal," I say.

He finishes, wipes his hands on the dish towel, and slings an arm around my shoulders as he walks past. "Come on. Let's take a walk. Get some air."

I hesitate, then nod. "Let me grab a sweater."

He disappears down the hall. I follow, pausing to look at the photos on the fridge, the jacket by the door, the half-read book on the counter with my name on the inside cover. I take a mental snapshot—everything in its place, everything as it should be.

He comes back with my favorite hoodie, the one I stole from him in college. He holds it out, helps me slide my arms in. His hands linger at my shoulders, and when I turn, he kisses my forehead.

"For luck," he says.

I smile, and it feels real.

We step outside, into the cold, clear air. He walks ahead, hands in his pockets, head tilted back to watch the sky. I follow, a pace behind, and let myself wonder—just for a moment—if maybe, somehow, we'll get the future we've talked about.

But I know better.

I watch the set of his jaw, the way he scans the street, the way his body moves between me and every possible threat.

I file it all away.

Just in case.

The house is quiet in a way that feels staged, like the world is holding its breath just to see what happens next. Lucas is in the shower, humming off-key, water thrumming against tile in steady, predictable pulses. I'm in the living room, sunlight striping the floor, dust motes glimmering as I flip through the half-finished wedding notebook with one eye on the hallway.

It happens so softly I almost miss it: a faint shuffle, the whisper of something sliding against wood. I freeze, senses flaring, every muscle remembering what it means to be prey. The sound is at the front door, not loud enough to be a knock—just a delicate scrape, then silence.

I set the notebook down and cross the room, my bare feet making no sound. I press my palm against the cool jamb and stare through the peephole: nothing. Nobody in the yard, no movement on the sidewalk, no sign of the usual mail truck or bored kids on bikes. I wait, count to ten, then slowly unlatch the deadbolt.

A wedge of white paper juts out from under the door, a tongue of threat. I kneel, heart in my throat, and pull it inside.

The paper is folded once, no envelope, no address. My hands shake as I open it, the ink blocky and all-caps, the letters dug in deep like someone wanted to gouge the meaning straight through the page.

IF YOU WANT YOUR MAN TO KEEP BREATHING

MEET ME AT THE OLD FIRE STATION

ALONE.

IF HE COMES, HE DIES.

MIDNIGHT.

SEE YOU THEN, SO, SO.

The world narrows to the sharp edges of the paper and the taste of bile crawling up my throat. I stare at the signature, at the nickname no one but my father ever used, and I want to scream or throw up or punch a hole through the drywall. But I don't.

Instead, I look down the hall, toward the bathroom where Lucas's voice echoes, mangled by the roar of the shower. He's singing something stupid and old, and for a second, I want nothing more than to walk in and climb in with him, let the day be normal for one more minute.

But there isn't time for that.

I move fast. The fireplace is cold, but there's always a pack of matches on the mantle. I light one, the sulfur burning my nose, and hold the note in the flame. The edges blacken, curl, then catch. I watch the words turn to nothing, the threat reduced to a single ashy coil. I crush it between my fingers, rub the residue into the grate until it's gone.

The bathroom door creaks open and a fog of steam billows out, warm and thick. Lucas pads down the hall in a towel, hair slicked back, skin flushed from the water. He stops when he sees me, and the sight of him—alive, unmarked, still somehow convinced he can protect us both—almost undoes me.

"What's up?" he asks, wiping condensation from his eyes.

I force a smile, muscles aching with the effort. "Just thinking about cake again."

He laughs, the sound rolling out easy. "I still say chocolate is the right call."

I let the smile linger, let him believe the world is still the shape we made it this morning. He doesn't see the matchbook on the mantle, or the way my hands are dusted with black.

He comes over, kisses me on the cheek, and heads for the kitchen. "You want some tea?"

I nod, and watch him go.

The clock on the wall is loud, each tick a nail in the coffin of the day. Midnight is less than twelve hours away, and I am already counting down.

I tell myself I am ready, that I have been ready since the first day I pulled on a uniform and ran toward the smoke instead of away.

But I have never been less sure of anything in my life.

Still, I do what I have to.

I brush the last of the ash from my fingers, wipe my hands on my jeans, and go to help Lucas make tea.

For now, I let him have the illusion.

Tonight, I'll save him, or I'll die trying.

Evening descends like a velvet shroud, soft and heavy and just a little suffocating. Lucas makes chili—his specialty, even though he always overdoes the cumin—and we eat it on the couch, bowls in our laps, feet tangled together under the throw blanket we both pretend not to hate. He finds a movie on TV, some dumb action thing with explosions and quips, and narrates every plot hole as if he's auditioning for Mystery Science Theater. I laugh at the right places, let my head drop to his shoulder, feel the shape of his ribs rise and fall with each joke.

It's almost easy to pretend.

Every so often, I glance at the clock. The hours bleed away in slow motion: seven, then eight, then ten. Lucas pours a glass of wine for each of us, teases me about how I hold the glass like a snob, and I tease him back about the grease on his hands from fixing the porch light. He leans in and kisses the tip of my nose, and for a second, I let myself believe this is real, that we are two people with nothing to run from but laundry and tax deadlines.

"I'm exhausted," I say around ten-thirty, voice thick as honey. "Let's just crash."

He stifles a yawn. "You sure? I thought you wanted to watch the rest."

I smile, tucking my feet beneath me. "I've already seen it." I haven't, but it doesn't matter.

He stands, stretches, and offers me his hand. "My lady."

I take it, let him spin me up, arms around my waist. He buries his nose in my hair and inhales, and it's so tender I almost break.

"You smell like cinnamon," he murmurs.

"Probably the wine," I answer, but my throat closes on the words.

We move down the hallway together, the house dim except for the lamp in the living room. In the bedroom, he peels off his shirt and flops face-first onto the mattress, limbs sprawled. I change into sleep clothes, moving slow, savoring every fold and tuck. I brush my teeth, wash my face, and when I look up at my reflection, I barely recognize myself. My eyes are red at the corners, mouth pinched tight, shoulders squared like I'm going to war.

I climb into bed, curling against his chest. His arms come around me, strong and warm. We settle into our groove, spooned just the way we've always liked, my back pressed to his front, his breath ghosting the nape of my neck.

"You good?" he asks, half asleep already.

"I'm perfect," I whisper.

His hand finds mine, lacing our fingers together. We lie like that, in the dark, listening to the wind in the gutters, the faint hum of the fridge, the occasional far-off bark of a neighbor's dog.

His breathing deepens, slows. The weight of him behind me, the security of it, is almost more than I can stand. I close my eyes and make myself remember it: the way he smells, the way his fingers twitch as he drifts off, the tiny snore that sneaks out when he's completely gone.

At 11:30, I open my eyes and check the clock again. My pulse is a drumline. I wait five minutes, then five more, just to make sure. When I'm certain he's asleep, I untangle our hands and slip from the bed.

I dress in the darkness: black jeans, black sweater, boots with the soft soles that don't squeak. My engagement ring catches on the fabric as I pull the sweater down, and I pause, fingers grazing the band.

The stone flashes, a tiny, defiant fire in the moonlight spilling through the window. For a second, I don't want to take it off. It feels wrong, like giving up.

But I do it anyway. I slide it free, cold metal against my skin, and set it gently on the nightstand. It glints back at me, a promise or a question. I run my thumb over the inside of the band, tracing the groove where his initials are engraved.

At the bedroom door, I turn back. Lucas hasn't moved, his face slack and peaceful in sleep. I watch him, memorizing every detail: the line of his jaw, the cut on his lip from biting it in concentration, the way his hair sticks up in the back. I want to climb in beside him, let the world end with both of us right here.

But I can't.

A tear slips down my cheek, hot and silent. I swipe it away and slip out.

I move through the house, every light off, shadows layered thick in the corners. I don't need to see to know where everything is—the keys on the dish by the door, my phone in the charger, the thin wallet I never bother to carry unless I have to. I collect them all, moving careful, methodical, every gesture rehearsed.

At the door, I hesitate. I look back one last time, at the living room where we ate chili, at the hallway lined with our dumb snapshots, at the pile of laundry waiting to be folded. I want to burn it all into my head, a map of the life I want to get back to.

Then I open the door and step into the cold, night air.

It slaps me awake, drives the last traces of sleep from my brain. The world is silent, sky cloudy and starless, the block deserted. I pull the door shut behind me, careful not to make a sound. The lock clicks home, a soft, final punctuation.

I start walking, every footstep a countdown.

In the distance, I hear a car, or maybe just the wind. It doesn't matter. I have a mile to go before the old fire station, and I know every shortcut, every alley, every place a threat could hide.

I move fast, steady. I don't look back.

By the time I reach the corner of Lincoln and Seventh, I'm numb to everything but the purpose driving me forward. I stop at the crosswalk, wait for a passing car even though the street is empty.

I touch my left ring finger, feeling the phantom weight of the band I left behind.

I will get it back.

I will see him again.

Or I won't, but at least it will be by my choice.

I turn the corner and head for the fire station, the wind howling low through the empty streets.

Tonight, I face the fire.

And this time, I am ready to burn.

20

Ring of Fire

SOPHIE

I COUNT MY STEPS. EVERY BLOCK BETWEEN HOME AND THE old firehouse is a slow calcification—bone growing over bone, making me heavier and harder the closer I get. The night is so quiet it feels rigged, like some god has paused the soundtrack just to watch how this ends.

By the time I reach the corner, my hands are numb and my mouth tastes like pennies. The building sits hulking and half-rebuilt, a skeleton half-patched with new wood and Tyvek, all of it wreathed in shadow. Every window is a blank eye. The front bay doors are chained shut, but there's a side door I know about, a splintered thing with a latch that's never really worked.

I check my phone—one last look, one last chance for a message from Lucas, or the cops, or the universe—but the screen is black. I turn it off and drop it in my pocket. I don't want to be found with it on me.

The walk up to the side door is the longest thirty feet of my life. The yard is overgrown with brittle grass and broken glass. Every step is a tiny confession: I am afraid. I am alone. I am going to do this anyway.

The door gives with a whine, the hinges screaming. Inside, it's colder than out. The air smells like char and ammonia, with a twist of something older—old paper, wet brick. My footsteps echo up through the empty shell. The station floor is blackened concrete, with one long crack running from the old kitchen all the way to the rear bay. I keep to the edge, letting my eyes adjust. Somewhere overhead, a strip of plastic flaps in the wind, beating a rhythm that sounds almost like a heartbeat.

I stop in the middle of the main hall, wait. Nothing. The silence stretches. For a second, I wonder if the note was bullshit, if I've left Lucas for nothing, if I'm just a bigger idiot than I ever wanted to admit.

But then:

"I knew you'd come."

The voice is familiar, but wrong. Slower, deeper than I remember. It comes from behind the rusted engine, the one they kept for parades even after it stopped running. A shadow peels itself away from the tire, and then Caleb steps into the light.

He's changed. Taller than I remember—taller than Lucas, maybe. His hair is buzzed short, face thinner, eyes recessed in a way that makes him look half-starved, half-hunted. His hands are bare, nails bitten to the quick, but he holds himself with the coiled patience of a snake at rest.

"Little So, So," he says, and the name lands on my skin like a wasp. "I was worried you'd bring a friend."

I keep my voice flat. "What do you want, Caleb?"

He grins, but it doesn't touch his eyes. "You never were much for pleasantries."

He moves closer, arms out at his sides, palms open. There's something off about the way he walks—not a limp, exactly, but a lopsidedness, as if one leg is half a second behind the other. He circles me, never breaking eye contact.

I stand my ground. I don't have a plan. I don't have anything but the knife in my jacket pocket and the hope that he'll keep his distance long enough for me to make a run for it if I have to.

"You look good," he says, and this time he smiles for real. It's a wolf's smile. "Better than the last time I saw you. Hospital, wasn't it? They gave you the private room."

He's close enough that I can see the sweat beading on his upper lip. Close enough to smell the iron on his breath. His gaze flicks up and down, cataloguing every flaw.

"You wrote the note," I say.

He shrugs. "Had to get your attention somehow."

I clench my hands into fists, feel my nails cut into my palm. "If this is about the past—about what happened to your mother—"

He laughs, sharp and echoing. "You think this is about her? I don't even remember her face." The laughter dies, and he steps in, close enough to touch. "I'm here for you, Sophie."

The way he says my name makes me want to back up, but I force myself to stay still.

He leans in, his voice a rasp. "You ever wonder what it's like, being invisible? Watching everyone live their lives, pretending the fire's not burning underneath? I used to watch you, you know. On the playground. At the firehouse picnics. You and Lucas, always together."

My skin crawls. "You were a kid. You could have said something. We—"

"We what?" he spits. "You didn't even know my name."

He pulls away, pacing a slow circle around me. His boots scrape on the concrete, each step measured.

"Lucas was the golden boy," Caleb continues. "Even when he messed up, everyone covered for him. You, too. Everyone loved you. But me?" He stops, turns, and his face goes flat. "I was the cautionary tale. The one the chief used as an example of how not to end up."

"You set a fire that almost killed people," I say. "You don't get to play the victim."

His lips curl. "Maybe I just wanted to see if anyone would notice. Maybe I wanted someone to stop me."

He keeps orbiting, never letting me out of his sightline. "Did Lucas tell you about the first time he saved your life?" Caleb says, voice gone dreamy. "You were ten. Your dad was drunk, left you in the car. Lucas pulled you out, carried you two blocks home, even though he was just a kid himself. You don't even remember, do you?"

I stare, mind racing. I can't remember it. I don't want to.

He sees the crack in my composure and pounces. "They never told you the truth. Not your dad, not Lucas, not anyone. But I saw. I see everything."

He's close again, reaching for my face. I jerk back, and he laughs.

"You're scared," he says. "Good. You should be."

I force myself to breathe, slow and deep. I glance at the back exit—twenty feet, maybe less. If I make a break for it, he'll be on me in three strides. I need him to get closer, or I need to distract him.

He must see it in my eyes, because he steps back, then seats himself on a toppled bench. "Sit," he says, patting the space beside him.

I don't move.

He shrugs, then leans forward, elbows on his knees, hands dangling. "Do you remember the time you came here with your dad, and he let you ride the truck? You pretended you were going to drive it all the way to the moon." He sniffs, almost sad. "I was upstairs. Watching. Wishing it was me."

I stay silent. Let him talk. Let him run himself out.

He shakes his head. "Doesn't matter. I just wanted to see you before it ends."

My voice is steady, finally. "Before what ends?"

He looks up, and his eyes are wet, but there's nothing human in them. "The cycle," he whispers. "The story. You, and him, and me."

He stands, walking toward the engine. He pulls something from behind the wheel—a can of lighter fluid—and sets it on the ground between us.

"Tonight, we make a new story," Caleb says. "One they'll never forget."

He kicks the can at my feet, the plastic rattling.

"Pick it up," he commands.

I don't move. He steps closer, and this time, I see the knife at his belt. My own knife is suddenly less comforting, but I don't flinch.

"What are you going to do?" I ask.

He grins again, wolfish. "We're going to light it up, Little So, So. Together. Like a family."

The word hangs in the air, heavy and obscene.

He moves in, slow, deliberate, and for a second I see the kid he used to be—the one who wanted to be seen, wanted to be loved. But it's buried under a mountain of rage.

"You can leave now," he says, almost kind. "Or you can stay and see what happens."

He's giving me a choice, but I know it's a lie.

I steel myself. "I'm not running."

He nods, almost approving.

"Good," he says. "Neither am I."

We stand there, two sides of the same old fire, waiting to see who will burn first.

The silence is brittle, but it won't last. Caleb stands a few paces away, watching me like he's waiting for some secret signal only he can hear. His eyes flick up to the rafters, then down to the can of fluid between us, then finally settle on my face with a flat, expectant calm.

I wait for him to make the first move. I need him to. If I lunge, I tip my hand. If I wait, maybe he'll get careless. But then he smiles—a thin, peeling back of lips that shows more teeth than warmth—and reaches into his back pocket.

He pulls out a phone and taps it. For a second, nothing happens. Then, over my shoulder, a bright rectangle flares into life on the back wall. I flinch, turning, and realize a cheap projector is clipped to the ceiling, its lens pointed directly at the peeling whitewash.

The first image is a close-up of a woman's face. Young, brown hair, a dimple at one cheek. She's holding a baby, maybe six months old, grinning into the sun. The image clicks to the next: the same woman, older, walking hand-in-hand with a boy who can't be more than eight. Another photo. The boy, older now, standing on a dock with a man I don't recognize—a beard, a ball cap, a look that's almost kind, if you don't notice the cold behind the eyes.

The photos cycle, each a little more battered than the last. A school portrait—Caleb, unmistakable, a sullen line for a mouth and eyes that look everywhere but at the camera. A Christmas morning, the same boy, sitting on the edge of a couch, unwrapping a fire truck, the kind you find at the dollar store.

Caleb's voice is soft. "You know what they called me at St. Agnes?"

I don't answer.

"Lost cause," he says, almost fond. "But I wasn't. I was just waiting for someone to remember I existed."

He steps closer. I back up instinctively, boots scraping concrete, but he keeps coming, moving with the weird, loping rhythm of someone whose anger has overtaken pain.

"You want to see the best part?" he asks. He raises the phone again and swipes.

The screen blips, then fills with a new image. It's a picnic, maybe from Twenty-five odd years ago. I know the park—Deadman's Hill, with the rotten swings and the old, painted fire hydrant. In the center: my father, looking younger than I ever saw him in person, one arm slung around the woman from the first photo. Caleb's mother. The other arm is wrapped around me. I'm maybe five, clutching a juice box, the pink straw sticking out like a birthday candle.

I stare at it, unable to move.

"That's not possible," I say.

Caleb's voice is steel. "But it is."

He closes the distance in three strides. Before I can react, he grabs my wrist—hard, so hard the bones grind—and twists. I cry out, low and involuntary, and he uses the leverage to whip a zip tie around both my wrists, pinning them behind my back. My brain is a carnival of alarms, but my body betrays me—I freeze, then kick, but he's faster, stronger, crazy in a way that makes him invincible.

He slams me into the closest bench. My knees hit wood, and pain lances up my thigh. He loops another tie around my ankles, cinching them tight. I try to rock back, but he shoves me down, his hand hot and wet on the nape of my neck.

"We're going to watch some family moments," he whispers, his breath sour at my ear. "Don't look away."

He lets go, then steps back, arms folded, the phone held up like a holy relic.

The photos start again. Each slide a piece of history I never knew existed: the woman—my father—me, sometimes together, sometimes apart. Then a shot of Caleb, maybe twelve, standing behind me at a parade, our faces both turned toward the camera. In the background, Lucas, arm slung around my shoulder, both of us beaming.

"You see it now, don't you?" Caleb says. "You always had everything. Family, friends, even the town's sympathy after your dad died. Me? I got a new home every year, and nobody even noticed when I disappeared."

I shake my head, more in disbelief than defiance. "My dad—he never—he wasn't—"

He barks a laugh. "He wasn't what? Capable? Trustworthy? Faithful? That's the thing about firemen. They all want to be heroes. But you can't save everyone, can you?"

The next photo is a Christmas tree, tipped over and burning. Caleb as a teen, grinning at the flames. There's a black scribble on the bottom—"Merry X-Mas, from the lost cause."

"You think I started the fires just for fun?" he says. "No. I wanted them to see me. I wanted you to see me."

The photo blips forward. Another shot—this time, my father and Caleb's mother, at a bar, faces close, his hand on her thigh under the table. Then, another: my father's handwriting, a letter. I squint, heart pounding, and realize it's a birth announcement. "Welcome, Caleb. May you always find your way home."

I can't breathe.

He steps in again, crouches so we're eye level. I can see the tremor in his hands, the sweat in his hairline.

"You're my sister, Sophie."

He says it like it's the punchline to a joke only he finds funny.

I close my eyes, shake my head, but the images keep coming. I try to think—try to reason, to find the flaw, the crack in the story

—but the photos are irrefutable, the timeline matching up in ways I never allowed myself to imagine.

A new photo. Me, at eight or nine, standing next to Caleb, both of us grinning, faces painted at the department picnic. I'm holding his hand, my father looming behind us, his smile stretched too wide.

Caleb leans in, his mouth at my ear. "The night I set the fire at the old station, I wasn't trying to kill anyone. I wanted to burn it down so you'd see what it felt like. To lose everything. To have nothing left but the ashes."

His hand closes on my shoulder, squeezing until my vision goes white at the edges. "But you never saw, did you? Even when you had nothing, people lined up to help you rebuild. They gave you money, clothes, a place to live. I never got any of that. Just more foster homes, more group therapy, more people telling me I'd end up dead or worse."

I try to pull free, but the zip ties bite deeper. I taste blood.

"Let me go," I say, my voice barely more than a croak.

He ignores me, stands, and paces a slow, triumphant lap.

"You know what the funny part is? I used to hope you'd show up at one of my placements. Maybe pretend to be my sister, just for a day. But you never did. So I decided I'd make you notice me."

He stops, turns, and his eyes shine wet in the glare of the projector.

"I thought killing Lucas would be enough," he says, matter-of-fact. "I thought you'd finally pay attention."

At the mention of Lucas, my mind snaps into gear. He doesn't know I left Lucas alive. He thinks I came alone, abandoned him at home. The knowledge gives me a sliver of hope, cold and sharp.

Caleb follows my gaze, smirks. "You're wondering if he's okay, aren't you?"

I say nothing.

"He'll come looking," Caleb says, and he almost sounds pleased. "But by then, it'll be too late."

"Well," he says, voice going flat. "Let's get this family reunion going."

He glances down at me, his eyes bright with something like pride.

"Don't worry, Little So, So. I'm not going to hurt you. We're family, after all."

He walks over to a battered workbench, opens a drawer, and pulls out a second can of lighter fluid and a box of matches.

"I just want to watch him try to save you," he says, almost giddy. "One last time."

He moves back to the bench where I'm tied, kneels, and strokes my hair with a gentleness that makes my stomach heave.

"Remember this," he says. "When it's over, and they ask you why, just tell them: you can't unmake family."

He stands, moves to the center of the bay, and waits.

I strain at the ties, panic clawing up my throat, but they don't give.

The projector cycles back to the photo of my father, arm around Caleb's mother, both of them smiling. It freezes there, a grim family portrait.

For a second, I think of all the times I wondered if my dad had secrets. If the weirdness, the absences, the sharp temper were just the cost of loving someone who spent their life in danger.

Now I know.

21

Rekindle the Town

SOPHIE

I'm strapped to a chair that used to live in the break room, back when the firehouse still had a break room and not just a forest of support beams and the moldy ghost of a vending machine. The ropes are new, hardware store grade, not the zip ties he started with. My wrists are already raw; the cord bites deeper every time I flex. The metal under my ass is cold enough to burn.

Caleb paces, slow, calculated, boot soles slapping the concrete like a metronome. The cavern swallows the sound and spits it back at me, louder than before. The only light is a battery-powered lantern lashed to a ceiling pipe, and it throws a single, greasy halo across the whole main bay. Behind Caleb, up on the scorched cinderblock wall, the spiral is burned in—big, almost sloppy, like he wanted it visible from orbit.

I focus on that spiral because it's easier than focusing on him. His face has sharpened in the past hour, all the soft left sucked away by adrenaline and whatever he's got brewing in his head. He doesn't look at me, not directly. Just keeps circling, glancing at the wall, checking the projector, the lighter, the door.

Every sense I have is cranked to eleven. My tongue is still fat with the taste of blood, and my hands have gone from pins-and-needles to full-on numb. My mind races: Lucas. Lucas is coming. If I can stall, if I can play this just right—

I test the ropes at my ankles. Nothing. Caleb notices anyway.

He stops dead, leans in until his face is inches from mine. "You're not getting out of this," he says, like it's a fact, not a threat.

I swallow. "My father would never—" I start, but the words catch.

He explodes into laughter. It's not loud, but it's so sharp it feels like he's laughing inside my skull. "Your perfect father," he says, pacing again. "Your fucking perfect father. I wondered how long it would take."

I grit my teeth. "You don't know him."

Caleb's hands ball into fists. He pivots, closes the gap between us in two steps. "I know more than you ever will."

He squats in front of me, puts his face at my level. "You want the story? You want the real version?"

I stare at the spiral behind him, and the more I look, the more it seems to pulse in time with my pulse.

"My father—" I try, but he cuts me off.

"Your father was a liar. A coward. And he's the reason we're both here."

He stands, paces again, then kicks a folding chair so hard it clatters across the bay and slams against the engine block. The echo bounces for a full minute.

He keeps his back to me as he says, "Your parents separated for six months. Did you know that? They never told you. Not even when you were old enough to put the math together."

My heart thuds so loud I almost miss the next part.

"During that time, your father had an affair with my mother. Only, she wasn't just some side piece—she was married. She had a son. Her husband thought the world of your dad. 'Best man I ever met,' he said, after Dad pulled his kid out of a burning car at the old IGA. Funny, right?"

He turns, and his eyes are black pinholes in the reflection from the spiral. "I'm the bastard. Your dad's little souvenir. My mom never told me until I got sick. Until I needed a kidney."

I blink. "That's—"

"Bullshit?" His voice cracks, goes high for a second before he chokes it down. "You ever get sick, Sophie? Like, really sick? The kind where they scan your whole family, praying for a match?"

I don't answer. I don't move. I just watch the way his hands tremble.

"I needed a transplant," he says. "I was seven. My 'dad' wasn't a match. My mom's only half-match. So she calls the real father, your dad, and he just... says yes. Like it's nothing. He comes to the hospital, he signs the paperwork, and that's that. A piece of him for a piece of me."

He wipes his nose with the back of his hand, then looks at me like he's looking through me.

"And then he left. He went back to you, and your mom, and he never looked back. Not once. But he saved my life. You know what that does to a man? To the husband who finds out he's not even good enough to save his own son?"

The edges of my vision blur. "No," I whisper.

Caleb smiles, and it's the saddest fucking thing I've ever seen.

My mouth is dry as bone. "You're lying."

He grins, all teeth. "Call the hospital. Go ahead. Ask them who donated. They'll tell you. They have to."

He leans in, voice gone soft. "You want to know why I started the first fire? Why I kept going?"

I say nothing.

He points at the spiral. "It's not about the fire. It's about watching the world burn the same way you did to me."

I look past him, at the wall, at the symbol. It's not just char and soot. It's got depth—layers, each one burned a little deeper, a little angrier.

He paces again, muttering under his breath, then spins, face inches from mine. "You still think he was perfect?"

I stare at him. "I think he tried. I think he did his best."

Caleb's eyes are wide and wild. "You're just like him," he says. "You think if you save one life, it makes up for everything else. But you can't save everyone."

He kneels, reaches for my face, wipes away a tear I didn't know was there.

"You're not a hero, Sophie. You're a product. You're what he made."

He pushes himself to his feet, and for a second I think he's going to hit me, but instead he just walks away, back turned, shoulders shaking.

I stare at the spiral until my eyes burn. I think about all the times Dad came home, hands shaking, eyes red, the nights he sat on the porch and didn't say a word for hours. The nights

Mom cried in the kitchen, the weeks he'd disappear and come back like nothing happened.

I think about the time I got pneumonia at nine, and he spent every night at my bedside, reading me stories in the dark, voice so raw I could barely hear the words.

I want to scream. I want to run. But all I can do is sit in this chair, wrists on fire, pulse thundering, as the truth rewrites itself inside me.

I am not who I thought I was.

And neither was he.

It's so quiet I can hear the blood in my ears, the flex and release of each heartbeat. Caleb has stopped pacing; now he stands statue-still, as if the air has hardened around him and he has to force each breath. When he does speak, his voice is different—mechanical, almost bored, but every word lands like a knife.

"You want to know the funny part?" he says, not looking at me. "I don't even hate you. I hated him. I hated how you looked at him, like he was the center of gravity. I hated how everyone else did, too. But you? I just wanted to be noticed."

He walks back to the projector and flicks it off, plunging us into half-darkness. The spiral on the wall glows faint, a memory of itself. I can't look away.

"My father," Caleb says, and for the first time there's no sarcasm, just the word, flat as a dead thing, "thought I was his. Until the tests. I remember the way he looked at me, like I'd grown horns overnight. I remember the silence. He didn't hit me, not then. Not until after the surgery."

I try to remember anything from that year. I was nine. Dad missed my school play—the only one he ever missed. He came home thin and pale, walked like his feet hurt, but said he'd just been working extra shifts. Mom was so gentle with him that whole summer, wouldn't let me ask questions. There were phone calls at night, voices pitched low behind closed doors. One time I caught her crying at the kitchen table, but she swore it was just the onions.

Caleb keeps talking, and the world narrows to his voice and the buzzing in my hands.

"She called him. She called your dad, and he said yes, right away. He didn't even tell his family. They took him in the back entrance, under a fake name. Afterward, he visited me in the recovery room. He gave me a toy fire truck." Caleb's voice cracks again. "He said to be brave. That everything would be okay."

He laughs, harsh and short, like he's choking on glass. "He lied."

The raw edges in his tone make my skin crawl.

Caleb sits on the floor, legs crossed, picking at the tape residue on his palms. "When I got out of the hospital, things were different. Dad didn't talk to me. Mom didn't smile. The whole house was like an empty bottle, nothing left inside."

He looks up at me, and the nakedness in his face is worse than any rage. "Three weeks after I was home, Dad found the paperwork. The real name, the forms. He found out I wasn't his. That's when he started locking me in the garage at night. That's when the burns started."

He shows me the inside of his arms—long, puckered scars, some faded, some fresh.

"He blamed me for everything. Said if I was his, I'd be stronger. Said I was a parasite, eating his wife and his money and now his dignity."

I think of Dad, standing in the garage with his hands in his pockets, the way he'd never let me touch his scars. I think of

Mom, chain-smoking on the stoop, waiting for the mailman even though she hated the mail.

Caleb's story drags on, each detail sandpapering away my version of the past.

"He started hurting my mother, too. I heard them, every night. Then one morning, she was dead. The coroner said overdose. I know better. He smothered her, then staged the pills."

I open my mouth, but nothing comes out.

"They sent me to a group home after that," Caleb says. "The police came, but they never asked the right questions. I told them what happened, but they said I was grieving."

The old smell of the station—the smoke, the chemical undertone—sours in my nose. I feel sick, like I could puke out my entire history.

Caleb stares at his hands, voice gone small. "Your father showed up at the funeral. Stood in the back. I wanted him to hug me, or even just look at me, but he left before the casket closed."

He glances at me, searching for pity and daring me to show it. I keep my face blank, or try.

"So, yeah," he says, standing and stretching his shoulders until they crack. "Your dad saved my life. And ruined everything else."

He walks toward me, and for a second I think he's going to untie me. But he just crouches, putting his mouth level with my ear.

"You think you know what loss is," he whispers. "But you've never lost yourself."

He stands again, this time looming over me, the light from the lantern carving shadows down his face. "You're lucky. You got the good parts of him. The courage. The loyalty. I got the left-overs. The rot."

His words drill into me, hollow me out. My lungs squeeze, and I realize I've been holding my breath for minutes.

"I didn't want to hurt anyone at first," he says, almost as if he's apologizing. "But nobody cared until I did. Nobody ever cared until things started burning."

I think about the night the old station went up, about the sick way my stomach dropped as I watched it burn from my bedroom window. I think about all the times I pretended not to see the pain in the people around me, because it was easier that way.

He turns his back to me, voice flat again. "You know what the best part is? After everything, they still named a wing of the hospital after your father."

He slumps onto the floor, like the weight of his own story is too much. "He's a hero. I'm the cautionary tale."

My own breathing goes shallow. I feel the world tilting, the spiral on the wall threatening to pull me in.

I force myself to remember the good parts: the sound of Dad's laugh, the warmth of his hand, the smell of coffee and engine oil and the cheap cologne he only wore for church.

But all of that is sliding away, replaced by Caleb's voice, by the story he's spun tight around us both.

I close my eyes and see the past in double exposure—the way I lived it, and the way it really was.

And I can't tell anymore which one is true.

Caleb's voice has lost its armor. The next words rattle out like broken teeth.

"You know what my dad called me, after he found out?" He doesn't wait for an answer. "The bastard son of a whore." He says it flat, like reciting a grocery list, but the words have weight. "Every day, over and over. Sometimes it was the only thing he'd say for hours. Sometimes he just... burned it in."

He rolls up his sleeves, shows me the skin inside his elbows again. Cigarette burns, perfect circles, all the way up to the crook of his arm. "He said it was so I'd remember what I was. Said he was doing me a favor."

He smiles, lips bloodless. "It worked."

The old firehouse is so cold now, I see his breath plume each time he exhales.

"It didn't matter what I did. School, sports, therapy. Nobody gave a shit. I was already written off. Until the day I realized I could write myself back in."

He looks me dead in the eyes. "I set the fire because I wanted to feel warm. I wanted the whole world to see what it's like, even for a minute. I wanted the pain to stop, and I wanted him to pay."

I see it, suddenly—the night the news vans showed up, the way the fire twisted up through the roof, the way neighbors lined the street, praying it wouldn't jump to the next house. I remember the way Dad stood with his back to me, helmet under his arm, and the way he looked at the flames like he'd seen them before.

Caleb keeps talking, voice barely above a whisper. "I didn't even mean to kill him. I thought he'd get out, or at least fight harder. I just wanted him to know how it felt."

He wipes his mouth with the back of his hand, almost misses, leaves a streak of spit on his cheek. "But he didn't get out. And you know why?"

I say nothing.

He steps closer, hands on the chair back, breath hot on my cheek. "Because your dad hesitated. He saw who was inside, and for one second, he stopped. That's all it took. He didn't even try."

I feel the words hit, low and hard.

Caleb laughs, a hollow echo. "He saved me, but he couldn't save his mistake."

I shake my head, but he cuts me off.

"You think he adopted me? Took me in, gave me a better life?" He spits on the ground. "No. I went to a foster home. And you know what they do to kids like me there?"

He doesn't wait. "They start with the beatings. Then they move on to worse. I learned to be invisible. I learned that pain is a currency, and I was always broke."

He paces, the ropes at my wrists grinding deeper. "Nobody cared. Not the teachers, not the social workers, not the town. They just called me a problem and shipped me off to the next place."

He stops, turns, and his face is a mask. "Until Detective Bennett."

The name lands like a fist.

"He came to see me when I was sixteen. Said he knew my story. Said he understood what it was like to be let down by the people you trusted. He promised to help me, if I just... helped him, too."

I stare, not breathing.

Caleb nods, reading my silence. "You want the truth? Bennett is the only one who ever listened. He's the only one who saw what I was, and didn't flinch."

He grins, a sick curve of the mouth. "He asked me to set fires. Small ones, at first. Test runs, he called them. Targets were always the same—places that mattered to someone, or had dirt on the department, or owed the wrong people favors. He said it was cleaning up, making the world a safer place."

He squats in front of me, all the heat gone from his eyes. "But when he found out your dad was the match, when he realized what that meant—he asked me if I wanted revenge."

He shrugs. "I did."

He stands, walks to the spiral, runs his hand across the char like he's reading a braille message from God. "I wasn't supposed to kill him, not really. But when I saw him, that last time, I knew he knew. He looked at me and he just... let go."

His voice is soft now, almost tender. "I thought it would feel good. It didn't. It just made me empty."

He turns, leans against the wall, and closes his eyes.

"All these years, I just wanted to matter. And the only way I could was by burning things down."

I feel the ropes cutting through my skin, but the pain is far away. My brain is a hurricane—images of Dad, of Lucas, of the way my life split in two and I never noticed.

Caleb pushes off the wall, walks back to me, kneels so we're eye to eye. "You don't have to forgive me," he says. "Just... don't lie about who he was. Or who you are."

He stands, brushes imaginary dust off his hands.

"We're the same, you and me. We're what happens when nobody tells the truth."

He crosses the bay, stands by the big roll-up door, staring out at the night.

I sit, shaking, the world split open.

I am not who I thought I was.

And neither was anyone else.

For a while there's nothing but the echo of his words, reverberating in the cold, burned-out shell of the station. I don't even realize I'm crying until I taste salt. Caleb stands by the door, every part of him in shadow except the whites of his eyes, which catch the lantern glow and reflect it back, alien and wet.

He breaks the silence. "I bet you wonder why you get to be happy." His voice is soft, almost gentle, like he's apologizing in advance. "After everything your family did. After everything you did."

I blink, breath catching. "I don't—"

He kneels, sudden and animal, sliding on the concrete until he's face to face with me. He puts a hand on my knee, not rough but not friendly either. "You do. You wonder every day."

He smiles, an actual smile this time, and it's so off-kilter it's almost worse than the rage. "You know the best part? Even after all the shit, after the fires and the funerals and the moves, you still had him. Lucas. You still had someone."

I look away, but he taps my chin, gentle as a lover. "But that wasn't right. Why should you get to keep your perfect ending?"

He leans in, close enough that his hair brushes my cheek. "You ever wonder about the note?" he whispers.

A chill runs down my spine. "What note."

He snorts. "The one that showed up on his car the night you broke it off with Lucas. The one that said 'She'll never be safe with you.'"

My mouth dries out. "You—?"

"I wrote it," he says, and his voice is so proud it's almost child-like. "I made sure he'd walk away. I made sure you'd feel just a fraction of what it's like to be left with nothing."

He draws back, surveying me, like a scientist admiring a new species. "It worked. You broke up. You left town. He spiraled, but he survived. You both did. I was almost proud."

He stands, stretches his arms over his head, bones popping in the hush. "But then you came back. And he followed. Like dogs, you always come back."

I stare at him, at the spiral burned into the wall, at the ropes binding my arms. My wrists are bleeding now, and every throb brings the room into tighter focus. I feel the world narrowing, whittling down to the last sharp point.

"Is that what you want?" I ask, voice unsteady but clear. "For us to end up like you?"

He laughs, full-throated and ugly. "No. I want you to know how it feels to have your life stolen from you by the people who claim to love you."

He starts to pace, turning his back on me. "You know what the cops always get wrong? They think arson is about destruction. But it's not. It's about change. It's about turning pain into something you can see. Something you can touch."

He pauses, head cocked, listening to something inside himself.

"You burned everything," I say, louder now. "And you're still empty. You think this is going to fill the hole?"

He spins, rage surfacing in an instant. “You don’t get to say that!”

I let the next words out slow, careful, the way Dad used to when he was coaxing a scared animal out from under the porch. “You’re right. My family wasn’t perfect. Neither was I. But I’m not going to let you turn me into a monster, too.”

His face goes slack, like he’s been punched. Then the mask snaps back, twice as sharp.

He lunges, grabbing my jaw, fingers digging in until I see stars. “Don’t patronize me. You don’t get to play the hero.”

“You’re right,” I say. “I’m not a hero.”

I bare my teeth in something that might be a smile. “But I’m not running, either.”

He recoils, then pulls back his fist. For a second, I think he’s going to hit me.

He does.

Pain explodes behind my left eye, and the room tilts. I taste copper, the world fuzzes at the edges.

But I hold on. I stay upright.

Caleb's screaming now, spitting words I can't even parse.

And in that moment, I don't think I will survive this.

22

Fire and Future

LUCAS

Somewhere in the dark, I surface. It's not the alarm that wakes me—it's the cold strip of empty mattress running the length of my left side, as if the shape of Sophie has just been cut out and vacuumed away.

I reach for her, hand slapping at nothing but the cold impression of her legs. For a moment, I'm still half-dreaming and in the dream she's just in the bathroom, or maybe slipped to the kitchen for water, or—my mind scurries for any normal explanation, every synapse trying to weld this to a routine night.

But there's no flush. No water running, no light under the door. The house is silent in that way it only gets at one a.m.—dead, expectant, holding its breath. The kind of quiet that means you've already lost.

"Sophie?" My voice, even hushed, sounds too big in the space.

No answer.

I twist up, rub the grit out of my eyes, and try to focus. She's always cold at night; she drapes herself over me like a blanket, knits her ankles around mine, snores soft in my ear. When she's gone, I notice. My body is still clocked to hers, every nerve firing distress before my brain's even up to speed.

Maybe she's in the living room, reading by phone light. Or fixing the front lock again—she never did trust the new deadbolt. Or, worst of all, standing at the window, scanning the street for a threat only she can see.

I check my phone. The screen burns my retinas. Nothing—no texts, no missed calls, no alarm set for shift.

I call her name again, louder. "Sophie?"

Still nothing. I listen harder, straining for any hint of her, the way her feet pad across hardwood, the husky note in her cough, the tiny gasp she makes when she's caught out of place. There's nothing but the hum of the fridge and the wind pressing against the eaves.

I flip back the covers, feet hitting the icy floor. The room is so black I'm half-blind, but I navigate by memory—six steps to the bathroom, three to the closet, five to the door. I check the bathroom first. Empty. The light switch clicks with a dead, echoing sound. I check the hallway, the guest bedroom, the coat closet, the laundry room. I open the garage door, scan the empty space, run a hand across the hood of her car. Still warm. The cold in my chest punches harder.

Back to the kitchen. And that's when I see it.

On the counter, under the glass dome that usually protects the good banana bread, sits a plain white envelope. My name on the front, nothing fancy, just block capitals, written with the same pen she uses to make grocery lists.

I don't pick it up right away. My hands are wet—when did that happen? I wipe them on my thighs, then rip the envelope open.

Inside, a single page. Her handwriting, loopy but tight, just starting to slant the way it does when she's scared or angry:

Lucas,

I love you. That's why I have to do this.

He called me to the heart of the problem, and if you come, he said you would die.

I'm sorry. I have to end it.

If I don't come back, please forgive me.

Sophie

That's it. No explanation, no "be careful," no next steps. Just the words, clipped and brutal.

The letter trembles in my hands. I stare at it until the words blur and double, as if they're being shouted through a heat mirage.

I go to the bedroom to get some clothes on, then I notice it, a glint on the nightstand that I didn't see before. I walk over, legs numb, and see her engagement ring, the fire-opal stone winking in the blue dark.

For a second, my heart just stops. Not metaphorically, not "skip a beat," just—nothing. Then it slams into overdrive.

I try to think, but my thoughts keep cracking in half: She left. She left because she thinks I'll die if I follow. She left because someone—no, because Caleb—threatened her, and she'd rather go than let me get caught in the crossfire.

A scream starts in the bottom of my spine and ricochets up my ribs. I smash my fist into the countertop, splintering the veneer and sending a coffee mug skidding into the sink. The pain barely gets through. I focus on the sting, use it to anchor myself, to stop from dropping right there and folding in on my own spine like an origami disaster.

I pick up the ring. The opal, even in this light, throws tiny flecks of orange and green against my palm. She loved this ring. Said it looked like sunrise through smoke, said it was the most beautiful thing she'd ever owned. I press it into my hand until I'm sure it'll leave a mark.

This is a game. A trap. He wants her alone. He's counting on her pride, her need to be the one who finishes what she starts. He knows she'll go if it keeps me safe.

But he doesn't know me.

I turn the note over and over, looking for any clue—an address, a code, a time. "The heart of the problem." What does that mean? Is it literal? Metaphorical? Is it—

It's the old firehouse. Where else would it be? Where everything started, where every lie and fire and heartbreak crumpled in on itself.

I pull myself together, focusing through the cold haze in my brain. If he's got her, he'll want to make it a show. He's not just after vengeance—he's after an audience.

I pocket the ring, grab the gun from the lockbox in the closet, check the mag, flick off the safety. My hands are steady, even as my vision pulses at the edges.

I stand in the middle of the kitchen, counting my breaths, slowing the rush of adrenaline down to something I can use.

I picture Sophie—her eyes, fierce and wild, her hands, always a little chapped, her laugh that starts quiet but ends up filling the room. I focus on her, on the promise I made, the one I tattooed into my bones every night she let me hold her: I will not lose you again.

I snap off the lights, slip on boots, and head for the door. The air outside is so cold it sears my lungs.

As I climb into the truck, I check the time: 1:17 AM. Every minute counts. I'm already late.

"Like fuck you're not coming back," I say to the empty cab.

I floor it, and the night opens its jaws for me.

The night is built for monsters. Every block I cross, I see them in the sodium glare of the streetlights—thrown long on the pavement, spindly and warped, each one threatening to slip through the windshield and into my chest. I don't flinch, don't slow. I ride the thin line between speed and control, redlining the old engine through every empty intersection.

I run the clues in my head like lines on a map: "the heart of the problem." It's not a riddle, not from her. It's a signpost, a direct line to the old firehouse, the place where everything started: her trauma, his obsession, and the last bad act that tied us all together. It's the only place that matters to any of us. Caleb wants a finale, a burn-off, something that leaves scars on the town itself.

I check the time again—1:21, four minutes since I left the house. In a town this size, four minutes is an eternity. Long enough for a knife, a fire, a bullet, a confession. I drive faster.

By the time I hit the edge of downtown, my hands are so tight on the wheel I can feel the bones grinding together. Every muscle in my body is coiled. Every bad memory is alive in my veins—fire drills, rescue runs, the unspooling of caution tape around a scene you already know ends badly.

At the last light, I kill the headlights, coast the last quarter mile with the engine low and the street black as a bruise. The firehouse sits at the far end, set back from the road, flanked by empty lots and a playground that's been condemned since I was a kid.

The place is a half-corpse, half-mirage. One wing is nothing but a ribcage of studs and loose insulation, the other still brick but shattered at the windows and tagged with angry, looping graffiti. There's a dumpster out front, overflowing with the trash of a hundred failed construction starts. No lights, no sign of a car, but I know better. He's here. And so is she.

I park two blocks out, ease the door closed, and jog the rest of the way under cover of the neighbor's dead shrubbery. I keep the gun in my hand, not drawn, but ready. I'm sweating through my shirt even though the wind is sharp and carries the tang of new rain.

I move slow, every step a calculation: Watch your corners. Don't silhouette against the floodlights. Don't trip over the blown-out glass. I get to the bay door first—still padlocked, but one side pried just enough to slip through. I crouch, listening.

There's a voice inside. It's not hers. It's lower, guttural, burning with that same old rage.

I move around the perimeter, keeping low, and find a crack in the wallboard where they never finished the patch. It's enough to see inside.

The interior's lit by a single lantern, casting long, greasy shadows over the charred concrete floor. The big spiral is still there, burned into the cinderblock above the main bay. Caleb paces below it, arms flailing, screaming at something—or someone—just out of my sight.

I shuffle right, peer around a rusted support post, and see her.

Sophie, tied to a chair, ankles lashed and wrists bound behind her back. Her hair's a mess, blood on her temple, but her eyes are locked on him—steady, undiluted, pure murder. She's not broken. Not yet.

He's waving a knife, jabbing the air between them. His mouth is a raw slit, every word a missile. I can't hear the specifics, but I know the cadence. He's working up to something, a finale.

I scan the rest of the space: a workbench with tools scattered across it, two gas cans by the old engine, a backpack at his feet.

No visible bombs, but I don't trust anything about this setup. He's got contingencies. He's always had them.

I check my options, running through the approach. The front bay is too open—he'll see me before I get two steps. The side door is closer, but it means crawling over glass and sheet metal. The best bet is to draw him out, get him to move, then get between him and her.

I back away, move to the north side, and set up behind the shell of the old generator shed. I keep the gun low, finger just off the trigger, and breathe slow and even, like they taught us in the academy: the way you do before a door breach or a confined-space rescue. The point is to not let the adrenaline run you. You have to ride it, steer it, or it eats you alive.

Inside, he's yelling louder now. I can hear words, bits and pieces: "liar," "never cared," "parasite," "product." The words hit me, because I know them—I've heard versions of them my whole life, in calls, in debriefs, in the mirror.

I catch a flash of Sophie's face: blood on her lips, but her jaw clenched and her eyes never leaving his. She's not screaming. She's not pleading. She's just... waiting.

I risk a peek over the cinderblock, lining up the next moves. There's a window, two meters up, barely big enough for a shoulder, but the glass is already shattered. If I time it right, I can pop the latch and slip in behind him while he's focused on her.

I steel myself. I run the scenario: If he's got a gun, I close the gap, go for the arm. If he goes for the gas, I shoot. If he runs, I follow. If he threatens her, I end it.

I check the ring in my pocket, the one she left behind. I roll it in my palm, focusing on the weight of it, the heat, the promise.

You do not get to keep her. You do not get to win.

I make the call, take the first step, and everything else drops away—the fear, the guilt, the doubt. All that's left is the mission.

I slide the gun into my waistband, grip the windowsill, and get ready to move.

I see her face again, and I know:

I will bring you back, or I will not come home.

Every instinct says run. Not toward the flames, but away—save yourself, salvage what you can, and leave the dead to the pyre. But that's never been my wiring. I climb the frame, the old mortar scraping my knuckles, and ease myself onto the crumbling ledge outside the bay window. Inside, everything is strobe and shadow, the single lantern spitting out more blackness than light.

I watch through the glass as Caleb rages in front of Sophie. There's a sick rhythm to it, the way he circles her, the way he glances to the spiral on the wall after every sentence, as if waiting for it to approve. In his hand is a black box—a detonator, sure as sunrise. Every few seconds he presses his thumb against the top, testing it, savoring the threat. My brain sprints: Is it a dead man's switch? Is it real? Is he bluffing?

Sophie doesn't flinch. Her face is busted up, but her chin is high and her eyes never leave his. She looks at him the way you look at a snarling dog behind a fence—pity, disgust, a little bit of hope that it'll tire itself out before it gets through.

He starts yelling louder, voice cracking on her name. He screams about fathers, about betrayals, about lies and being forgotten. I can't get all the words, but the cadence is the same as every rage-monologue I've ever defused on a call. The escalation is coming—he's running out of things to blame, and when that happens, violence is next.

He pivots, and that's when he hits her. The crack of knuckles on bone is loud enough to vibrate the window. Her head snaps to the side, blood spraying from her lip. She goes slack for half a second, then spits the blood at his shoes.

That's my girl.

I slip the gun from my waistband, line up the shot. But there's no angle—he's always behind her, using her as cover, even in the middle of his tantrum. If I go through the window, he'll have a straight line on her before I can close the gap.

I wait. Watch. Let the scenario build. My hands are steady, my breath is steady, but my heart feels like a grenade with the pin half-out.

Caleb turns his back to her, stalks toward the workbench. He grabs the gas can, unscrews the lid, and starts sloshing it onto the floor in an arc that points directly toward Sophie's chair.

She starts talking. I can't hear her, but I read her lips: "It doesn't have to be this way."

He ignores her, pours the rest of the gas in a ring around them both. He flicks open a lighter and holds it over the puddle, grinning.

23

Matchstick Moments

SOPHIE

My first memory is of a firehouse.

Not the one that's burning now—not the one where I'm tied to a metal chair, ribs crushed against the cold steel, lantern light stinging my retinas and gasoline choking my throat. No, the old one: a place of order, of men with sooted knuckles and coffee breath, a space so thick with safety that you could forget the world outside was always in the process of burning down.

Maybe that's why, when I open my eyes to the full shock of the present, what gets me isn't the pain. Not the numbness in my hands, not the way the rope slices my wrists, not even the migraine bloom in my left cheek where Caleb's knuckles split the skin. What gets me is the betrayal of the old familiar. This is the place I thought would never betray me. It's where my father came home every night.

Now it's a tomb.

The main bay is stripped bare, a husk. What used to be a shrine to town heroes is now a game board, every piece rearranged for maximum humiliation. There's the spiral, burned into the cinderblock above the roll-up door, thick and slick with fresh soot. There's the engine—now gutted, cables uncoiled and laid out like entrails. The lantern, lashed to a pipe overhead, paints everything in sick, jaundiced yellow. And there's Caleb, pacing the perimeter, boots hammering the cracks in the floor, hair stuck to his scalp with sweat.

He's a live wire. He circles me, always just outside of reach, never quite making eye contact unless he's sure I'll be the first to blink. The lighter dangles between his fingers, sometimes flipping open, sometimes snapping shut, always in motion. He's dumped gas all over—on the floor, the old desk, the feet of my chair, even the sleeves of my jacket. When he flicks the lighter, the smell jumps, thick as vomit.

But he doesn't ignite it. Not yet.

Instead, he rants. Not loud, but unbroken—every sentence packed tight with the kind of logic that only makes sense when you've gone too far to turn back.

"You remember how you used to laugh at me?" He's not talking to me, not really. He's addressing the ghost of someone else—a father, a teacher, the voice that used to tell him he'd never amount to anything. "You remember how everyone looked past me, like I was already a ghost?"

I don't answer. My mouth is dry and my lips are split, but mostly I just want to give him nothing. He wants a reaction. I won't give it.

He throws the lighter, hard. It bounces off the wall and clatters to the ground. He kicks it, but then immediately snatches it up, like he can't stand the idea of not having it in his hand.

He starts again, a new circuit. "You know what it's like, Sophie? Being the mistake? It's not just the foster homes. It's not just the group therapy. It's the way everyone looks at you and sees what they want to see."

He spits the last word, then wipes his mouth with the back of his hand, leaving a smear of blood from my earlier bite.

He stops in front of me, just far enough that I can't kick him. He stares at me, eyes too wide, whites raw and red.

"You think you're better than me," he says, a twitch in his cheek. "You always did. Golden girl, fire chief's daughter. You could have had any life you wanted. I had one chance, and he—he fucking took it from me."

There's a tremor in his hands. He tugs something from his pocket, and for a second I think it's a knife, but it's not.

It's a black plastic box, rounded at the edges, with a single red button in the center. It looks like a joke, like a prop from a prank show. But the way he holds it, reverent and shaking, tells me everything I need to know.

"Dead man's switch," he says, waving it in front of my face. "Simple tech. I let go, it blows."

I glance at the gas cans, the wires trailing across the floor, the greasy stink of fertilizer in the air.

He grins, eyes glassy. "Poetic, right? You and me, together in the end. Brother and sister."

He steps back, raises the box in a slow, theatrical gesture.

"Reunited in ash."

He lets the moment linger. I keep my expression flat, but inside, every pulse is a scream. If he really means to do it, there's nothing I can do—nothing but try to keep him talking, keep him off-balance, keep him from deciding that this is the second the story ends.

I look for options, but I'm lashed down good. The chair legs feel bolted to the ground. The ropes are nylon and new, hardware store special. My hands are going to be useless. The only advantage I have is that he wants me to listen.

So I do. I watch him, track every step, every twitch. I wait for the opening, the little break in the rhythm.

That's when I see movement at the far end of the bay. It's a flicker—a shift in the shadows, almost a trick of the lantern light. But it's real. I see the glint of an eye, the set of a jaw I know better than my own.

Lucas.

My heart does something dumb and traitorous, but I force it down. If he's here, he's got a plan. He always does.

But Caleb is sharp. He's been waiting for this, I realize. He's been hoping for an audience.

He starts talking again, louder this time, projecting to the corners of the bay.

"You know what I love about fire?" He raises the lighter, flicks it open, lets the flame dance for a second before snapping it shut again. "It doesn't care who started it. It doesn't care who's innocent. Once it's burning, it just wants more."

He's walking the edge, eyes bouncing between me and the spot where Lucas hides.

I need to keep him focused on me. If he sees Lucas too soon, it's over.

So I say, "Why didn't you just tell me?"

The words come out raw, but it's enough to snap his attention back. He freezes, lighter poised mid-air.

"What?"

"If you wanted a sister so bad, why didn't you just tell me? Why all of this?"

He looks at me like I've asked him to recite the digits of pi.

"I tried," he says, voice cracking. "You never listened. You never saw me."

I shake my head, fighting the ache in my neck. "You never tried. You never came to me. You just set fire after fire, and waited for someone else to figure it out."

He flinches, and I see it—the raw, ugly pain under the performance.

I push harder. "You could have been anything, Caleb. You could have been family."

He stares at me, mouth working, but no sound coming out. Then, all at once, he rushes forward. He's on me, down on one knee, hands gripping the arms of the chair so hard I can hear the metal creak.

"That's all I ever wanted," he says, and this time it's not a threat. It's a plea.

I look into his eyes. I see the same color as my father's.

"Then let go," I whisper. "Let it end."

He blinks, fast, and I see the shift—the war between wanting to die and wanting to be forgiven.

He leans in, close enough that I can smell the sweat and the old tears.

"I went to him," he says, so quiet I almost miss it. "I went to your father. I told him I wanted to know my sister."

He pulls back, tears on his cheek now, hot and furious.

"He said to stay away from you," Caleb spits. "He said you'd be better off never knowing about me."

The words hang between us, heavy as wet rope.

I hear a scrape behind Caleb—the smallest sound, but enough to make him tense.

He turns, slow, and for a second the world shrinks to the size of a breath.

Lucas stands in the doorway, gun drawn, jaw clenched so hard I can see the veins in his neck.

Caleb stands, and with the same sick grace as before, he raises the dead man's switch.

Lucas stops, hands in the air, eyes never leaving the box.

Nobody moves. Nobody even breathes.

"Don't," I say, voice cutting through the space.

Caleb laughs, a sound so raw it hurts. "Don't what, Sophie?"

"Don't kill us both. Don't do what he did."

Caleb looks at the switch, then at me, then at Lucas.

He smiles, and it's the saddest smile I've ever seen.

"Too late," he says.

He tightens his fist.

The world stops.

Caleb's thumb hovers over the button. He's shaking, every tendon in his arm lit up, but he doesn't press it. Not yet. I breathe in through my nose—gasoline, old mold, burnt sugar—and out through the split in my lip. Lucas doesn't move. He stands framed in the lamplight, hands spread, gun loose at his side but not pointed, voice steady as the grave.

"Caleb," he says, and the sound of his name in Lucas's mouth does something ugly to the air. "You don't want to do this."

Caleb bares his teeth. "You don't know what I want."

Lucas takes a half-step, slow, measured, cop-style. "I know you want someone to see you. I'm seeing you right now. I'm here. You win."

A twitch, a laugh—then Caleb's attention flicks back to me. "Is this how you thought it would end, Sophie? The hero, come to save you?"

My wrists are on fire from the rope, but I keep working at the knot. One more twist, one more flex, and I might get some slack. I need to keep him talking.

"I don't need saving," I say, teeth gritted.

He snorts, then hitches his chin at Lucas. "Tell him that."

Lucas's eyes meet mine, and for a second there's just the two of us, like the rest of the room is underwater. He gives the faintest nod—like he's telling me to hang on, to buy him one more second.

I give it to him. "You think you're the only one who was hurt?" I spit at Caleb. "You think trauma is a contest? Get in line."

He laughs, high and glassy, but I see the way his grip loosens, just a little. He's listening.

Lucas takes another step, and this time I let my eyes flick to him for just a split second—too fast for Caleb, I hope, but not fast enough.

Caleb sees it. He explodes, pure reaction. In one motion, he's behind me, hand snaking around my throat, the box jammed against my cheek.

Lucas's gun comes up. "Let her go," he barks.

Caleb tightens his grip. "You're going to shoot?" he says. "Risk hitting your little princess? I don't buy it."

He pulls me back, chair legs shrieking across the concrete. The spiral on the wall spins in my peripheral vision, a black hole swallowing everything else.

"You see it, don't you?" he whispers in my ear. "You always had someone to pull you back from the fire."

His voice breaks on the last word. Lucas is less than ten feet away, but it might as well be ten miles.

Caleb's grip is iron. The switch is jammed so hard against my face I can feel the cold sweat on his palm. I keep working my wrists, feeling the first thread of the rope start to give.

Lucas tries again, voice low and calm. "It doesn't have to go like this, Caleb. You've proved your point. Let her go and I'll stay."

Caleb laughs, the sound vibrating my skull. "Stay for what? So you can play savior again?" He spits on the ground, the glob landing near my boot. "You always think you can save her. Or fix me. Or both."

Lucas lowers the gun, just a fraction. "You're right. I can't fix you. But I can listen."

Caleb's breathing is ragged. He's shaking, but his hand never leaves the box. "Nobody ever listened. Not until I made them."

There's a split-second of something—regret, maybe, or just exhaustion. I feel his grip loosen, infinitesimally. I yank my wrists, the pain blinding, but the knot shifts. If I can just get one hand free—

Lucas moves. He's on Caleb in a heartbeat.

In Lucas's lunge my chair is toppled over smashing my body into the floor with a large thud.

The concrete is cold against my cheek. The air in here is burnt toast, sweat, gasoline, and blood. The taste of copper rides up the back of my tongue as I push myself upright, shoulder screaming. Time has collapsed to a single, pounding moment: Caleb and Lucas locked together, neither willing to let go, each determined to drag the other down with him.

They crash into the battered engine, knocking loose a rain of rust flakes and memory. Caleb moves with the brutal economy of a cornered animal—no finesse, just leverage and pain. Lucas, for all his training, is running on fumes and a kind of desperate faith that there's still something to save.

Every collision sends shockwaves through the bay. The spiral on the wall seems to spin with each impact, keeping score. My wrists are raw, nerves singing, but the rope is looser now. I brace my knees, dig my heels in, and use the pain as a wedge.

A gunshot cracks the air. It's not the one in my hand–it's the memory of the one Lucas had, the one Caleb's boot just punted across the room.

It spins across the floor, coming to rest not five feet from my face.

I see it, glinting like a dare.

The ropes dig deeper as I twist, but I don't care. There's no air left in the room; all of it is in my lungs, fueling the kind of effort that would rip my arms off before the knot gives. I claw for the tape, the cords, anything, fingernails scraping skin. The left hand goes numb, then hot, then nothing.

But I get free.

I don't even realize I'm screaming until my own voice drowns out the grunts and curses and the wet, choking sounds of the fight. My hands are slick with blood—some mine, some not—but I crawl, half-blind, to the gun.

It's heavier than I remember. For a second, I think I won't be able to lift it. But then I do.

I stagger to my feet, the world spinning.

"Hey!" My voice cracks, but it lands. Both men freeze. Lucas is pinned under Caleb, one arm wrenched at a wrong angle, but he's alive, eyes locked on mine. Caleb is breathing in heaves, wild, mouth open, spit on his chin.

He turns.

He sees the gun.

He smiles.

"Do it," he says. "Come on. Finish it."

His hand is empty. The dead man's switch is somewhere in the wreckage, or maybe still in his pocket. I can't tell. I can't risk it.

I line up the shot.

The sound is biblical—like the start of the world, not the end.

Caleb's head snaps back. A small, perfect hole blooms in his forehead, just above the eye I inherited from our father. The light in it goes out.

He topples, boneless, onto the floor.

The silence that follows is absolute.

Lucas groans, rolling onto his side. I drop the gun. It clatters across the concrete, echoing off the empty walls.

I fall to my knees, the pain finally catching up, and sob until I can't breathe.

Lucas crawls over, dragging his useless arm, and gathers me in. His heart hammers against mine, both of us shaking so bad we might come apart. Neither of us says anything. There's nothing left to say.

We sit like that, the two of us, covered in blood and sweat and everything that made us who we are. Across the floor, the dead man's switch winks a slow, defeated red.

I think about the spiral. About how it always looked endless, but was really just a trick—a loop that couldn't hold you if you fought hard enough.

The fire is out.

We're still here.

For the first time in my life, I believe that might be enough.

24

Burned By You

LUCAS

There's a kind of hush that always follows the sirens—the silence of everyone deciding what version of the story they're willing to live with. The old firehouse is choked with cop lights, the blue and red strobing across blackened brick and spent life. I'm not sure who pulled us outside, or how I ended up on the steps with Sophie half on my lap, wrapped in a scratchy wool blanket, her pulse flickering through the thinnest skin at her wrist.

Her eyes are open, but she's somewhere else. I run my thumb across her knuckles, trace the blood and grime and the line of her veins, as if I can thread her back into this world with enough gentle pressure. The paramedic—one of the new ones, face unlined, voice pre-faded for tragedy—offers us water, an IV, maybe a sedative. I wave him off. Sophie just keeps staring at the parking lot, lips pressed so tight the blood's fled to the corners.

A detective in a windbreaker with a clipboard kneels in front of us, trying for kind but landing on perfunctory. His mouth is saying words but all I hear is "explain what happened." I answer mechanically, the way you do after a car crash: the facts lined up, no emotion in the delivery, all the horror stripped out. Name, rank, event, body count.

I say, "He had a dead man's switch. He meant to blow the whole place, but it was either faulty or a ploy, but we didn't know that. Sophie got free. She saved us both."

Detective's mouth goes tight, jaw working like he's chewing a rubber band. "You fired the weapon?"

"I did," she says.

He doesn't ask if she regrets it. He doesn't have to.

Sophie flinches under the blanket, as if she's just now registering the cold. I pull her closer. She's so small in the heavy wool, bones gone bird-light, breath shivering.

“Hey,” I whisper, pushing the hair from her cheek. “Stay with me. We’re almost out.”

She blinks, focus returning with the slow, reluctant force of a sunrise after a bad night. “He’s really gone?”

I nod, throat clamped. “You don’t have to look back, Soph. You never have to look back.”

The corners of her mouth tip up in something not quite a smile. She leans in until our foreheads touch, the place where my skull split on the cinderblock years ago pressed to the new scar above her eyebrow.

A camera flashes across the street. News van, local affiliate. I turn my body to block her from view, wrapping the blanket tight around both of us. Sophie’s hands are ice. I take them, rub heat back into the fingers, counting under my breath—one, two, three, four, five, six, seven, eight, nine, ten. I don’t stop until she pulls free, rolling her shoulders with an effort that looks like it might break her.

“I want to go home,” she says, and the words are so soft I think I’ve made them up.

I nod. “Let’s get you out of here.”

Detective is back, this time with a pen instead of a gun. "Just a few questions for the record," he says, not unkindly. "Then you're free to go."

Sophie straightens. "Ask him first," she says, nodding at me.

The detective does, rattling off the same questions, never looking directly at my hands, never mentioning the red splatter on my jeans. Sophie listens with the intensity of a hostage. Her face doesn't move, but her eyes jump from detail to detail: the cop's hands, the stains on my shirt, the shape of her own name scrawled at the top of the form.

When it's her turn, she answers in clipped sentences, voice hollow. "He had me tied to the chair. He was going to burn the building. He talked about my father, about his own childhood. It wasn't about me. It was never about me." She says it like a confession, as if the detective is the priest and I'm the sinner.

The detective writes it all down, every word, then closes the pad and says, "Can I call someone for you?"

Sophie shakes her head. "No family left. Just him," she adds, tipping her chin at me.

The cop looks at me with something like pity. I look away.

"Can I take her home?" I ask, not bothering to hide the desperation in my voice.

He hesitates, then nods, scribbling something on a business card. "We'll need you both for a full statement, but that can wait. Get some rest. She'll probably want to see a doctor."

I pocket the card, then stand, bringing Sophie up with me. She wobbles on the step, blanket nearly tripping her, but I catch her waist and steady her until she can stand on her own. Every muscle in my body aches, a rolling, rolling throb. But the only thing that matters is the way she leans into my side, trusting me to hold her up.

We pass the ambulance, the EMTs hovering but not intervening. "You okay?" one asks, eyes flicking to the blood on my temple.

I nod, then turn to Sophie. "You good?"

She doesn't answer. Instead, she looks back at the firehouse, at the spiral burned into the cinderblock, now lit up by a thousand forensic flashlights.

She shudders. "It's over," she says, so quiet I almost miss it. "It's really over."

I help her into the truck, make sure the blanket is tucked around her shoulders, then climb into the driver's side. The world outside is a flickering pulse—cop lights, ambulance strobes, the camera flashes from the news van. But in here, it's just the two of us. The smell of gasoline lingers, sharp and mean. I roll down the window, let the cold night air slice through.

Sophie puts her head against the glass, eyes shut, breathing slow. I watch her, memorize every line of her face, every fleck of blood and sweat, every inch of her that made it through.

I start the engine. The radio kicks in, static and bad country, and I kill it with one slap.

My hand is still on the shifter when she says, "Lucas?"

"Yeah?"

Her voice is a rasp, but steady. "Promise me you won't let go."

I wrap my arm around her shoulders, pull her in until we're knotted together. "Never," I say, and I mean it.

The truck rumbles down the block, away from the lights, away from the spiral, away from the worst night of our lives.

I keep my hand at the small of her back the whole way home.

The drive home is a blank stretch—my memory only records the pressure of my hand on her knee, the way she tenses at every cross street, how the headlights make her bruises look like they're written on her skin in black ink. When we finally reach the house, I kill the engine and just sit for a second, not moving, not breathing, waiting for the world to admit that it's over.

Sophie doesn't move either. She's tucked against the door, blanket pooled around her shoulders, eyes fixed on the neighbor's porch light like it's a lighthouse and she's the last ship off a dying planet. When I reach across to help her out, she flinches —not from me, but from the cold, from the effort of being touched after so much violence. I tuck the blanket tighter and help her out. She doesn't say anything.

Inside, the house is exactly as we left it: mug rings on the counter, half a banana bread, her wedding notebook, my pile of bills. I want to erase it all, give her a fresh start, but I can only manage the basics.

"Come on," I say, voice low and even. "Let's get you cleaned up."

She shrugs out of her coat, leaving a spatter of blood on the sleeve. The fabric sticks to her arm. I want to say something soothing, but my voice won't work. Instead, I steer her to the bathroom.

The light is brutal—makes her look like a crime scene. Purple is blooming along her jaw and her left temple, her wrists raw and swollen from the ropes. I help her sit on the toilet lid. My hands are too big, too clumsy, but I use them anyway, peeling back the blanket and the flannel shirt beneath. She holds herself rigid, jaw clenched.

"Sorry," I whisper, as I tug the cuff over her knuckles.

She laughs, a broken sound. "You're not the one who should be sorry."

She's wearing a tank under the shirt. The skin along her ribs is already turning yellow at the edges, the deeper bruising fresh and angry. I press my fingertips to the spot just under her arm, feeling for any fracture. She hisses but doesn't stop me.

"Nothing broken," I say, trying for clinical, but it comes out like a prayer.

She looks up at me, eyes wet but not leaking. "You want to take a shower?" I ask, feeling idiotic. "It'll help. Maybe."

She nods, once, but doesn't move. I help her stand, work the tank off over her head. Her body is a map of every bad thing that's ever happened to her, but all I see is the way she keeps her chin up, the way she refuses to fold.

I strip down too, not for comfort, but because I can't bear to leave her alone even for a second. In the shower, the water comes out cold for the first minute. She flinches and shudders, but I ease her in, arms around her waist, the two of us pressed so tight there's not even room for air.

She sags against my chest, forehead to my sternum, and finally, finally, the tension breaks. She starts to sob. Not loud, but deep, full-body, as if she's vomiting out every awful thing she's ever swallowed.

"I killed my brother, Lucas." She says it like a curse, over and over, until her voice goes hoarse. "I killed him. He was my brother."

I don't have words for this. Nothing I say will fix it. So I just hold her, water pounding down, hands locked around her back, keeping her together by brute force.

After a while, she stops crying. She just stands there, hands balled in my hair, shivering.

I lather the soap in my palms and run it down her arms, her back, the sticky blood at her shoulder. She doesn't look at me, but she doesn't push me away. I rinse her hair, finger out the glass and the grit. When she can finally stand on her own, I step back and turn off the water.

She lets me dry her off, lets me swaddle her in towels, lets me guide her to the bed and sit her down like a china doll that might break if you look at it too hard. I find the first aid kit, dab at the split above her eye, tape a gauze pad to her elbow.

She says nothing, not even when I gently tug a shirt over her head, or when I kneel to get socks on her feet. Her skin is still cold. I wrap the thick comforter around her, tuck it under her legs, and sit on the edge of the mattress, just breathing.

She looks at me then, really looks. "You don't have to do all this," she says, voice tiny.

I cup her face in my hands, careful not to touch the bruises. "I know," I tell her. "But I want to."

She closes her eyes, and for a moment, I think she's drifted off.

But then her hand snakes out, fingers looping around my wrist. She doesn't let go.

I stay like that, perched at the edge, her hand on my wrist, as if the whole world could fall apart and we'd still be tethered.

When she finally sleeps, I pull the comforter tighter, then sit in the chair by the bed and watch the rise and fall of her ribs. I don't dare leave.

The night is so quiet, I can hear her heartbeat, steady and insistent, pounding out the message: Still here, still here, still here.

I try to stay awake, but the night keeps pulling me under. I lose time, then find it again in the shape of Sophie—her arm flung out across the mattress, her breathing deep and thick, her hair a river across the pillow. The clock blinks 2:48 AM, then 3:16. I watch the numbers mutate, each one proof that the world is still moving forward, that nothing is frozen except the two of us in this room.

At some point, she stirs. Not the half-conscious shuffle of someone turning over, but a full-bodied jolt, like she's surfaced from a nightmare and doesn't trust the air. She sits up, comforter sliding off her shoulders, hands curling into fists in her lap.

I get up too, careful not to startle her. I keep my distance, sitting on the edge of the mattress with my back to her, head bowed.

"You awake?" I ask, knowing she is.

She nods, then shakes her head, then nods again. "I don't want to sleep," she says. "It's worse in there."

I reach back, palm up, an invitation. After a second, she slides her hand into mine. Her skin is still cold, but the grip is all muscle, all intent.

We sit like that, in the dark, hands joined, not talking. I feel the words building in her, each one a weight she can't put down until it's said.

"He told me everything," she finally says, voice just above a whisper. "About my father. About his mother. About the kidney, the hospital. All of it."

I keep my eyes on the carpet, the ugly pattern that runs from one corner to the vent. I don't know how to answer, so I don't.

She goes on: "He said my father knew, and didn't do anything. That he just—walked away. Like it was a bad habit he could quit any time. I never thought of my dad as a coward. But now it's all I can see."

She lets out a sound that's halfway between a laugh and a sob. "It's so stupid. All these years I thought he was a hero."

I squeeze her hand, hard enough to hurt. "He was your hero," I say. "He saved people. He tried."

She shakes her head, loose hair blurring her face. "He saved everyone but the ones who needed him most."

The silence after is long and sharp. I feel like I'm bleeding from the inside out.

Then she turns, pulling her knees up, hugging them to her chest. She's backlit by the blue haze from the hallway, and for a second she looks like a ghost, all ribs and angles and hurt.

"Maybe if he'd been honest, none of this would've happened," she says. "Maybe Caleb would've had a real family. Maybe he wouldn't have—" She bites it off, teeth snapping shut on the word.

I want to argue, but what's the point? There's no fix, no undo.

I crawl to her side, wrap her up, tuck her against me until she relaxes by degrees. Her head fits just under my chin. I rest my cheek in her hair, the tang of smoke and antiseptic still in it.

We stay like that, wrapped in each other, for a long time.

"Do you hate me?" she asks, after an hour or maybe a year. "For what I did?"

I shake my head. "He was going to kill you. There's no world where I'd want you to take that chance."

She pulls back, just far enough to look at me, eyes ringed in black, shot through with something that could be love or terror or both.

"I still did it," she says, voice flat.

I touch her cheek, gentle as I can, thumb on the bone. "You did what you had to. You survived."

She leans into my palm, eyes closing.

"I feel empty," she says. "Like there's nothing left. Like I burned up everything."

I tuck the blanket around her, fold her into my lap, and rock her slow, like a child. "You're still here," I tell her. "You're still you."

She shivers, then turns, burying her face in my neck. For a minute, I think she's going to cry again, but instead she goes quiet, body melting against mine.

We stay like that, entangled, until the first light starts to creep through the window.

Her hand drifts up under my shirt, palm flat against my ribs. The touch is soft, but hungry.

"I don't want to sleep," she repeats, but the words sound different now—less desperate, more alive. "I want to feel something."

I don't ask what. I don't have to.

She shifts, slow and deliberate, swinging a leg over me. The blanket pools at her waist, and for the first time in hours I see her whole—every bruise, every scrape, every mark left by the night. She isn't trying to hide any of it.

She leans in, lips finding mine, and it's not a gentle kiss. It's furious, insistent, teeth and tongue, and the taste of old tears. I kiss her back, hands tracing the length of her spine, mapping every ridge, every ache.

She pushes me down, straddling my hips, eyes locked on mine. There's a challenge there—a dare to look away, to be disgusted, to flinch. I don't. I couldn't if I wanted to.

She pulls my shirt over my head, then her own, and the cold air hits us both, raising goosebumps. I trace the bruises on her arms, the yellowing around her ribs, the fading blue of her wrist. She lets me look, lets me touch, lets me memorize every square inch.

"You don't have to," I start to say, but she cuts me off with a hand on my mouth.

"I want to," she says, voice low and raw.

She grinds against me, a friction that's equal parts pain and need, and I respond in kind—palms on her hips, fingers bruising, holding her steady as she moves. The sheets twist around us, damp with sweat and old blood and the smell of our bodies. She rides me slow at first, then faster, chasing some animal thing that neither of us can name.

When she comes, it's with a gasp, head thrown back, hair wild. I follow her over the edge, arms locked tight around her waist.

After, she collapses on my chest, boneless and trembling.

We lie there, catching our breath, hearts hammering.

She laughs, a shaky, startled thing. "That's... not what I thought would happen tonight."

I stroke her back, slow circles, grounding us both. "Me neither."

She tips her chin up, eyes meeting mine. "Still here?"

I grin, even though my face hurts. "Still here."

We stay like that, tangled and silent, as the sun edges up over the neighbor's roof.

It feels, for the first time in months, like we might be okay.

Maybe not tomorrow, maybe not next week.

But we'll get there.

Together.

Epilogue

The first thing you notice is the light.

Not the cold blue of sirens, not the flicker of flames behind a cracked window, not even the harsh glare of a thousand cell phone flashes. No, what fills the air outside the new firehouse is softer—morning sun sluicing through freshly cleaned glass, catching on the polished brass, spangling every window and badge in sight. It's the kind of gold that makes the world look slightly better than it is, the kind that lets you pretend, just for a moment, that nothing bad has ever happened here.

I'm standing at the podium, front and center, with the town's new logo laser-cut behind me and a sea of faces stretching all the way to the curb. I grip the edges of the microphone like it might lift off and drag me with it. My hands are steady, but the tremor inside isn't nerves, exactly—it's the weight of not wanting to fuck up a moment that actually matters.

The firehouse itself looks almost nothing like the building I grew up in, but if you squint, you can see the bones are the same. They left the old archways on the south side, patched and power-washed, so the ghosts could find their way home. The rest is plate glass and brushed steel, so modern it almost hurts, but every corner is softened by plaques and memorials and painted tiles done by local schoolkids. The front lawn is green and freshly mowed, ringed with flags and bunting and so many balloons you could mistake this for a child's birthday instead of an anniversary celebration for a rebuilt town.

A hum spreads through the crowd, the low, eager chatter of people ready for something to happen. In the front row: the mayor, in a suit he'll sweat through by the second paragraph; next to him, the city council, dressed like they're headed to a church picnic. I catch glimpses of the old fire crew—some in full dress, others in faded t-shirts, bellies soft but faces hard. There's Lillian, my mother, standing as straight as the support pole in our first home, her hair silver and tight to her scalp, her mouth a thin line that means she's already said four prayers and is bracing for a fifth.

The back rows are thick with kids—elementary schoolers sitting cross-legged, older ones fidgeting, bored out of their skulls. A knot of high school volunteers lounge against the side of the new engine, their eyes half on the speakers, half on their phones. I spot Sarah, waving from the far end, her hair tamed into a French braid for the first time since the eighth grade. She has a little girl on her hip, who wriggles and shouts my name the moment she sees me looking.

They told me to keep it under five minutes. They told me, "Don't get too personal." They handed me a script on city letterhead, every word stamped and sanded until it was safe to print in the Gazette.

I fold the script, stuff it into my pocket.

"Thank you all for being here," I start, voice steady and just loud enough to catch the back fence. "It's an honor to see so many old friends and new faces in the same place—especially with the building still standing."

A nervous ripple of laughter; a few people clap, either out of politeness or habit.

I let my eyes scan the faces again, and for a second, just a second, I can almost see the day my father brought me here the first time. I was five, maybe six, scared out of my mind by the echo of the hoses and the clang of the lockers. He'd hoisted me up, set me on his shoulder, and told me, "You don't ever have to be afraid of fire, kid. Just don't turn your back on it."

I blink it away, focusing on the here and now. "When they asked me to speak, I thought about what this place used to be—what it meant to the people who worked here, and to the families who lost someone to it." I swallow, not for drama but to keep the ghosts from catching in my throat. "A firehouse is more than four walls. It's more than a job. It's a promise. It's the idea that, no matter how bad things get, there's always someone ready to step up."

The sunlight is in my eyes now, hot and blinding. I shift, letting it outline the crowd. The retirees, the teachers, the skeptics who once said the town would never recover. And just left of the dais, standing at parade rest in a suit so perfectly pressed it's probably held together by prayer and starch, is Lucas.

He's not in the department's new colors, not today—he wears his old captain's bars, the ones that somehow never fit right on anyone else. He's holding a baby, our daughter, cradled in a front carrier that makes him look both ridiculous and impossibly soft. Her tiny fist is balled up, clutching his collar; her eyes are fixed on a point somewhere above my head, already distracted by the next shiny thing.

The sight of them—Lucas standing tall and unflinching, the baby so content she might as well be asleep—sends a bolt through me that's equal parts terror and something fierce, maybe even pride. I think, if I died right now, I'd die knowing I left something behind that mattered.

I go on. "A lot of you know the story. Two years ago, this place was nothing but char and rubble. A fire took it. That fire took a lot of things—homes, livelihoods, lives. It took the truth, too, for a while. Secrets got swept up in the smoke and carried off, and for months, all we could do was sift through the ashes and wonder if anything was worth saving."

People aren't talking now. Every face in the crowd is either locked on me or on the gaping hole in their own personal history. The mayor dabs at his forehead. My mother bows her head and folds her hands.

"But fire doesn't just destroy," I say, letting the words hang. "It forges. It transforms. It reveals what truly matters. That's why we're here—not just to celebrate a new building, but to celebrate the fact that, after everything, we're still standing. Stronger. Smarter. And maybe a little less willing to turn our backs on what needs fixing."

A few heads nod. A couple of the old-timers even clap, slow and steady.

"I won't pretend it's all better," I add. "Some wounds don't heal, not really. But today, for the first time in a long time, I think we can say we've earned this second chance."

Now there's actual applause, not forced but real. Some people even stand. In the lull that follows, I look at Lucas. He gives me a small, crooked smile, the kind that means "I told you so" and "I love you" at the same time.

I clear my throat. "So let's dedicate this house to those who never got a second chance. To those who gave everything, even when the odds were bad. And to those who never stopped believing that a better day could still be built out of ashes."

The last line lands, clean and sharp. I let it echo for a beat, then step away from the mic.

I can't see the ghosts anymore. Just the faces of the living, upturned and shining.

Behind me, the new station glimmers in the sun, every window ablaze.

It looks, for once, like hope.

There's a sweet spot, just after a speech lands but before the crowd has figured out what to do with itself, where you can see every possible outcome flicker across a hundred faces. The first to recover are always the ones with an agenda—press badges and politicos, those perpetually in need of a sound bite or a handshake. They close in on the dais, blocking any hope of a graceful exit.

I'm mobbed by the time I make it halfway down the steps. The mayor intercepts me first, all smiles and damp handshakes. "You did the town proud, Sophie," he says, his palm so clammy I worry he'll leave a film on my skin. "Wouldn't be here without you, kiddo."

"Thanks," I manage, working to keep my expression polite. The mayor's wife is next, her eyes glassy with tears—real ones, or at least good enough to pass as real. "Your father would be proud," she says, pulling me in for a hug that's both desperate and oddly political. I pat her back, hoping that's enough.

Council members follow, each with a variation on the same line: "You've come a long way," "Takes guts to speak like that," "Glad you're still standing." Their voices blend, a chorus of bureaucratic approval.

Someone hands me a bouquet. It's wrapped in cheap cellophane, stems already leaking at the bottom. The smell is so sharp and green it almost cuts through the haze of perfume and aftershave. I tuck the flowers under my arm, careful not to crush the petals.

Old neighbors are next—the ones who used to glare at our house every time my dad staggered home late, the ones who once called my mother's casseroles "too spicy." They press in, shoving babies forward to be admired, introducing grandkids by name, as if I might still remember them from birthday parties I haven't attended since I was twelve.

Through the crush, I keep my eyes on Lucas. He's standing off to the side, letting the rest of the town flow around him like water around a rock. His uniform is perfectly pressed, every stripe and bar in place. But it's the baby strapped to his chest that makes him look more human, more breakable. Stella is awake, big blue eyes scanning the world with the same wary skepticism I feel.

I want to be over there. I want to put my head on his shoulder and let the rest of the day burn away. But there's a gauntlet to run first.

A woman with trembling hands and a voice like shredded silk grips my elbow. "I lost my son in the old fire. You spoke for him today." She squeezes once, then moves on, leaving a whiff of lavender and cigarettes.

A teenage boy with a mop of curly hair pushes a battered firefighter's helmet into my arms. "Found this in my grandpa's shed," he mumbles. "Thought you should have it." I take it, blink hard, and mutter "Thank you" before he sprints away.

Someone from the Gazette shoves a microphone under my nose. "Any words for the next generation of firefighters?" she asks, voice sharp with caffeine.

I glance at Lucas, at Stella's impossibly tiny hands peeking from the carrier, and say, "You save what you can, and you let the rest go."

She nods, satisfied, already turning away for the next quote.

A woman I vaguely recognize as the town's top gossip blocks my path, pinching her lips into a red slash. "I was wrong about you," she says, as if it's the hardest sentence she's ever constructed. "I said you wouldn't last a year back in this place. Guess you proved me wrong."

I want to thank her, or at least offer a peace treaty, but she's already gone, vanishing into the shifting tide of bodies.

I make it to the edge of the crowd, past the food tables piled high with barbecue and sheet cakes, past the cluster of kids swarming the antique fire engine. The engine is covered in construction-paper hearts and scribbled signatures, the aftermath of some PR stunt I missed in the lead-up to today. I spot Emily, Lucas's sister, wrangling a pair of toddlers who are taking turns trying to climb the truck's cab. She catches my eye, gives me a thumbs-up, and mouths "Call me!" before one of her charges attempts a kamikaze leap off the running board.

Lucas is waiting, right where I left him. He's holding Stella like she's made of spun sugar, one big hand cradling her head, the other splayed protectively across her back. The sunlight catches the blond in his hair, making him look younger, almost boyish. His gaze is locked on me, and there's so much in it—pride, relief, something private and wild—that I almost break stride.

I step up to him and he pulls me in, bouquet and helmet and all, until our bodies fit together the way they did before everything went wrong. He kisses my forehead, then my hair, then finally my mouth, soft but unyielding.

"You killed it," he whispers against my ear, voice low and thrilled. "I've never been prouder."

He shifts, letting me take Stella from the carrier. She's heavier than I expect, her body warm and squirming, fists flailing at the sudden change. I press her to my chest, inhale the scent of her—milk, sweat, something like vanilla and heat. She's perfect. Her eyes are all Lucas, but her chin, set stubbornly even in sleep, is pure Grant.

I study her face, tracing the little lines of her nose, the whorl of her ear, the tiny dimple in her left cheek that only appears when she's on the edge of a full-scale meltdown. She stares up at me, blinking, and for a moment I can't remember any pain, any loss. There's just this: the impossible, ridiculous fact of her.

Lucas watches me, a smile pulling at the corner of his mouth.

"She didn't cry once," he says, like it's the most impressive thing either of us have accomplished.

"She gets it from me," I say, though we both know that's a lie.

He laughs, reaches out, and brushes a strand of hair from my face. His hand lingers, thumb tracing the line of my jaw. It's the same gesture he used the first time he kissed me, back in the locker room, with the world ending all around us.

"Want to escape?" he asks, glancing at the mob gathering for the next round of speeches.

"More than anything," I say, and he nods, already plotting a route through the buffet and out toward the playground.

But before we can move, my mother appears at my side. She's wearing her best dress, the one she saves for funerals and Easter Sunday, and her shoes have left twin scars in the grass. She looks at Stella, at me, then at Lucas.

"You did good, Soph," she says, voice a little rough.

I nod, afraid if I talk I'll lose my composure entirely.

She reaches for Stella, but stops, hand hovering. "May I?"

I pass the baby to her, watching as she cradles the bundle with the expertise of someone who's done this a thousand times. For a second, I see her as I did when I was a child—strong, unbreakable, the center of gravity for a world I could never quite control.

"She looks just like your father," she says, so quiet I almost miss it.

I want to disagree, to say something about chins and stubbornness, but my voice cracks.

"Thank you," is all I manage.

My mother kisses Stella's forehead, then hands her back to me. She squeezes my arm, once, hard, then vanishes into the crowd with the certainty of someone who's already accomplished her day's work.

A band starts up at the far end of the lawn, horns blaring out a version of "Sweet Caroline" that's off-key but earnest. Kids dance, spinning in wild circles, their laughter tripping over the music. The scent of barbecue drifts on the air, mixing with the sharpness of mown grass and the tang of sunscreen.

Lucas and I find a patch of shade by the engine, settle onto the grass. He pulls me in until our legs tangle, then leans back, propping himself on one elbow so he can watch both me and Stella at once.

For the first time in forever, I don't feel the urge to run, or to look over my shoulder. I let myself breathe, let the noise and color of the crowd wash over me.

Stella fusses, and I shush her, rocking her gently. Lucas reaches over, his hand covering mine, anchoring us both.

"You think she'll remember any of this?" he asks, nodding at the balloons, the crowd, the riot of celebration.

"Doubt it," I say, smiling. "But maybe she'll remember the feeling."

"What feeling?"

I look at him, then at our daughter. "The one where you're exactly where you belong."

He kisses me again, this time slow and deep, and I let myself fall into it, the rest of the world fading to a dull, happy blur.

We stay like that for a long time—me, him, the baby, the sound of kids and music and the low murmur of a town finally at peace.

It's not perfect.

But it's enough.

Most crowds thin from the edges, but this one evaporates from the center—once the speeches are over and the cake is cut, people drift toward the familiar: the picnic tables, the lawn chairs, the safety of their own front porches. I watch them peel away in clumps, the parking lot slowly filling with the hum of engines and the soft punctuation of car doors closing.

Lucas and I linger, Stella drowsing in the sling against my chest. The warmth of her body, the steady pulse under her soft skin, anchors me better than any drug I've ever tried. The grass is wet under my feet now, the shade no longer necessary, and the air is threaded with the clean, wet promise of rain.

There's a hush, similar to the one after the sirens, but this time it's not about loss. It's the lull that comes with a job finished, a battle survived.

I stand, legs stiff from sitting, and shake the grass off my jeans. Lucas leans back, arms crossed behind his head, watching the sky turn from blue to a faint, bruised lavender. He's never been one for big crowds; even now, with most of the town gone, he keeps his eyes on the horizon.

He must sense my shift, because he sits up and brushes my shoulder. "You good?"

"Yeah," I say, meaning it. "Just need to walk a little."

We cut across the lawn, skirting the edge of the playground where a lone kid spins herself dizzy on the old merry-go-round. The band is packing up, their laughter carrying above the clatter of folding chairs. In the distance, someone revs a chainsaw for the cleanup crew, and the noise is comforting in its ordinariness.

The new firehouse looks different from this angle—less fortress, more cathedral. The windows are tall and uncurtained, the bays wide enough to fit two rigs side by side. I trace the outline of the building with my eyes, then stop in front of the main entrance.

Inside the lobby, mounted on the wall opposite the doors, is the new memorial. It's not fancy—just a line of framed photos, names etched in brass below each one. Fallen firefighters, going back a century. Some in black and white, some yellowed from age, some fresh and slick from the printer.

I pick out my father's photo instantly. They chose the one from his last award ceremony, the only time I ever saw him wear the dress blues without looking like he wanted to crawl out of his own skin. His jaw is set, his eyes fierce and stubborn. The nameplate below reads "Michael Grant, Chief." No dates. Just the title, the role he never quite escaped.

For a second, I wait for the punch in the gut. The ache, the anger, the old reel of questions I used to run every time I saw his face. But it doesn't come. Instead, there's a small, quiet pride. Not in the man he was, or the man he tried to be, but in the fact that he's here at all, locked into the town's DNA alongside the rest.

I nod at the photo. "Miss you, asshole," I say, just loud enough for the glass to catch it.

Lucas stands behind me, hands loose in his pockets, letting me have the moment. He's gotten good at that—being near without crowding, knowing the difference between rescue and respect.

"Ready to go home?" he asks, voice gentle.

I shift Stella on my hip. She's asleep, her lips pursed in a perfect bow, lashes so long they look painted on. I kiss her forehead, careful not to wake her.

"Yeah," I say. "Let's go."

We walk toward the lot, shoes crunching gravel. For a moment, the world narrows to just the three of us, wrapped in the last light of the day. Lucas brushes my hand with his fingers, linking them, and I let him pull me close.

The past isn't gone. It never will be. The weight of the brother I never really knew, the father who left more questions than answers, the way fire can both save and ruin—those things still exist. But they don't define me now.

I'm mother, wife, survivor. A keeper of the flame, but no longer its prisoner.

As we reach the car, I glance back at the firehouse. In the lobby, the memorial wall catches a stray shaft of sunset, the faces glowing gold for just a heartbeat.

It hits me, then, with a certainty that's both terrifying and electric: I would burn down the whole world for these two, if that's what it took to keep them safe.

But for now, I don't have to.

I buckle Stella into her seat, slide into the passenger side, and watch as Lucas starts the engine.

He grins at me, hand resting on my knee. "Home?" he asks.

"Home," I say, and this time it means everything.

As we pull away, the shadows stretch long behind us, reaching for the firehouse, for the past, for everything we've survived.

We drive into the future, the sun setting at our backs.

And this time, I'm not afraid.

Also by Laci Mae Wyld

Vow of Redemption

Haunted by a debt he never wanted, former Navy SEAL Lieutenant Mason Phillips is thrust back into a world of shadows and danger when a ghost from his past calls for help. Emelio Zentarra, the arms dealer who once saved Mason's life, has been brutally murdered, leaving his daughter Yelana as the unexpected heir to a treacherous empire.

Yelana harbors resentment towards Mason, blaming him for her brother's sacrifice years ago. Their initial animosity ignites a spark of undeniable attraction as they navigate a web of deceit and peril within the Zentarra Organization. With enemies closing in and betrayal lurking at every turn, Mason and Yelana must confront their shared past and uncertain future.

As danger escalates and trust becomes a scarce commodity, Mason grapples with his true motives while Yelana faces a heart-wrenching choice between loyalty to her family legacy or embracing a love that could either save her or shatter everything she holds dear.

In a world where loyalties are tested and love comes at a cost, will they find redemption in each other's arms or will the shadows of their past consume them both?

Beneath These Ruined Walls: Whispers in the Highlands

In a quest for solace, Fi MacPherson's journey to the Scottish Highlands leads her to the haunting ruins of Sutherland Castle. A chance encounter with a Highland warrior, who fades into thin air before her eyes, initially seems like a mere illusion.

Yet, as his presence lingers in her dreams and his touch ignites a fire within her, Fi is thrust into a realm where time blurs and souls entwine across centuries.

As Fi unravels the entangled memories of Isla—a woman torn between two brothers in a bygone era—she realizes that she is destined to relive their tragic tale over and over. Lachlan, the loyal and fierce warrior, and Hamish, his jealous and vengeful brother, are forever linked with her fate.

I Do...Hate You

In the heart of a city ruled by crime, survival means embracing the darkness within.

Meli Vasquez, a fierce and clever young woman, has long been confined to a life of servitude within the walls of a notorious crime family's stronghold. When the ruthless and feared Corbin Argyros, known as "The Executor " for his lethal efficiency, unexpectedly claims her as his bride to fulfill an ancient family decree, Meli is thrust into a world of opulence, danger, and power beyond her wildest dreams.

To Corbin, Meli's defiance is an intriguing challenge, her sharp wit a valuable asset. But to Meli, he is nothing more than a monstrous captor with haunted eyes and hands that stoke a dangerous fire within her. Their fiery clashes soon give way to forbidden passion, blurring the lines between loathing and longing.

In Corbin's brutal world, where compassion is weakness and love is a liability, Meli and Corbin realize that their unlikely partnership may be their most potent weapon yet. As betrayals mount, they must stand together against all who seek to tear them apart.

Content Warning: Contains explicit language and sexual scenes, including light choking, oral sex, manual stimulation, sexual violence, murder, kidnapping, torture, physical and sexual abuse, and themes of parental death.

Mark Me

35-year-old Mica Greer harbors a talent for intricate designs and a shield against emotional entanglements. But when Nyah Summers, with her haunting past and hidden pain, walks into his life, the flames of change flicker to life.

In a bold stand against Nyah's abusive past, Mica's defiance sets off a spark that neither of them can ignore. Drawn together by shared scars and unspoken desires, their connection deepens as they navigate the shadows of their histories.

Offering Nyah refuge within his sanctuary and a role in his creative world, Mica finds himself unraveling the layers of his own defenses. As their bond intensifies from friendship to something more, they must confront the looming threat of Nyah's vindictive ex-lover.

Experience a tale where redemption emerges from chaos, and the brightest flames are forged from the depths of darkness.

Good Girl To Goddess: Dancing with Desire

Cast aside on her birthday for not fitting in a mold, Elara James sheds her timid skin and overnight becomes a bold enchantress. Guided by her loyal confidante, she swaps modest clothing for daring outfits and quiet behavior for a fearless, take-no-prisoners attitude.

For six months, Elara indulges in fleeting affairs and casual flings, vowing to avoid emotional entanglements to protect her heart. One golden rule guides her nights: never stay until dawn.

Then enters Ryker Davis—confident, commanding, and undeniably captivating. In the heat of passion, he awakens her submission to his every whim. But beyond the bedroom, he reveals a tenderness that challenges the barriers guarding her heart.

As her former lover seeks reconciliation and her closest friend leaves town, Elara faces her deepest fears alone. Will she embrace the vulnerability that comes with true desire, or retreat into the safety of emotional distance?

Betrayal of Blood

In a whirlwind of betrayal, Sarsha Mitchell's once-promising future implodes when she catches her fiancé, James, entangled with her very own sister. Reeling from the heartbreak, Sarsha takes flight, leaving the shards of her shattered dreams behind. With her picture-perfect life in ruins, she seeks solace on an impromptu getaway to their abandoned honeymoon destination with her loyal confidante, Jess.

From the sun-kissed shores of Perth to the dazzling allure of the Gold Coast, Sarsha attempts to outrun her anguish amidst carefree escapades and electrifying nights out. Just as the shadows of her past threaten to engulf her present, a chance encounter at a club propels Sarsha into an unexpected charade with a mysterious stranger named Riley.

As sparks ignite between Sarsha and Riley during their fabricated romance, healing begins to seep into her wounded soul. However, upon their return to Melbourne, old wounds are ripped open anew as James refuses to relinquish his hold on her heart while envious desires stir chaos within her own family.

Supported by Riley's unwavering presence and unwavering gallantry, Sarsha finds the courage to confront the toxicity suffusing her familial bonds. Yet just as hope blossoms for a brighter tomorrow, a cruel act of revenge orchestrated by James and Megan threatens to shatter everything they hold dear.

In a race against time and treachery, Sarsha stands vigil by Riley's bedside, clinging to hope amidst the turmoil. Together, they uncover the depths of deceit woven by those she once trusted most. With Riley's love paving the way towards redemption and renewal, Sarsha severs the ties that bind her to darkness and steps boldly into a future brimming with promise.

www.ingramcontent.com/pod-product-compliance
Lightning Source LLC
LaVergne TN
LVHW030907080826
845145LV00010B/2795

* 9 7 8 1 7 6 4 5 1 6 9 3 8 *